Don't go in there alone....

For several seconds Bree listened to the voice of reason urging her away. She didn't want to die. But the logic in that seemed so absurd. A woman didn't die in a small-town hospital lab in the middle of the night ...

Most women didn't get to be the widow of a KGB mole, either. Gritting her teeth, Bree pulled her key from the lock and the lab door swung open. She could see that the door to the walk-in freezer was ajar, and moved quickly to close it.

She caught movement behind her and, before she could react, felt one brutal shove that sent her crashing down onto her knees in the freezer. At the same time the shadow of a bladed instrument hurtled toward her.

She hurled herself away from the violent shadow, too late realizing she was not the target at all. An ax smashed against the safety handle on the inside of the freezer door. She struggled with every bit of her strength, but with a resounding echo, the door slammed shut.

ABOUT THE AUTHOR

As the author of *Prince of Dreams,* one of the four titles in Harlequin's Dreamscape promotion of paranormal romances, Carly Bishop finds the demands of romantic intrigue to be a very gratifying contrast. An avid reader all her life, Carly takes special pride in creating characters who risk it all for the emotional brass ring. Carly lives in Denver with her husband and twelve-year-old daughter, Sarah.

Books by Carly Bishop

HARLEQUIN DREAMSCAPE
PRINCE OF DREAMS

Don't miss any of our special offers. Write to us at the following address for information on our newest releases.

Harlequin Reader Service
P.O. Box 1397, Buffalo, NY 14240
Canadian address: P.O. Box 603,
Fort Erie, Ont. L2A 5X3

Fugitive Heart

Carly Bishop

Harlequin Books

TORONTO • NEW YORK • LONDON
AMSTERDAM • PARIS • SYDNEY • HAMBURG
STOCKHOLM • ATHENS • TOKYO • MILAN

To Sharon, Kay, Jasmine and Lee—who, along
with all of Rocky Mountain Fiction Writers, have
made the journey its own reward.

Harlequin Intrigue edition published September 1991

ISBN 0-373-22170-3

FUGITIVE HEART

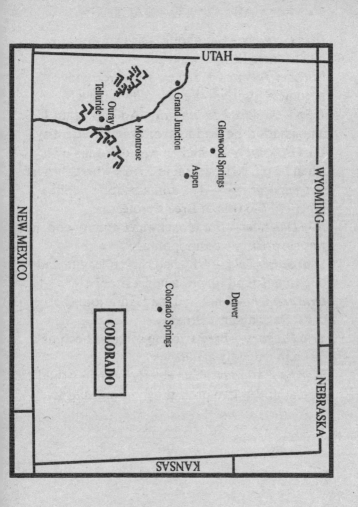

CAST OF CHARACTERS

Bree Gregory—She should have known how much worse things could get.

Michael Tallent—He knew why Bree had become a fugitive—he just didn't like it.

Henry Davidson Reinhardt—An important U.S. ambassador, he died to protect Bree's identity.

Carl Blessing—He had an agenda of his own when he put Michael on to Bree's whereabouts.

Patrick Marquet—The ambassador's nephew inherited the role of Bree's protector.

Roy Danziger—For a backwater county cop, he was surprisingly cosmopolitan.

Tom Sutterfield—Why had this colleague and one-time friend turned against Bree?

Oral Jenner—What had made him join the conspiracy against Bree?

Eric Gregory—Bree's young son had become a pawn in a deadly game.

Martha Halladay—The elderly woman would stop at nothing to protect her young charge.

Prologue

Confetti, he thought. Ugliness into confetti with a flip of his liver-spotted wrist.

In the small hours of the still-scorching Middle Eastern night, His Excellency Ambassador Henry Davidson Reinhardt stood over the document shredder in his private quarters. Girding himself against the onset of the inevitable pains in his chest, he held the months-old newspaper clippings for the last time. Even now, the headlines chilled him to the marrow. THE TRAITOR'S BRIDE. A MOLE'S ACCOMPLICE.

By dint of pure will, the ambassador forced himself to complete the destruction of the documents before him, final payment for the simple pleasures he'd garnered of late. He thought now of the choices he had made. He had never sired children of his own, never, in fact, married. No woman to warm his muffins in the morning, his bed in the night or his heart, ever. No one. The causes of world stability might well regret his passing; only his goddaughter, Sabrina Jean Huntley Preston, the object of worldwide vilification, would truly mourn his death.

His heart fibrillated wildly. He shivered and felt his chin quivering. Yet, he would not be robbed of this last earthly pleasure, of giving Sabrina a way out. At the eleventh hour of his own life, he held her fate in his hands. He switched the shredder on. It hummed to life and, one by one, unspeakable clippings and piles of documents churned through it.

How simple the pleasures of a dying man. One week ago, Sabrina—Bree to the few who knew her well—had delivered a son. He'd been with her, holding her hand, hearing her cries, her pain and ultimately, her triumph. In all his fifty-nine years, he had never been so touched. He'd been the first to know of her pregnancy; he alone knew who had fathered the child. Now he fed the voracious shredding machine all official documentation that the woman known as Sabrina Preston had ever lived or ever sought his help in arranging her escape, and finally, every evidence of the new identity he had concocted for her.

Bree Gregory.

All his plans had come to fruition. He'd put Bree Gregory and her infant son on a private jet some twenty-three hours before, and now his nephew, Patrick Marquet, would see to Sabrina's survival. Grim satisfaction eased the tight lines of distress from around the ambassador's lips.

When at last he finished, the ambassador removed the small vial of nitro tablets from the pocket of his elegant, teal-blue silk smoking jacket. He ambled, slowly and in pain, to the patio doors that opened onto the magnificent embassy gardens.

He looked up and studied the stars, constellations that were more familiar to him than those in the hemisphere from which he came. It was time now. Time to remove the last link between that unspeakable epithet, "A Mole's Accomplice," and Bree Gregory—himself. *How horribly convenient,* he thought, that his heart would give out within weeks in any case.... That pronouncement made this final act easier by far. He emptied the vial into his hand and hurled the tablets into the night.

He began walking slowly, then a little faster, away from strange emotions and his all-too-human needs. He pushed on, farther and farther into the gardens. The heat of the night and the cloying scent of the blooms forced upon the desert environment mocked him.

The pain built in him, stride for stride. Uncertainties shrouded his thoughts. Too late, instinct warned him that he'd made a serious error in judgment. Entrust his beloved Sabrina to the care of Patrick Marquet? The choice of a guardian had come down to the most obscure of the ambassador's connections. Would his weak-spined nephew be able to protect her?

He had pleaded Michael's cause with Bree; he'd *known* her best chances lay with the man whose son she bore. But with the edge of hysteria lacing her voice, Sabrina had refused. *Every tie with the past must be cut, even . . . even Michael.*

Fears clouded the ambassador's mind and made him tremble. Such doubts were as foreign to him as the tenderness he'd only recently discovered in himself.

The pain in his chest sharpened and shot down his left arm. He felt full, as if he might explode from within. He stumbled and cursed and dropped to his knees. At the last moment, he cried out.

And when he died, when it became known that Sabrina Preston had disappeared and when the news reached Washington, D.C., hours ahead of a formal press announcement, one man's heart would break. Another man would howl in outrage.

Chapter One

Survival. A simple matter, so basic that it went without saying. An agent never exposed his back, no matter how far removed from the field. *Aces and eights,* he thought. *Wild Bill Hickok died of a bullet in the back holding aces and eights. A dead-man's hand.* Of course, there were more ways than one to die. Michael Tallent wondered if he was about to learn another.

Stale, smoke-filled air wafted upward toward a six-bladed ceiling fan, and the late winter sun streamed through hazy windows, casting rainbows onto the floor. And there in the corner of the Buckhorn Bar stood a vintage jukebox. Michael's eyes were drawn again and again to its boxlike shape, its glossy dome, its fifties-era flair.

He drained the tumbler and scraped the legs of his chair against the age-darkened hardwood floor as he rose from his position of observation. With the long-legged bearing of a man who knows how to blend in with his surroundings, Michael wore jeans, a polo shirt that revealed bulky triceps, the requisite Tony Lama boots. His Stetson and jacket hung from an old brass hook on the wall by the table. Laramie, Wyoming was a cow town, a university town and unabashedly, a frontier town. Western macho was always in season.

Michael ordered and paid for a second club soda, then, perversely, sat where his broad back made one hell of a target. He'd lost everything a man watched his back for—a wife, a baby daughter, his best friend—and then the one woman who might have made him care once more.

He had no intention of letting clandestine habits consume him again. He told himself Blessing could come and go with his desperate secrets and veiled innuendoes. But when the old man entered the tavern, Michael's guts twisted, and sweat broke out on his upper lip.

Head of the fearsome U.S. naval intelligence operations, Carl Blessing quite literally held in his gnarled hands the security of the western hemisphere. His coming to Wyoming was a little like the mountain come to Mohammed. Michael wondered what the old man could have to say to him now.

But he knew. Bree had been found.

Blessing paused to order a Scotch, straight-up, tossed a five spot on the hard oak patina of the bar and then wandered in Michael's direction. Their eyes met and locked. Blessing eased himself into a chair. Michael lit a cigarette, inhaled and blew smoke rings at the quietly whirring ceiling fan.

"It's been a while, Michael."

"Not so long. Not long enough." In spite of himself, Michael felt churlish. Bree had been found; he didn't want to hear about it.

Blessing swallowed straight Scotch as if it were water, and his eyes, a blue to rival the wide-open Wyoming skies, cut Michael no slack. Years of top-secret dealings were evident in the quiet rasping of his voice. "I have information for you."

Michael's eyes hardened. "We have nothing to discuss. I'm no longer privy to your kind of information."

"You know why I'm here, Michael."

Michael drew hard on his cigarette. He suspected, yes. He had cared, once, about Bree Preston. Cared...very much. Now, caring came real hard.

Blessing stalled, as much for effect as to appease his curiosity. "You've attained tenure here, teaching linguistics?"

"For what it's worth." In no more of a hurry than his old boss, Michael let his eyes wander to the tavern windows. It had begun to snow. How typical of Wyoming. Sunshine one moment, a blizzard the next. *Tenure.* He was a man without a family or the comforts of any home. Tenure in hell was all he'd achieved.

Failing daylight made seedy, peeling wallpaper appear still shabbier. Other meaningless details drew his attention. Dust balls and peanut shells on the floor. The jukebox reflected over and over again in chipped, beveled mirrors.

He must've seen a jukebox in half the bars and all the truck stops he'd ever been in, but Michael's eyes, every facet of his attention riveted on *this* barroom juke. A kid, maybe twenty-one and bearing no physical resemblance to Joe Preston, plugged the jukebox with a quarter, selected a country-western she-done-me-wrong song and crowed along with Hank Williams.

In another time and another place, Joe Preston would have punched out the D-5 or J-9 selections—neither would have been country tunes, more likely the Beatles. Still, something in the kid's flair, his abandon, his flourish triggered in Michael the image of Joseph Allen Preston.

Fair-haired all-American boy, Notre Dame halfback, collector of vintage jukes and junkers, loving husband to Bree, Michael's own best friend. Preston had turned out to be the single most daring mole—a foreign agent brought up from birth to give every appearance of being a true and loyal American—ever planted in U.S. intelligence.

Joe Preston was dead, and his widow, Bree, seemingly vanished from the face of the earth. Michael had spent five fruitless years searching for her in every blind alley from Cairo to Virginia Beach.

He fixed Blessing with a hard stare. His arm rose from the shoulder as he slugged down the contents of his glass, steeling himself against the truth. The woman who might have made him watch his back again had been found. "Say it, Carl."

Blessing stared into the swirling amber liquid in his glass, his thumbs stroking at the moisture. At last he pulled a five-by-seven photo out of his breast pocket, a candid shot of a woman climbing out of a '77 AMC four-wheel drive Eagle.

Breezy. Sabrina Jean Huntley Preston. Matron of honor to Michael's bride, Daisy, godmother to Michael's baby daughter, Abbie. The truth was, Bree Preston had been Daisy's best friend and yet had managed to rub Michael the wrong way at every encounter.

She'd been his only salvation when Daisy and Abbie drowned—the same afternoon baby Abbie went off the breathing monitor she'd lived with since birth.

Six months later, when Joe Preston was arrested for treason and Bree came under suspicion and extreme prejudice herself, Michael had been there for her.

Bree. Michael found himself unprepared for the lurching inside or his throat constricting against the smoke. He fought against caring with everything in him. "So you've found her. It's no concern of mine."

"She's in grave danger."

Michael crushed out his cigarette. "Of what? A fatal rumor?"

Blessing drew a deep breath. The look in his eyes would brook no black humor. "I'm quite serious."

"So get her out of it."

"Impossible." Blessing studied Michael through eyes quick to spot pretense and quicker to cast judgment. "I grew up in the Kentucky horse country. Watching the ponies taught me a great deal about flying in the face of the odds. The odds, Michael, are ninety-nine to one that pulling Bree out will only precipitate another crisis another time. This has to be dealt with. Now."

"Why?" Michael demanded harshly. "Why should anyone chase her that far or for so long?"

"The *why* almost never matters."

Michael kicked a chair out from under the table, then drew it aside with the tip of his boot for a footstool. "Let her run."

"It's not that simple."

"It never is."

Blessing drew from his pocket a fistful of photos. With the ease of an accomplished poker player, he arced the six of them across the table, the corner of each covering the edge of the next with remarkable precision. Michael looked at a virtual catalog of strangers. It wasn't the faces he noticed. Across each, accomplished by some eerie, Machiavellian photographic trick, a skull and crossbones was engraved.

Blessing thumped them, one by one toward Michael, naming each in turn. "These people will die if Bree is pulled out—or if she runs."

Michael turned ashen, felt numbed. "How do you know that?"

From another pocket, Blessing withdrew a commonplace one-touch recording Sony M-740 tape player and shoved it across the table. Michael flipped it open and read the label on the miniature tape inside. "Rules of the Game." Michael's eyebrows raised in silent question.

"This came in the same package with the photos," Blessing said. "Delivered to my home by public courier."

Michael drew a stunned breath. Only on the highest level of the old intelligence saw, "need-to-know," were the residences of men like Carl Blessing known. It was a flagrant slap in the face of the entire intelligence community for a public courier to have delivered those photos to Blessing's home.

If Michael had wondered why Blessing gave a second thought to Bree Preston's dilemma, he had his answer. The threat to her was a threat to Blessing's entire operation.

"I assume you've checked the point of origination, run voice prints—"

"Everything. The package originated in Denver, but that's all we know. No voice match was found by our computers, no syntax similarities identified, no fingerprints. Nothing of any forensic significance."

Michael put the small earplug to his ear, pushed in the middle gray button and steeled himself to listen.

"Greetings, Michael," the harsh whisper said. "Vengeance is mine. Preston is dead. Long live Preston." Michael flinched at the soft, almost demented laughter before the scratchy voice continued.

"You don't see it that way, of course, and so you must stop me. The rules are simple and few. One, stick around to the finish—*all of you,* or the good folks in the photos will die....

"Two. Take your time—start that house you always wanted to build, and don't forget the playroom. Get to know your territory. An unprepared adversary is no adversary at all....

"Three. No uninvited guests, Michael, just you and me and the whore Sabrina, huh? That's all. Catch me if you can, friend, because if you don't, she's history. Dead, Michael, right along with her bastard brat. You, on the other hand, will live to appreciate your losses...."

Slouched in the wooden chair, Michael straightened. His throat was suddenly as dry as the winter-parched Wyoming terrain. "What 'bastard brat' is he talking about?"

Blessing reached into his coat pocket again and produced another photo—of a boy, six, maybe seven years old—on a park swing. "Sabrina Preston's son."

"Bull!" Michael swore. "Preston wasn't capable of fathering a child."

Carl's lips twisted into a crooked, certain smile. "No," he agreed. "Adolescent mumps left him sterile. That leaves only one possibility, I should think."

The child was Michael's son. Realization blistered in him, and his hands shook as he remembered the only night he might have conceived a child with Bree.

From the first, she had been taken into protective custody, which only meant that as the wife of a traitor, she was as suspect as Joe Preston himself. There was a body of evidence implicating Preston's wife. Michael had been allowed twenty-four hours with her—to break her down, he was told, in a perverse version of the old good-cop-bad-cop routine.

It hadn't happened that way. When the federal prosecutors sent Michael in, he could only hold her.

Images of Bree assailed Michael, stark and poignant. The sensation of her thick, sable hair caught on his whiskers like some rare linen. The scent of her. The look in eyes the color of morning glories, haunted with the need to believe that she hadn't been a dupe to Joseph Allen Preston's treachery. The sprinkling of freckles across the bridge of her nose made less subtle by pallor and shame. And her naked legs... Holding her had become more. So much more.

She was gone the following morning. He found out months afterward that she was in the protective custody of her godfather, Ambassador Reinhardt. Michael had expected her to return. Instead, she'd disappeared and the ambassador had died.

If she had a child of seven, the boy was his. She had to know what that would have meant to him after losing his baby daughter. Michael kicked at peanut shells on the floor. "Where are they?"

Blessing leaned away from Michael, reeling under the intense, unnerving change in his eyes that went from a muted shade of battleship gray to cold, hard ice. Michael's voice, always soft, was a whisper against the granite-hard language of his body. Irrationally, Blessing felt intimidated. "Grand Junction. Colorado." He gathered the photos and tape player, rose and gestured for Michael to follow him out of the tavern.

The wind blew like billy-hell. Everywhere, pedestrians leaned unnaturally into the gusts. Blessing followed Michael's lead onto Ivinson Street, where ancient evergreens blocked the biting cold wind.

"I was against your search for Bree from the beginning. Call it an old man's superstition—call it seat-of-the-pants— I don't give a rat's A. Sabrina Preston was never meant to be found. A blown cover is an invitation for trouble."

"I know that."

"You never understood the first thing about it," Blessing said flatly. "You were strictly ivory tower, Michael."

"An innocent in a den of thieves, merrily cracking codes, is that it?" he demanded harshly. "*I'm* the one who discovered Preston's KGB connections."

"Granted. You nailed him to the wall. But after Preston died in the firebombing of the transport on the way to trial, something happened between you and Bree. You cooked up this little happily ever after with the widow Preston. You thought you could mop up the mess her life was in. You were wrong."

Michael's throat swelled reflexively. He'd been so sure that he could shield her, protect her from the gruesome fact that she'd married a traitor. So sure that he had come up tilting at windmills? Michael's jaw locked in self mockery. *Lieutenant Colonel Don Quixote*.

They passed through a knot of university buildings. "I'll tell you this very frankly, Michael. Whoever sent those photos is as great a threat to national security as to your Bree. That threat is very real."

They stood at last in Prexy's Pasture. The grounds should have had a more dignified name, like Harvard Yard or the Memorial Quadrangle. This was not much more than a humble pasture, and Blessing was the mountain come to Mohammed. When Michael looked again, Blessing's eyes had filled with tears.

"Don't kill the messenger, Michael."

He had never known Blessing to betray the smallest show of emotion other than anger; the old man's tears raised serious doubts in Michael. Doubts that he had been told even half of whatever Blessing knew or suspected of Preston's avenger. Still, he hugged the old man's now-fragile shoulders.

Blessing handed Michael the package. "You'll go?"

Michael stuffed the goods into his coat pocket and nodded. It would have been easy to suggest to himself that it was for the sake of national security that he would go, only nothing much had been easy his whole life.

He would go to Grand Junction, knowing he'd gone to protect the woman who had scorned and then betrayed his trust, and the son she had stolen from him.

He would go, knowing there *were* a hundred and one ways to die. You could die in your sleep. You could die of grief. You could even die laughing.

The truth might kill Michael Tallent.

BREE GLANCED UP FROM THE blood-bank microscope to check the time. Her eyes blurred and watered as her focus changed. She squeezed them shut before peering again at the clock. Ten-twenty. Where had the hours gone?

The blazing July sun had set hours before, and now only a quarter moon and a few street lamps softened the darkness outside the open windows of the Mesa County Hospital lab. Nothing relieved the sweltering heat. Bree lifted damp tendrils of hair from the back of her neck and silently cursed the nonexistent air conditioning.

After crossmatching eight units of blood for the patient with bleeding esophageal varices, she'd put in close to a sixteen-hour day. She removed the last of the crossmatch slides from the stage of the microscope and tossed it along with a dozen small test tubes into the bio-hazard trash. The clatter of glass on glass splintered the silence. Bree shuddered, feeling a chill.

Was it the quiet? The dark? Or simply her own bone-tired body starting at the ordinary sound? She'd pulled shifts like this before and had spent endless hours over the past six years in the late-night solitude of the lab. So why the jitters tonight?

It was Patrick, she thought, going through another of his jealous, controlling phases. He'd called seven times in the hours between four and eight o'clock. *Do you know where your son is, Bree? Who he's with? What they're doing?* In all the years since the ambassador had sent her to the protection of his nephew in Grand Junction, Patrick had never been this restless or demanding.

The phone rang again now, shrilly interrupting her thoughts. Bree snatched the receiver off the hook and answered. Thankfully, it wasn't Patrick, but the operating-room circulating nurse. Would Bree deliver two units of whole blood to the O.R. on her way out?

Bree drew a deep breath to settle her jitters. "Of course. I'll be there—ASAP." If it would get her out of here as soon as possible, she'd start the blessed units running herself.

She signed the blood out to the O.R., and then grabbed her purse from the desk. In less than two hours, she'd be off call and off duty for three whole days. It couldn't come soon enough.

Toting the little picnic cold-keeper, Bree walked into the outer, nonsterile area of the O.R. The radio played Streisand, and no one inside the suite heard Bree's knock. She swung the door in and the surgeon glanced up. "It's about bloody time," he cracked.

Bree had little professional regard for Tom Sutterfield, but his son was Eric's age and she knew the man very well outside the hospital. His pun was clearly an invitation to a tension-relieving exchange. "In trouble, Tom? Sounds like a personal problem to me," she shot back. "But I've bailed you out again."

Mary Lipscomb, the scrub nurse, went stiff with pretended shock. Sutterfield barked at her for a clamp and winked at Bree from above his mask. "It's ready?"

Bree nodded.

"Hang it." Bree shot Mary an encouraging glance with the last of her energy and turned to leave.

Moments later, on her way out to the circular drive in front of the hospital, Bree reached for the keys to her battered, four-wheel-drive Eagle and shouldered her purse. The automatic door swished closed behind her and she heard the lock click solidly into place. Finally, she could go home.

Idle for the first time in hours, her thoughts turned back to Eric. The summer was half over and she hadn't had a full weekend off to spend with him in weeks.

How she loved that uncomplicated little boy! She had no more idea how to turn a toy tank into a robot than how to defend a soccer goal or tie a proper fly. But those were just the innocent, commonplace pursuits of any seven-year-old kid. It seemed to her that they had led a blessedly normal life. Until lately.

Patrick's increased, unwanted attentions were only one symptom. Since May, a wariness had pulled at her, like the threads of her life were slowly unraveling. She'd felt... shadowed, as though someone watching from an indefinable distance saw her every step, knew where she'd been and where she'd go next.

Then there was Eric and the fishing trip that had inspired all Patrick's angry calls this afternoon. Although Martha Halladay was always at home for Eric, and had been from the day Bree had gone to work, he'd been spending more and more of his days with his friend Billy Kendall and Billy's dad.

This morning Bill, Sr. had called Bree at work, asking to take Eric fishing for the day. She'd had serious reservations, but Eric wanted to go so badly.... How could she refuse him the chance at things a million other seven-year-olds did every day?

The traffic light at First and Broadway turned red, and Bree braked to a stop. A dozen times, a hundred times over the years she had thought, *What should I do, Michael? If you were here, what would you do?* Such questions were silly, of course. If Michael were here, *he'd* take his son fishing.

Eric was beginning to have needs she could never fulfill. The realization had been slow in coming, but it had only been a matter of time.

Preoccupied when the light turned, Bree was a little slow pulling into the intersection. A car horn blasted behind her. Jerked out of her thoughts, Bree gripped the steering wheel to keep from trembling. Unaware that anyone had pulled up behind her, she stamped on the pedals, but her foot slipped off the clutch and the car lurched forward and died.

She reached for the keys and glanced into her rearview mirror. Her fingers froze on the ignition key. The car behind her was a '65 Mustang, the same one Eric had pointed out to her at the market last week, and in the McDonald's drive-in the week before that. The coincidence shredded her composure.

Grand Junction was small. The Mustang was a classic Eric recognized. How many other less-noticeable cars might she see three times in two weeks? Annoyed at her own overblown dismay, Bree turned the key and the Eagle came to life again.

She started out across the intersection, west toward The Ridges, where she lived. The Mustang matched her pace and followed, crossing the railroad overpass and then the Colorado River behind her. Bree swallowed hard and forced herself to breathe deeply. In . . . hold . . . out. She slowed to a turtle's-pace ten miles an hour. Rather than pass her, the Mustang slowed, too, long enough for her mind to register the Colorado license plate. UFQ-9307.

UFQ-9307 edged perilously closer. Bree bit back a cry, jerked the steering wheel sharply to her right, putting the car on the road shoulder, and then pulled a U-turn in the middle of the highway. An eighteen-wheeler came over the hill behind her and the air horn blasted the driver's protest of her maneuver.

Bree pushed the accelerator to the floor. The truck's lights flashed in her mirror. She could talk to herself all night about how small a town this was, about coincidence, but it was hard to ignore the Mustang duplicating her switch-back behind the truck in her rearview mirror.

Her fingers ached from gripping the steering wheel. *UFQ-9307.* She had no chance of losing the Mustang if its driver meant to stick with her. No chance at all, unless—unless she could get to the police station. Bree's heart began hammering. Two miles—less, maybe, and her pursuer would surely give up. Who could it be?

Bree forced another deep breath in and out of her lungs. The light on the other side of the river was green; she slowed anyway, which earned her the nasty blare of the trucker's air horn again. She kept slowing until the light changed from green to yellow. At the last moment, she sped through the intersection. The trucker ground to a halt and the Mustang was stuck behind.

The moment of relief over her success in eluding the Mustang faded fast. Angry enough now to report the incident and demand the Mustang's owner be stopped, she drove toward the police station. Without using her blinker, she turned south on Sixth to Ute, back to Fifth, then south again. She left the Eagle in a no-parking zone, ran for the door and threw one glance back over her shoulder. A Mustang rounded the corner to the northwest of her and drove slowly, tauntingly to a position behind her Eagle.

UFQ-9307.

A shaft of pure fear shot through Bree at the blatant action. How dared he risk discovery in front of the police complex? For one numbing moment, she thought the Mustang's driver capable of reading her mind. How else could he have known that she'd come to the police station? Her heart knocking crazily, Bree flung open the door. Where else could a woman alone go in the middle of the night for help?

She found the desk sergeant preoccupied with a magazine of questionable taste. Her keys clattered on the counter, and Bree took one more calming breath. "Excuse me?"

Whether irritated at the interruption or embarrassed, the sergeant slapped his magazine down. "Yes?"

"UFQ-9307. A black Mustang, 1965 I think. I'd like to know who owns it—and report being followed."

The sergeant—Farraday, according to the tag above his badge—turned to his computer monitor. "Who's asking?"

"What?" For the first time, Bree considered what it might mean to her precious anonymity to register a complaint. Her name would go into official police records, and records made her dangerously vulnerable. A driver's license and Social Security number were record enough of her existence.

"Your name, ma'am. If you're going to lodge a complaint, I have to have your name."

It took her one split second too long to decide he could easily check any alias she could throw at him—one split second her credibility rested on. She had no real choice if she wanted the Mustang and its driver stopped. "Gregory. Bree Gregory."

She gave him the rest of the information he required—her address, employment, reason for being on the streets alone this late at night, the license-plate number she'd given him before. "UFQ-9307. A '65 black Mustang."

When he punched the information into his computer, Bree tensed. He sat there for a long time, just staring at the screen. Bree fidgeted, thinking she ought to call home and let Martha know she'd be delayed a little longer. A call in the middle of the night would probably alarm more than reassure her.

Farraday finally glanced up from his monitor, his expression no longer slightly bored, but challenging.

Bree's chin went up. "Well?"

"Ma'am, how do you know you were being followed?"

"How do I know?" Did the man think her a complete moron? "Because he *followed* me. Because he was close enough that I *saw* his license plates," she snapped. "Because I pulled a U-turn in the middle of the highway and he came right after me!"

"Ma'am, the car you describe belongs to a county sheriff's deputy. Are you seriously going to stand there and tell me an off-duty officer of the law was on your tail for the hell of it?''

UFQ-9307 was a cop?

A county cop. Bree understood in one blinding flash of insight that if she pursued this complaint, she would only draw unwanted attention to herself. She hadn't truly thought of herself as a fugitive in years. Now she could think of nothing else. Why had she been followed? Why now?

Impatiently, Sergeant Farraday knocked his knuckles on the counter. "Well? Are you going to sign a complaint?"

Bree swallowed. "No. I . . . no."

Farraday leaned back, rocking in his chair, more kindly now that she'd backed off. "Go home, lady. Get some sleep. Maybe things'll look different to you in the morning, huh?"

"No, sir, I doubt that very much." UFQ-9307 had followed her and meant her to *know* he was following her.

She wouldn't file a complaint, but neither would she forget it. She needed a name to go on, to measure the trouble she was in. Surely there must be less conspicuous ways of getting that information.

NO ONE FOLLOWED HER HOME. No headlights in her rearview mirror, no threatening honks of a Mustang horn. Bree switched on her turn signal and swiped at a random tear of relief.

Then she turned onto Thistle Ridge Road and noticed the absence of Martha's car, which should have been parked in front of the house. *Drive,* Bree, she thought. *Just drive, up the short incline into the driveway.* She got out of her Eagle and then hesitated. Where in God's name was Martha?

The night was extraordinarily quiet but for crickets and fireflies and tiny, swooping bats. Her hands felt clammy against the stifling heat. *Move, Bree.*

She climbed the stone steps up the steep, desert-scaped terrain of her front yard. A half-dozen chameleons skittered out of sight, mocking her own hesitant pace. *It's okay…. Eric is okay.* Surely if she hadn't been so tired, such nameless fears would never arise. But where was Martha's car?

Silently, Bree eased open the screen door—Martha would have locked the solid oak door and bolted it, as well. "Martha?"

"Quiet, Bree. You'll wake up Eric."

Patrick. The screen door slammed shut behind her. "What are you doing here?" she ground out. "Where is Martha?"

"I sent her home, Bree. She was tired. It's almost midnight."

Bree wanted to scream; she knew perfectly well what time it was. Instead, she crossed the living room, switched on a red clay beanpot lamp and sank onto the couch. "Don't ever do that again, Patrick. Martha knows she can sleep here."

She waited for an apology, but he sat in the overstuffed rocker with raw-boned fingers laced over his slight paunch. Faintly Slavic cheekbones and a high forehead made him look somehow…accusing. "Where have you been? We need to talk."

"Nowhere. The hospital." Sometimes his brand of caring wore her out. She simply didn't have the energy to get into an argument now over how she constantly invited trouble. "I'm going upstairs to check on Eric."

Patrick rose from the rocker and intercepted her at the stairs. He took both her hands in one of his and caressed her silvery-blond hair with the other. "He's asleep, Bree."

The warmth of his breath next to her ear made her recoil from the intimacy. "Patrick, please. I need to check on him."

"Fine." He spun away and strode to the liquor cabinet. "I'll be waiting."

Bree stared at his retreating back. Patrick was tall and underweight. His lean muscles bunched in anger under a light-yellow polo shirt. He'd done everything his uncle the ambassador had asked—and more. She'd given him all the gratitude in the world, but her gratitude was all she owed him. With or without his help, she and Eric would have survived.

Bree forced her tension-knotted fingers to relax, then climbed the stairs to Eric's room. Picking her way across the toy-strewn floor, she opened the window a bit further and then sat down on her son's bed.

All she'd ever wanted was a chance to raise Eric far away from spies and traitors and those who would paint her with the same brush, the ones who condemned first and asked questions later. Eric would never suffer for her mistakes.

She eased a lock of his hair off his forehead, sable-colored, like her own before she'd bleached it as part of her transformation into Bree Gregory. Although Eric had her fair, lightly freckled coloring and blue eyes, she would never see Eric without some part of her acknowledging Michael's features—the slender nose and rich, full lips, a jaw that would square as he got older and eyebrows that seemed to overwhelm his little face. She touched Eric's cheek and bent to kiss his forehead.

"Mom...?"

"Yes, sweetheart, I'm home," she whispered. "You go back to sleep now, okay?"

"Mom? You weren't worried about me, were ya? I'm sorry if goin' fishing worried you."

Bree swallowed hard and shook her head. "No, darling. Not really."

"How come he sent Gramma Martha home?"

"*Gramma* Martha?"

"Yeah. Mike says she's as good as a gramma, and every- body but me's got one. She said I could, too. . . ."

Most children had not one but two grammas, and aunts and uncles and cousins. And a father. "Who's this Mike who's so smart?"

Eric yawned. "Billy's dad works for him, 'n' he said next time we'd go fishing by ourselves—y'know, just us two guys."

Bree's fingers went motionless in her son's hair. "Eric—"

"I'm not lying! He did, Mom!"

What business did a stranger have offering such a treat to someone else's little boy? "I didn't think you were lying, sweetheart. But I don't even know Mike. We'll have to see about that."

She caught the barest hint of resistance in his eyes before Eric flung his arms around her neck. She wanted him safe; Eric just wanted to make this friend on his own. Swallow- ing her fears—Eric shouldn't have to cope with her instinc- tive recoil from strangers—Bree smiled and kissed her son good-night.

Downstairs, Patrick handed her a snifter of brandy.

"Eric is very upset that you sent Martha home. I'd still like to know why."

"I told you, Bree, we have to talk. Your options are run- ning out. Eight years is a long time to live a lie."

Chapter Two

Moments passed while Bree paced the living room, seven steps from the stairs to the picture window; ten steps over the braided hooked rug she despised to the front door Patrick had so casually left open. The door to the house Patrick owned.

There's a lie for you, she thought. *Eric thinks this is his home. The school thinks his father is dead. Martha knows nothing of the truth. And Patrick thinks I could grow to love him, given time enough.*

Hers weren't the little white lies of harmless social cover-ups or the forbidding black lies the traitor Joe Preston had perpetrated. Hers were sepia lies, like old photographs. Boring and brown and safe . . . the lies she lived merely to survive. *Was I wrong, Michael? Forgive me if I was wrong. So help me God, I didn't know what else to do.*

She plucked a dried brown leaf off the philodendron by the kitchen entry and then sank onto the burgundy leatherette couch. The leaf crumbled in her hand. Were all the lies crumbling about her now, the very lies that had once been her only salvation?

Patrick stood with his elbow perched on the banister, his snifter swinging in his fingers. She saw him suddenly as a carrion bird hanging around for the spoils—and then felt badly. The fight in her seeped away; anger was replaced by weariness.

"I have to live with them, Patrick. I never had any options to begin with."

"But you did! You have this way of thinking things can't get worse, Bree, but they can. Eric's running wild—"

She stiffened against the criticism. She'd spent half her adult life thinking exactly how much worse things could get, but it was Eric she defended. "He's growing up, that's all."

"He needs a father, someone to control him, someone to make sure he walks the straight and narrow. I deserve a chance with you. But you won't see it, will you?" Patrick swirled his refilled snifter until it began to slop over the lip and onto his fingers. He didn't notice. "You won't believe that your lies could still fall apart, but they *will*."

"Patrick, I don't know what you're talking about! Is this about my letting Eric go fishing with Bill Kendall?"

"I saw the four of them walking into McDonald's today, Kendall and his kid, the other guy and Eric," Patrick taunted. "You should see how Eric looks at *him*. You should see how he takes Eric by the shoulder like he's *his* son, like he has every right to the boy."

Foreboding, fears she had no trouble identifying, stalked at the edge of her consciousness.

Oh, Michael... She tried to remember a time when she could see the kindnesses of strangers as a welcome and precious thing, but she couldn't. Not with a faceless creep stalking her or with Patrick spying on Eric. And not with a low-life stranger acting as though he had any right to her son.

A chill swept over her flesh.

Somehow, she managed to send Patrick away, next door to his own, other house. Somehow, she managed to undress in the darkness and to shower, aching for warmth to banish the worry, the tight, awful certainty that her life,

Eric's life, had begun to spin wildly out of control. But the chill clung to her like frost on a blade of desert grass, refusing to melt even in the oppressive heat of the July night.

FOR THE THIRD TIME IN AS many hours, Michael stood at the miniature stainless-steel sink in his camper, dousing his unshaven face with lukewarm water. Aching for the simple luxury of a cool shower, he soaked a cloth, ran it over his arms and torso and then threw it into the sink. Why in blazes didn't he just chuck this Spartan life-style and move into the Hilton?

Because, per the instructions on the tape, he had begun building his house. Because he needed to go out and hammer the place together or pound out his frustrations—he couldn't have said which took priority. Mostly, though, the place was within walking distance of his son.

He'd have rather built his dream house amid stands of spruce and aspen, in a place scattered with lupine and Indian paintbrush and wild asters. He'd settled for the edge of an old peach grove with columbine and raspberries. Eric loved raspberries....

Michael hoisted himself onto the cramped bed space, wrestled with the three pillows in the too-short bed and kicked the covers over the edge. Tempted to peruse Blessing's dossiers one more time, Michael thought instead of the wild luck that had led him to hire Bill Kendall.

Out-of-work contractors were a dime a dozen all over Colorado. Michael had talked with half that many, and Bill Kendall was no more or less qualified than the next to pour a concrete foundation. The guy was a football jock with bad knees only two years off the Denver Broncos line-backing squad. But the day Kendall delivered his bid, he had his son along for the ride—a kid named Billy who had a pal named Eric.

Michael had hired Kendall on the spot.

Bill Kendall poured the foundation, which, all-told, took four days, and on one of those days, he brought both boys with him. All day long, Michael's heart pounded in his chest while a kid named Eric whose mom was named Bree, trailed shyly after him.

His son. When Kendall submitted his bill, prepared to go drum up another job, Michael asked him to stay on. What Kendall knew about framing a house Michael neither knew nor cared. He cared only that Eric might tag along with Billy another day.

Michael spent most late afternoons and the long nights waiting, watching—"learning the territory"—watching for anyone who might show undue interest in Bree or Eric, or anyone with more than a passing interest in the fact that his house was by now well begun. Watching for an unknown adversary.

Throughout it all, Michael considered himself lucky. Kendall could handle a hammer, and Eric, fascinated with the geese Michael kept around to ward off vandals, came more days than not. And today, Michael had taken his son fishing.

Tonight, he had to wonder when the peace would be shattered.

He slid off the makeshift bed of his camper, pulled on a pair of worn Levi's and a T-shirt, and kicked open the aluminum screen door. Murmuring to the two pairs of geese—*Eric's* geese, Michael thought now—he locked up and struck out in the direction of Thistle Ridge Drive.

It took him twenty minutes to hike over the hills to a vantage point on the barren bluffs well above Bree's house. And the one next door—Patrick Marquet's house.

Michael took his pack of cigarettes from the sleeve of his T-shirt and lit one. Blessing's dossiers painted Marquet as a weakling, complete with monumental insecurities and towering greed—a dangerous combination, given the need to protect Bree's cover. Was it Marquet who had set Bree up to be discovered? Possibly. Probably. Almost certainly unwitting....

Marquet could have no rational motive for destroying Bree; but someone else did. Someone clever enough to entice Michael to Grand Junction, patient enough to wait until he'd invested in building a home, and undoubtedly delighted to see that Michael had fallen hard for the seven-year-old he knew without question to be his son....

He knew which was Eric's window. For several moments, he thought of the weeks he'd spent with his son, odd moments and precious few long hours. He thought about those times to avoid thinking of Bree.

He'd put off revealing himself to her, but he'd seen plenty of Bree from a distance. Her hair was bleached a silvery blond, and to have kept Eric's existence from him, Michael thought, she had a heart of stone. He no longer knew her. It was merely a biological accident that she was the mother of his son. An accident, nothing more.

Michael lit his last cigarette off another. The time had come to reveal himself to Bree. Tomorrow. His guts twisted. How in God's name would he handle such a confrontation? How would she?

He hadn't thought he'd give a damn.

BREE WOKE FROM AN exhausted sleep to the slap of Caruso's plastic pork chop against the back of the house. The basset hound bayed at the toy, and Eric's laughter rippled after his pet. Her head throbbed, but a half smile touched her lips.

How Eric loved that dog. More than making the Peanut Butter Fish recipe with the trout he caught...more than the clatter he made with a playing card clothespinned to the spokes of his bike...more than the latest Nintendo challenge.

Such simple, innocent pleasures. *Eric and his friends think they've invented fun, Michael.*

Eric's noisy, normal antics made it hard to imagine that last night could have been as bad as it was or that her life could be edging toward disaster. Yeah, the black Mustang had been following her. There was no way to misinterpret that, but she'd handle the problem. With three whole days off work, three days to spend with Eric, everything would work out. Maybe they could go to her mountain cabin above Ouray, she thought. Eric would like that.

Bree slipped out of bed and into a comfortable old patchwork terry robe. Skipping lightly downstairs and through the kitchen, she thought, *Enough is enough.* She hadn't made it this far and this long to let one minor crisis throw her.

"Hi, sport." She slipped through the screen door and sat down on the back porch, feeling a welcome shiver go through her from the cool, shaded concrete. "How's old Caruso?"

"Hi, Mom. Don't say that—you'll hurt his feelings. Caruso ain't old!"

"Caruso *isn't* old."

Eric rolled his robin's egg blue eyes, full of feigned innocence. "Ain't that what I said?"

"Noooo, it *ain't.*"

Eric grinned. "You off today?"

"Three, count them, three whole days! What would you like to do?"

"Yippee!" His face lit up with the unexpected pleasure and then, slowly, his broad smile faded. "You mean, like, go somewhere? Nawww. Can't we just hang around home?"

"Stay home? This from my seven-year-old dynamo? Come here, you, I want a hug."

Eric turned briefly to wrestle the pork chop from Caruso and sidearmed it to the back reaches of the cactus garden. Bree felt her brow furrow as Caruso bounded after it. She'd never seen Eric throw so well or so far. He ambled over to the porch and plunked down beside her. She reached easily around his spare, bony shoulders and her fingers lightly stroked an equally knobby knee as she drew him close.

Her cheek rested on his sun-warmed hair. The little-boy scents of dirt and a pet dog took her breath away. So precious, and so soon, not a boy at all. He snuggled for a moment and then bent down to examine the pink, polished nails of her bare toes.

"How come girls paint their toes, Mom?"

"Hmm. Because toes are basically ugly? That was a pretty decent throw there."

"I been playing catch with Mike. He says—" Eric's eyes flicked toward hers, full of a childish alarm. His lips pursed shut and his glance darted away. Until this moment, there had been nothing in Eric's life he hadn't clamored to tell her.

Mike. *Well, Mike,* she thought. *I'll thank you for your kindness, and thank you kindly to leave my son to me....* "You want very much for me to like your friend, don't you?"

Eric sat sullenly, grasping handfuls of dirt and throwing them. "I wish I could do that—know what *you're* thinking all the time. Gramma Martha says it's a natch-ral wonder the way you always know what we're thinking."

"I think you do know what I'm thinking, sweetheart. I think you know what I'm thinking right now, for instance."

"That we better talk about Mike. What about him?" Eric twisted away from her and whistled for Caruso. An honest-to-heaven, two-fingered whistle.

Did Mike teach you that little chunk of male lore, too, she wondered bitterly. "Like who is he, where he comes from."

Why a grown man seeks the company of someone else's son. "Stuff like that."

"He's just a guy, Mom. Billy's dad, Mr. Kendall, met him first. Isn't that okay? I mean Mr. Kendall is a grown-up and he put in the foundation on Mike's house. Billy and me were just along. He's Billy's friend, too. Besides, *you* said I could have a friend of my own, didn't you, Mom? Didn't you?"

Something intangibly rebellious in his childish insistence pulled at her. He needed her approval and at the same time, fought against needing it.

"I'm not saying that you can't have a friend of your own. But I'm your Mom, you know? Even if Mr. Kendall works for Mike, I need to know him, too. If I don't know who you're spending time with, I wouldn't be a very good mom, now would I?"

Eric's jaw jutted stubbornly out and he swallowed back a retort. It was the first time she'd ever noticed his Adam's apple bobbing so manfully. He shook his head and batted the pork chop from Caruso's hopeful jaws. "Can we eat now? I'm hungry."

She recognized his ploy. "Not till we're finished here, Eric."

"What, Mom!" he yelled. He tore away from her and ran halfway across the yard. "What's there to talk about?"

Eric's reaction seemed to her overwrought. She hadn't begun to understand how important this man had become to Eric. Was it possible Patrick was right this time?

Silent, stiff-legged and tight-lipped, Eric's wiry body radiated anger at her. The sun rose by degrees in the sky, and Bree felt the tension rising in herself. They hadn't been at each other like this since the day she'd put Eric's baby bottles away forever. There was a lot more at stake here than a battle of wills.

"My way," she warned softly. "It's got to be my way or no way at all, sport."

Eric ground the toe of one battered Reebok into the grass, refusing to look at her. A long, tense moment passed, and then another before he flung himself into her waiting arms. Her eyes fell shut and relief flooded through her.

Please God, she thought. *Please let Eric's Mike be someone I can trust with him....*

PATRICK MARQUET STOOD brooding at the oversized picture window in his living room, sipping at freshly ground, newly brewed coffee. The beverage suited him very well because it was a rare blend, because it cost twenty-three dollars a pound, and because its aroma, strong and rich, matched his image of himself.

This morning, however, nothing truly suited Patrick. All this, he thought bitterly, letting his eyes sweep over his elegant possessions, artifacts and modern treasures and luxurious furnishings. He could give all this and more to Bree if she would just have him. He lived like royalty. No one knew, of course. From the outside, his domain looked like any other bland tract house.

"But *I* know." He lived better than half the wretches who had hounded him out of Hollywood, and he would gladly, even joyously, have shared it with Bree. But the boy ruined everything, time after time.

Abruptly, he swung away from the window, trod across plush turquoise pile carpeting and peered into the fading silver of an antique cheval glass.

She could have it all. Where was the pleasure in hoarding it? Instead, she lived like ... like a pauper, paying him half her pitiful wage for rent. Instead, her cornflower blue eyes filled with some sort of condescending sorrow when all he wanted was to love her. Instead, she wrapped herself up like a mummy in her relentless devotion to Eric.

Ungrateful female, he railed. But then a pang of disloyalty bit at his heart. He was quite madly in love with her, and she was not ungrateful, just ... misguided. She had every right to be confused, married to a traitor and betrayed—worse still, condemned to a fugitive existence.

Hurriedly now, for he had an appointment of some importance, Patrick carried his Gorham china cup and saucer into the kitchen, grabbed the keys to his Mercedes, the one luxury he allowed the outside world to see, and bustled out to the garage.

The sound of Eric taunting that damnable baying hound intruded on Patrick's thoughts as he pulled away. His thumbs drummed incessantly on the steering wheel as he pealed off down the street. Always, it was the little brat who rocked the boat, who commanded Bree's attention, who spoiled Patrick's carefully scripted seduction scenes.

He guided the cranberry-colored Mercedes through the early-morning traffic on the highway. As always, the driving calmed his nerves, and within ten minutes, he sat in the Crème de la Croissant.

He came to the extraordinary little shop both because of its pastries—they were exquisite, light as cloud wisps and as delicate to a discriminating palate as his own fine blends of coffee—and because he had met Roy Danziger here.

Most of the Mesa County sheriff's officers frequented the greasy spoon across from the County Court House, but not Roy. Satisfaction flowed over Patrick like warm whipped butter over a fresh croissant. He was not without friends or resources, and Roy was his ace in the hole. In this city full of what Patrick thought of as unconscionably witless, unrefined dullards, Roy owned and drove only vintage cars, drank only vintage Pinot Noir at the Bookcliff Country Club and frequented only a select few superior establishments, such as this.

Patrick couldn't believe his incredible luck in finding, much less befriending, such a man in this backwater hellhole, but Danziger appealed to his writer's finely-honed sense of the elegant reversal. Like a wolf in sheep's clothing, Roy was a sort of Renaissance man in the plebeian position of a local deputy.

Roy had even remembered immediately the most subtle plot points in Patrick's triumph, his magnificent *River of Sins* screenplay. Roy Danziger could even name the categories of the nine Oscar nominations for *River,* including Patrick's own for Best Original Screenplay. And it was Roy who had made Patrick see the light at last, the path to his own restoration to glory, and Bree's. He'd write *the* script to end all.

Bree's story had every element of a smash success. The world's most dastardly villain, the beautiful, monstrously wronged heroine, and a hero of epic proportions. Patrick didn't think it in the least self-serving or egotistical to cast himself in the role of hero. He *was* her savior. Hadn't she once said as much herself?

First, Patrick had to get rid of the man who bribed the brat's affections with the likes of outings to McDonald's. Patrick *had* to reclaim Eric's good graces. That's where Roy came in, Patrick thought as he parked his Mercedes and entered the café. Danziger, with insights that astounded Patrick.

Still in uniform, Roy Danziger approached Patrick's table and clasped his hand in greeting. "Patrick, my friend, how are you doing? How's the screenplay coming?"

Patrick made a sour expression, thinking of last night's debacle with Bree. "Not well, I'm afraid. The brat is thick as thieves with his so-called friend, and Bree doesn't have the chutzpah to put a stop to it." His voice crept down to a pained whisper. "We quarreled about it last night."

Roy cast him a sympathetic, cautioning glance as a waitress drew near with his pastry and coffee. "She's not going to ignore it, is she?"

"No. She said she'll go meet the guy today and then we can all quit worrying."

Roy smiled. "Then all is not lost, surely?"

"Not yet, maybe. But the kid is stubborn. I'm not sure he'll stay away even if Bree tells him to." Patrick shrugged, unable to convey his frustration. "Any ideas?"

"A few, but they'll depend on Bree and not the boy."

"On Bree? But I thought you said I should get in with Eric—"

"Patrick, Patrick," Roy soothed, "you've got to use *all* your resources."

Resources, he thought, reassured now. *Yes, I'm not without resources.* His heartbeat began to quicken. "Do you have something?"

Roy smiled. "Something big, my friend. Really big."

Unable to contain his mounting excitement, Patrick's hands began to shake and he slopped some coffee over the edge of his cup. Patrick was enormously gratified that Roy had the good manners to pretend not to have seen it, just as Patrick pretended not to notice the chronic rasp of Roy's voice. "What?"

"I checked the construction permits in the county offices. Your enemy has a name, Patrick. It's Michael Tallent. Tallent was Joseph Preston's best friend."

He paused, nodding acknowledgement of the shock spreading through Patrick like wildfire. "Think about it, my friend, because here comes the *denouement* of your screenplay." He pronounced the word with such flourish Patrick was hooked. "The forces of evil, so to speak, the villain of your script is Eric's friend, not the dead Preston. Think of the irony, Patrick. Think. Preston is dead. She's been hiding from *Tallent* all these years. How do you think she'll react when she's confronted with him?"

A kaleidoscope of possibilities streamed past Patrick until, at last, he latched on to the significance of Roy's information. His heart thundered in his chest and his fingers shook. Triumph was within his grasp. In a matter of hours, confronted with the man from whom she had fled, Bree would cut and run again, straight into Patrick's waiting arms.

Roy got up, picked out a couple of fruit-filled pastries from the artful display case and then tossed down his cigarette. Fascinated by the élan of such a crude action as stamping out that cigarette butt on the highly polished white tile of the establishment, Patrick regarded Roy with awe.

"The kid will probably need a little pick-me-up." Roy tossed the sack of pastries on the table. "Let 'im eat cake."

"MIKE'S EVEN GOT GUARD dogs! Guess what they are, Mom."

The floodgates open at last, Eric couldn't seem to tell her enough about Mike. Bree shifted into reverse and backed the Eagle down the driveway.

"Real guard dogs?"

"C'mon, Mom. Just guess."

"Dobermans? Weimaraners? German shepherds?" Each guess brought a smug shake of his head. "Tell me then."

"Geese! They're geese, Mom, and they're the best." He sat forward and his eyes sparkled as he rotated his arms from the shoulders, palms out, in a backward circle. "They go like this to keep you away, and hiss like this—wsssh, wssssh!"

"Really? Geese that go wsssh?"

"Yeah. Mike says he read about them. The army even uses them to guard long stretches of fence far out on their bases."

"Why does he need guard geese?"

"To keep vandals away. He's got a lot of tools and lumber there."

"Oh. Is the house he's building so grand?"

"Well, it's not a mansion or anything, but he says it'll be special. It'll have three fireplaces and a Jacuzzi and a playroom that takes up the *whole* attic."

A playroom? Why does a man alone need a playroom, she wondered. *To tempt a boy? For Eric?* But instantly, she felt silly and paranoid. He probably had a wife and ten kids waiting somewhere in the wings.

"He says he's been thinking about building his house for a long time."

"I'll bet. Now where do I turn?"

"Just keep going. See, the turnout is down there where there never was one before. See?"

"Down by the orchard?"

"Yeah. There's even an old field of raspberries down there. You have to pick through a lot of weeds to get any of 'em, but it's real neat. Here. Turn here."

Bree glanced in her rearview mirror and then slowed. The turnoff from the other direction would be a simple veering off; this way, it required a U-turn.

"There," Eric pointed. "You can pull up next to the trees."

Bree guided the car next to a scrub oak, then shut off the engine and set the emergency brake. "Well, sport, this is it."

"Yeah. Will you like him, Mom?"

Butterflies seemed all at once to career wildly in her stomach. For all her stern, motherly insistence, the moment had arrived and she felt more vulnerable than she had in a long time. *He needs someone, Michael. I never dreamed of the things I wouldn't be able to be for him.*

"I'll try, sweetheart. I'll really try. Let's go."

She opened her car door and low-lying branches scraped and squealed against it, then slapped at her ankles as she climbed out. "Do you think he knows we're here yet? Can he hear us rattling around up here?"

"Naw. It's a ways down. But the geese do." Eric came around the back of the car and took Bree's hand, guiding her through the tangle of grass and brush. The little-gentlemanly gesture, so like him, touched her.

"Won't he hear the geese wsssshing?"

The high-pitched whine of a rotary power saw came alive. Eric grinned and shook his head. "He'll have his Walkman on. It's real neat, too, Mom, 'cept that he listens to some real old junk like you do."

"Old junk, huh? Like the Beatles?" She poked him in the side, teasing, and he skipped away, nodding and grinning.

"Yeah," he taunted. "Old as the hills and twice as dusty."

Eric took her hand again, then, and they walked together down the ruts made by countless delivery trucks through ancient peach trees until Bill Kendall's Ford pickup came into view. Behind the truck were the framed outlines of a steeply pitched roof. Pine timbers forming the rafters gleamed in the sun.

Bree breathed a little easier. The rich earthy scent of the orchard and freshly cut native grasses clung to air already shimmering in the blistering heat. These were the scents she associated with Grand Junction and with safety. Only the shrill sound of a power saw was different, but a man building a home could hardly be a threat.

Eric dashed off hollering for Billy. The older Bill glanced up from the plywood subfloor he was laying and waved in greeting.

"Ho, Bree! So you came down to see where the kids've been hanging out." He hefted his hammer and shoved it into a strap hanging from his tool belt.

"I thought it was about time, too. I haven't met this guy and Eric is so enthralled."

Bill nodded, then sank down between the studs of a load-bearing outside wall and unscrewed the lid to a plastic water jug. A beefy man, Bill's redheaded, sunburn-prone complexion made a shirt essential in the sun. Bree waited while he wiped his face on a sleeve and drank deeply.

"That he is, but then, so is Billy. Mike's good people, Bree, and I for one am glad he came along wanting to build. Had a long stretch with no job, myself, so it kind of takes the pressure off in more ways than one." He hesitated for a moment. His expression turned awkward, almost embarrassed. "Look, Bree, maybe it's none of my business, but I think Mike has done the boy some good. It can't be easy, raisin' a boy alone."

Bree acknowledged the difficulty with a quick nod, but refused to indulge the unexpected tears. The whine of the power saw sputtered and then picked up again in earnest. Bree glanced in the direction of the noise and watched as the man she supposed was Mike guided the saw through a sheet of plywood.

"Isn't it a little strange, building here? I mean with the economy and all so bad on the Western Slope, he could pick up a beautiful house anywhere in town for fifty cents on the dollar."

"Reckon so, but this is where he wanted to live."

Bill shaded his jade green eyes and watched Billy and Eric racing around, letting out war whoops as four geese, in mad pursuit, hissed and threatened with their wings just as Eric had described. A grin creased Bill's face and dominated his ruddy, sunburned features.

"Will the boys survive it, do you think?" Bree asked.

"Oh, yeah," he reassured her. "They love it."

But it wasn't the boys who drew her attention. The man who so enthralled Eric was naked to the waist and sweat gleamed in the midmorning sun on powerful shoulders and muscles bunched against the strain.

One knee bent on the sheet of plywood, his other leg stretched back, straining at the thighs of dusty, worn jeans. His narrow hips swayed to the music of his Walkman in a movement so unconscious, so natural, it was purely sexual to her eyes.

She could almost hear the music; she could feel the sensual, undulating beat. Flushed and oddly warm, feminine desire so long denied coursed through Bree so fast it left her weak. *The sun,* she thought. *It must be the sun.*

But in secret places where a woman knows, she knew the sun was not to blame.

Her eyes flicked guiltily toward Bill, but he was laughing at the antics across the clearing. She followed his gaze, and there stood the boys, swinging their little butts, making outrageous fun of the man's unconscious movements.

The whine of the power saw died and the high-pitched, infectious sound of the boys' laughter rang out. Mike jerked the power cord toward him and unplugged it from its extension. Bill whistled raucously and both boys stuck two fingers into their mouths and followed suit. Bree found herself clapping wildly with the three of them.

He raked the Walkman onto his shoulders, planted his hands on his hips and turned to bow. Bree smiled. But when he turned fully, his head cocked ever so slightly, and his shadowed, piercing gray eyes met hers, then Bree heard her own heartbeat echoing in her ears.

Michael... Oh, my God... Michael.

Her fingers, numb and cold as the running water in the riverbed of the Colorado, pulled at her cheek. Her eyes fell shut. Shockwaves rocked her body and she couldn't seem to remember how to breathe or swallow.

Her eyes were drawn back to Michael. Not an apparition, but a real man with a tool belt dragging on jeans that rode low already. This was not the memory-Michael to whom she'd confided every achingly personal shred of her life, but Eric's father in the flesh. Not a lifeless form with a permanent Polaroid smile in a picture taken long ago, but...Michael.

He turned away, picked up a rag and mopped his face and chest free of the splinters of plywood. Tension thick as sawdust choked the air around them. The fun wilted in the heat and the laughter strangled in all their throats. The thunder of a sudden, unexpected squall echoed off the far-away Bookcliffs.

Only the geese carried on, foraging in the grass. Michael swallowed hard. Shock at the sight of Bree registered in his scatter-shot thoughts. It wasn't supposed to have been like this, not in front of Bill Kendall, and certainly not with Eric and Billy looking on. Or himself sweating and half naked.

He could smell her perfume and he nearly choked on poignant, half-starved memories. *White Linen*. The scent was a part of her, like flax to the fabric. With granitelike resistance, Michael fended off the images of linen and any admiration for this woman's fragile, elemental strength.

She'd stolen his son.

He let the rag fall to the ground. His hands went to the buckle of his tool belt. He jerked at it and let it fall away. A rush of sparrows in the trees filled the silence.

Bree swallowed and gooseflesh swept over her skin. "Eric, get in the car."

"No!" he hollered. "You promised!" Flushed now with confusion, he ran around the plywood sheet and stood between them, looking from one to the other. "What's going on, Mom? How come you're bein' so rude?"

"I said, get in the car now, Eric. Now."

Her eyes flashed with panic and anger. "Eric..." Her warning tone was strident, but her voice cracked under the strain.

Eric glared at her and refused to move. Bill reached out to touch her shoulder.

"Bree?" Bill looked from one to the other of them, and then to Eric.

Eric screamed, "What is it with you guys?"

"Eric," Bree moaned. Her own eyes brimmed now with agonized tears.

Michael bent to retrieve his shirt and crammed his arms into it, then left it hanging open. He had to do something, anything to stop the panic in his son. He knelt and gathered Eric's rigid little body against himself. "Eric, I promise you it'll be okay. Will you trust me? I knew your mom from a long time ago. We were friends, and we'll...we'll be friends again."

Eric's tears dried up, but his body trembled and his chin quivered. He bit his lip, and his eyes demanded the promise once more. Michael let him go, then placed his hands firmly on Eric's shoulders.

"Man to man. I promise you, Eric. Your mother and I will be friends again. I wouldn't lie to you. Will you go get some new saw blades with Billy and his dad? Give your mom and me a chance to talk about this?"

Taking the balled up Kleenex Michael offered him, Eric nodded, then turned to Bree. "Mom?"

Bree nodded woodenly. What choice did she have after the promises Michael had just made? "An hour. No more."

His eyes hard on Bree, Michael took Eric by the hand. "An hour. Bill, would you mind?"

Looking unspeakably relieved, Bill said, "Billy, Eric, let's get out of here for a while."

Eric seemed unwilling to go in spite of having agreed, and Bree knelt down to hug him. "Go on, Eric. We'll... I'll be okay, and you will, too."

She swallowed and turned to Bill. "Take care, please."

Bill squeezed her shoulder in reassurance and then led the boys away. She heard the truck's engine turn over; she heard the gears shift into reverse. And then she heard Eric through the open window. "You promised, Mom. Remember, you promised...."

Chapter Three

Electric with distant lightning, the very air magnified the tension between them after Bill's truck had gone. Thunder clapped a few miles away. Anvil-headed clouds blotted out the sun.

The rain began without warning, coming down in sheets. Michael grabbed Bree by the hand and ran for the west side of the house where the roof was on and provided some protection against the downpour.

Bree stepped up through open wall studs and, pulling her hand from Michael's grip, she sank to the floor. Michael crossed the bare plywood floor, reached into his shirt pocket for a cigarette and lit it with a wooden match struck against his belt buckle. He stood with his back to the rain, and his left hand braced against a window header.

Fleetingly, Bree noticed his stance, his blue cambric shirt hanging awry, away from his naked chest. His eyes studied her, waiting.

A thousand questions clamored for answers, but she needed time to adjust to his being here. Eight years later, still she needed time.

"My God, Michael, what have you done in coming here?"

But he didn't answer. Her apprehension thick as ditch water, Bree couldn't think how to start. She plucked at a

loose thread on her sandal. "Are you . . . have you left naval intelligence?" The question was a far cry from the one
she needed most to ask. *How did you find me?*

Michael nodded slowly. "I stayed on. Five years. Spent
most of it searching for you." He flicked ashes onto the
ground, inhaled and fixed his attention again on her. "After Reinhardt died, your trail was stone-cold dead."

Thunder clapped again and Bree shivered. "It was sui-
cide, Michael. He gave up his life to protect my . . .
whereabouts."

Give her this, Tallent, at least this, he thought. "He was
dying anyway, Bree. He had an inoperable heart condition.
According to the embassy physician, he had only days left
to live, maybe a few weeks."

Bree swallowed and, for a moment, closed her eyes. "You
went to the embassy?"

"Yeah." His gun-metal gray eyes merely watched her, and
he offered nothing else.

She straightened, resentful of his condemning silence.
"Eric—"

"Is my son. Even Kendall saw the resemblance just now.
What kind of woman keeps a man from his child, Bree?"

"He never asked about his father—"

Michael swore. He spun away and grabbed an ax, letting
it slip in his hand from blade to the handle's end and back
again. "What should Eric have asked you? 'How come I
don't have a dad?' Or how about, 'Are you lying to me
about my dad?'"

Her chin rose, defying Michael's questions on Eric's behalf. "He's never needed anyone but me. Never." The ax in
Michael's hands brought all her anger roiling to the sur-
face. "Do you know what you've done?"

"No," he snapped. "Why don't you tell me? What have
I done besides befriend my own son?"

"You've... you've forced Patrick into a jealous rage for one! He can't understand why Eric comes here or why I let him go fishing with you.... How am I supposed to deal with that?"

"Patrick?" Michael sneered. Bree didn't know about Blessing's dossiers, including the one on Patrick Marquet, and so she couldn't know how much he knew of the man. Or how little he cared *how* she dealt with Marquet's jealousies. Michael began slivering a scrap of wood and the ax bit dangerously close to his fingers. "What is Patrick to you?"

"A friend," she railed. "Just a friend. He's Henry's nephew, and he was here in Grand Junction when I came. He's always helped me.... He may be a little too possessive, but I've always been able to trust him."

"Like you weren't able to trust me?" Bitterness poured out of Michael. If she'd trusted him years ago, none of them would be in this damnable mess.

Bree stared steadily into Michael's eyes. "It wasn't a matter of trusting you. I won't apologize for taking refuge with my godfather, Michael. Things were very... ugly. I didn't know I was pregnant with your baby, and I haven't really trusted anyone since Henry died."

"It's not the time you spent with Reinhardt I resent, Bree. It's the months—the *years* without my son since then."

"So you found a way to get to Eric behind my back! You've undermined everything I've worked so hard to instill in him. It's not right, Michael. You've no right!"

"Fear, Bree," Michael spat. "Out-and-out fear. That's what you've instilled in him. Do you know how long he hung around here with Bill and his boy before he even worked up the courage to speak to me?"

"It wouldn't have been like that if you'd come to me first."

Michael rubbed the ax handle against his throbbing temple. He ought to tell her right now that her cover was blown, how much worse, how *dead* she and Eric would be if he hadn't come. At the moment, the only thing he gave a damn about was setting Bree straight on the subject of his son.

"Did you think I'd come say, 'Bree, *pretty please,* could I see my son?' After all these years?" Michael laughed harshly, but his voice was ominous and low. "I don't need your permission to be with my son, Bree. Live with it anyway you can because I swear, if you so much as *think* about stealing off with him again, I'll hit you with federal kidnap charges."

An icy dread settled over her. He'd never forgive her. She drew a deep breath and tried to stanch the threat of tears. "What do you want from me, Michael?"

He looked at her as if she'd asked the most stupid question of all time. "From you? Once, I thought I wanted it all." His eyes spoke of promises he'd have made, the exile he would once have endured with her. Just as quickly, his eyes clouded over and he slowly shook his head. "Now? Nothing."

"From Eric, then," she demanded. "What do you *want?*"

"I want to teach Eric to use a hammer without blackening his thumb. I wanted to shoot basketballs in the driveway with him. I want him for my son." And he wanted it all without the threat of some hell-bent assassin threatening all their lives, but he couldn't tell her that.

His ax bit viciously into the scrap of pine as he thought of the years he'd spent searching for Bree. "I only want what you've had all along, Bree, all to yourself." Michael's eyes strayed through the pouring rain to the nearest raspberry patch Eric had single-handedly demolished. "I am his father. He needs me whether you want to believe it or not. *Me,* not some wimp like Marquet that he can't look up to and never has.''

"You can't have him, Michael. He's mine. He's all I've got.''

It was as close to begging as she'd come, he knew. If he had a measure of respect for her strength, however, he had none for her faithless heart of stone. Did she think *he* had one damn thing besides his son? Even one?

"There's nothing you can do about it, Bree,'' he warned, "at least, not without destroying him.'' His deep-seated outrage, pent up so long, erupted, and Michael threw the ax—sidearming it just as Eric had thrown Caruso's plastic pork chop. The blade bit into the header across the framed room and hung there, quivering with unspent force.

Bree cried out and Michael regretted his violence, but her eyes were trained behind him, and Michael turned. The pouring rain had deadened the sound of Kendall's return. The big man crossed the clearing with worry and agitation written all over him. In tears, Billy trailed behind.

Eric was nowhere to be seen.

Bree scrambled to her feet just as Bill stepped through the studs and wiped his face with a sopping sleeve.

"Bill?''

"Bree . . . Mike . . . God, I'm sorry. Eric ran off. We were standing in the hardware store, and Billy, here, made some snot-nosed remark. Eric took off like a bat out of hell, and by the time I got outside, he was gone. I watched the highway real close, but—he couldn't have made it back here yet, or home, either—''

"Oh, my God! Bill! Are you saying you don't know where Eric is?'' Bree cried. "He's just a little boy! How could he get away from you that fast?''

"Hang it all, Bree, I wish I knew—I called the cops right away. . . .''

The police. Of course, he'd have called the police. For several seconds longer than it should have taken her body to move, Bree stood, poised to run, to find Eric herself before someone else did.

For one desperate moment, Michael thought about the demented maniac bent on vengeance and Eric's terrible, childish vulnerability, and knew that the boy had been snatched. Fear slammed into him, but just as suddenly, he realized what an obscene coincidence it would take for Preston's avenger to have caught Eric running from Kendall. But Bree bolted and Michael snared her wrist.

"Let me go! I have to find Eric.... I have to—"

"Damn it, Bree, just wait a minute. Think. Where would he go?"

Bree fought him. "How should I know where he'd go?" she cried. "He's never in his whole life even threatened to run away!"

UFQ-9307 flashed through her nearly frenzied mind. If she hadn't been followed or felt trapped by Patrick and then threatened even by Michael, maybe she could have stood there rationally and thought where Eric might run. She struck out at Michael with furious, impotent blows until he pulled her in his arms so close that her flailing fists were caught tight between their bodies.

"Breezy, stop, please." He felt her body go slack against him and knew she was on the edge of her control. The tiny breath of surrender from her nearly broke him. How had they come to this? If she'd raged at him like a mother bear protecting her cub, he'd have known what to do. He touched her hair and wondered if he'd ever get the chance again.

His arms tightened around her in a gesture meant only to comfort. Her cheek rested against his bare chest matted with black hair threaded with silver. She heard the unsteady beat of his heart and smelled the honest sweat and sawdust on Michael. For one shameful moment, she soaked up the exquisite feeling of Michael Tallent's arms around her—shameful because somewhere out there, her little boy was cold and scared and getting drenched.

Torn by the impossibility of their situation, Michael stroked her hair and murmured soothing, gentling sounds. "Easy, babe, take it easy. We'll find him."

Determined to do so, Bree nodded and closed cold fingers over his shoulders.

"I never meant it to be like this. I would never hurt Eric, Breezy."

"No." She believed him. Her throat felt as choked and parched as the desert. *Michael.* He'd called her Breezy.

His voice gritty with emotion because after they found Eric he'd have to tell her it wasn't only him she had to fear, he promised her they'd find Eric.

"Now," she said. "We have to find him now."

Michael said nothing, only nodded. Bree's body stiffened again as she drew away from him. He caught shadows of dark distress in her eyes, and then turned to Bill, who'd stood by uncomfortably.

"Would you mind sticking around while we go look for Eric, in case he shows up here?"

Drawing his own little boy closer, Bill agreed. "Hey, man, that's the least I can do. Suppose I use the phone in your camper to call my wife? Cindy could hop in the car and—"

"I'll call Martha first," Bree interrupted, thinking Eric's sitter could drive to her house and wait there for Eric.

Their calls were made and every conceivable base covered before Bree and Michael headed for her car. Michael drove toward town while Bree searched the roadside for any sign of Eric.

They searched for hours. Every nook, cranny and wood storage bin in the lumberyard where Bill had taken the boys to buy the saw blades—and every hill, gully and outcrop for five miles around. Stopping every hour to call Martha,

whom Bill and Cindy Kendall had promised to let know if
Eric turned up, they searched for several more hours until
the rain began to ease off and the sun began to go down.
Real fear began to take ahold of Michael around dinner-
time; Bree's fear multiplied with every passing hour.

They searched together and apart, split up to cover more
territory. They combed the parks within walking distance,
the schoolyards, the homes of every friend Eric ever had, the
hospital where Bree worked, the eddies along the river where
Michael had taken his son fishing and Bree's own neighborhood. It wasn't until the sun had set that they turned
onto Thistle Ridge Drive and discovered a police vehicle
with its lights flashing in the near dark—parked in front of
Bree's house. A uniformed officer stood on the porch,
talking to Martha through the screen door.

Michael watched the color drain from Bree's face, and
understood for the first time what living lies had truly cost
her. The police—the threat of discovery any law officer
represented—were enough to send her over the edge; that
the police had Eric in their custody or had come across his
body—Michael refused even in the privacy of his own mind,
to complete that thought—put her into shock.

Before Michael could bring the Eagle to a stop, nose to
nose with the police car, Bree flew out the passenger door,
screaming for Eric. His little head popped up from behind
the dash of the squad car and he jerked frantically at the
locked door while Bree tried to open it from the outside.

The officer ran down the driveway and put a restraining
hand on his shoulder. Bree turned on him, and Michael was
right behind her. "Let him out of there, now!" she cried.

"Ma'am—"

His voice a commanding murmur not to be misunder-
stood, Michael cut short the cop's stalling tactics. "Let the
boy out and then we'll answer your questions."

Distractedly, overwhelmed with the evidence of Eric's safety, Bree watched the middle-aged officer. He obviously outweighed Michael and probably had the letter of the law on his side, but he didn't so much as blink before reaching for his keys. Eric scrambled into her waiting arms the moment the door opened.

He'd never held her neck more tightly. Bree buried her face in her child's rain-soaked hair, and tears of sheer relief spilled onto her cheeks.

Michael's head dropped with his own relief and sense of deliverance. Until this moment, he had not known how great his own fear had been or how tightly drawn his control.

"Are you this boy's father, sir?" the cop asked.

Michael hesitated. Bree's head snapped up, and for a second, their eyes met. "I'm his mother. This is our home, and I'd like to take Eric in and get him a hot bath and—"

"Well, I'm glad to let you do that, ma'am, but I've gotta warn you, this boy spent several hours alone out on the streets. State law requires kids under twelve to be under adult supervision—"

"He is," Bree snapped.

"At all times," he continued, holding up his hand to ward off Bree's anger. "It's the law, ma'am, and I'm required to warn you that if your son ever turns up alone on the streets again, the department will be forced to take a serious look at a referral to Social Services."

Though he couldn't possibly understand all the implications of the officer's words, Eric began breathing as though he'd cry again, and Bree snapped at the man and his stupid assumptions. "If you'll excuse me, I don't need to listen to this—this *drivel* while my son catches a cold." She loosened Eric's hold on her neck, stood and began leading him toward Martha, who waited at the front door.

Halfway up the drive, Eric turned. His chin quivered as he looked back at Michael and then tugged at Bree's hand. "Please let Mike come in, Mom. Please?"

Her eyes flew to Michael's, and she saw no choice. "Of course, sweetheart. Mike will come in and have some dinner with us after your bath. Okay?"

Given this precious inch, Eric went for the mile. "Can Mike help with my bath, too?"

He'd been through hell today. How could she refuse him so simple a thing? Bree fended off her equally simple jealousy and agreed.

The policeman offered Michael one final warning, then climbed into his car, shut off the flashing red lights and left. Michael walked up the drive, took Eric's other hand and the three of them walked together into the house that Patrick owned.

Bree had no doubt Patrick witnessed the entire scene.

MICHAEL PULLED ON the dry pair of jeans and the shirt that Bill Kendall had delivered to Bree's house in a brown paper bag, and then sat on the floor of the bathroom with his back to the wall, allowing Eric to run down. Given the trauma of his day, it was no wonder the kid was wound up like an eight-day clock.

Eric chattered on and on about his escapades as though they were just that—childish adventures. Michael thought he might never tire of listening to his son, but the fact was, Eric was dangerously vulnerable. Somehow, without scaring him, he had to make Eric understand that he couldn't run off like that ever again. Someone, somewhere—Preston's demented avenger—could be lying in wait for just such a chance as Eric's running away would provide.

But Eric brought the subject up himself. Splashing his cloth in the bath water, he squeezed it out with two mighty little fists. "Running away was a pretty dumb thing to do, huh?"

Michael cleared his throat. "Yeah. How come you picked such a dumb thing to do?"

"Because Billy said my mom didn't want me to have a dad."

"What were you talking about when he said that?"

The little tremor in his chin belied Eric's careful nonchalance. "All I said was you *could* be my dad if my mom said it was okay."

Michael's heart twisted in his chest. "Maybe it'd be better if you didn't talk about who your father is for a little while. Your mom might get the wrong idea."

Eric looked skeptically at Michael. "My mom never gets the wrong idea. She's...to-it-tive. Least, that's what Gramma Martha says."

Intuitive. *Yeah, sure.* In spite of himself, Michael condemned Bree's behavior in his soul. "*In*tuitive, you mean?"

Eric's head bobbed vigorously. "Yep. *In*tuitive. That means she always gets the right idea."

Michael had once thought his mother had eyes in the back of her head, too. Which didn't account for Bree. Ten years ago, Daisy had told him Bree was the most intuitive woman she'd ever known. But Bree had had one spectacular failure—falling, like everyone else, hook, line and sinker for Joe Preston's monumental lies.

"Yeah, well, buddy," Michael advised, "better forget the whole thing for a while, okay?"

"Forget what?" Bree asked, appearing in the doorway.

Eric blinked both eyes tightly at Michael in his version of a conspiratorial wink and grinned. "I forgot, Mom."

Bree glanced from one to the other of the men in her bathroom, and her eyes lit on Michael, who drew his legs up, propped his wrists on his knees and shrugged.

"Me, too."

For a moment Bree's heart swelled with bittersweet pleasure for the teasing "did you forget too" routine between them. "Okay, okay, so you both forgot. But you better not forget about never, ever running away again, sport. Clear?"

Again Eric grinned, and held up the dirty washcloth. "Clear as mud, Mom!"

Shaking her finger, Bree went to help Martha get off now that Eric was safely home.

At seventy-two, Martha was a retired Latin teacher, and the talents in her gnarled fingers had always far surpassed changing infant diapers. Taller than Bree by a few stately inches, Martha had brown eyes that were the soul of compassion.

"I couldn't love that child of yours more," Martha said, "if he were my own grandson! Whatever possessed him to run away like that, do you think?"

Bree helped Martha on with her sweater. "I don't know everything, yet—he was upset. I'm sure he won't do it again. Are you certain you won't stay for a bite of your casserole?"

"Quite, dearie. I've simply no appetite left these days, and today of all days—no, thanks."

Bree sympathized. Though Martha's pheasant casserole smelled enticing, Bree had no appetite left herself. But food was not on either of their minds, and Bree braced herself for the question she knew Martha wanted to ask.

At the door, the elderly lady turned and peered into Bree's tired eyes and the question spilled out. "Who is this Michael, my dear?"

"He's Eric's father, Martha."

Martha smiled gently. "I thought as much. Eric looks a good deal like him."

Bree couldn't force a word past the lump in her throat, but the telephone ringing saved her the necessity. Martha patted her on the cheek. "It's a good thing for a boy to have a father," she declared. Bree watched for Martha until she got into her old Pontiac, then answered the call.

"Bree? It's Mary Lipscomb."

Bree recognized the scrub nurse's voice. "Mary! Hi." Bree tilted her head to shoulder the phone receiver and began setting the table in the kitchen—three places. Mother Bear, Baby Bear and...Papa Bear. Weary. So silly... "What can I do for you?"

"Nothing, Bree. I just wanted to warn you—it's all over the hospital that you're in big-league trouble. The administration is in a dither over your flip remarks about bailing Sutterfield out last night."

Bree laughed. She doubted very much that Mary had a clue to what constituted big-league trouble. Marrying a KGB mole was big-league trouble, not to mention living it down in exile forever after. By comparison, exchanging sassy barbs with a surgeon was a tempest in a teapot.

"Bree! This really isn't funny. I'm telling you, it's all over the house—every ward, every staff lounge. Sutterfield squealed in high places!"

Her attention half caught up with the deep-voiced laughter and childish peals of pleasure emanating from Eric's room, Bree poured Eric's milk. "Look, Mary, I'm sure this is all just some enormous practical joke—you were there. You saw Sutterfield. Did he look incensed to you?"

"No, but the man is respected far and wide for his lightning mood swings."

And not much else, Bree thought. Although Tom Sutterfield had a first-rate bedside manner, Bree thought very little of his surgical finesse. But Sutterfield, like Bill and Cindy Kendall, had a son in Eric's class at St. Stephen's, and he'd given Bree copies of dozens of pictures of Eric taken during activities sponsored by the private parochial school.

Still, arguing the merits of the hospital grapevine with Mary could accomplish nothing. Bree was bone tired, and besides, Eric had come sailing down the five-foot banister in a clean set of jeans and a nice shirt. Bree hugged him while she watched Michael tucking a fresh blue cambric shirt neatly into fresh, faded jeans in her kitchen. The subtle intimacy of it stunned her.

"Listen, Mary, thanks. I didn't mean to discount your warning—I'll come back prepared for whatever happens. We'll talk then, okay?"

By the time Mary hung up, Bree had the casserole in hand and Eric plucked the receiver from her shoulder while she served the food. "Eric, honey, you could have gotten right into your pj's—"

"A man oughtta come dressed decent to dinner, Mom."

"Oh, well—" Confused, Bree hesitated. Her little boy was growing up fast around the man who was his father. Michael's small smile gave Bree another curious pang in her heart. "A man's gotta do what a man's gotta do, I guess. Will you have some wine, Michael? There's tea or coffee or, well, milk, of course—"

"Milk would be fine, Bree," he said softly, perversely pleased in his heart that his presence made her a little nervous.

"It's whole milk—for Eric—probably not so good for you, but—"

"Wine, then."

"I didn't mean you shouldn't have milk, I just thought—"

"Criminy, Mom! Just give 'im the milk, okay?"

Feeling like an idiot for the minor trembling in her hands, Bree passed Eric the gallon jug from the dairy. "How about *you* give him the milk, Mr. Wiseguy?"

Smugly, Eric poured Michael's milk. And then the three of them sat down to dinner. Only Michael and Bree understood the significance of this first meal together. Eric said grace, thanking God and all the angels in heaven for Mike's having supper with them. Michael's "amen" was appropriately solemn. Bree's was tardy.

Before long, Eric fell asleep at the table, and Michael carried their son to bed. Tempted to follow, Bree shoved a bit of rice around on her plate. She knew Michael must crave this moment alone, the chance to tuck in his sleeping child. The chance to do what a father does. Which didn't make it any easier for her to sit there alone in the kitchen.

By the time Michael returned, Bree had stacked their few dishes in the sink and turned off every light in the place. The house stayed cooler with the lights off, but the brutal truth was that she simply couldn't face the ineffable joy in Michael's expression for such a simple pleasure as putting his son to bed.

She sat in the darkened living room and watched Michael slowly descending the steps with his paper bag and Eric's battered old skateboard in his hands. She was surprised that he hadn't spent a little more time in Eric's room, and something of her bewilderment must have reached him.

"I can't make up for the years with one night, Bree."

His tone conveyed only the truth, unadorned with his earlier contempt, and he obviously expected no response. Nor did he seem surprised that she'd left the place in darkness. He sat down on the last step, dropped the paper sack and fingered the rough, splintered edges of the skateboard.

"I didn't think they made these things out of wood anymore."

Relaxing a little, Bree answered, "Eric picked that one up at a neighbor's garage sale. It has to be thirty years old."

Michael nodded. "If you've got some sandpaper around the place, I'll smooth off these splintered places."

"Tonight? It's late, Michael. Maybe you should go home. I don't have any sandpaper anyway—"

"Who is Sutterfield?" With his thumb, Michael spun the wheels of the skateboard.

"Tom Sutterfield? A surgeon. An acquaintance. But what has he got to do with anything?" A tendril of alarm began rising in her. Had Michael overheard her conversation with Mary?

"What does he look like?"

"He's tall, blond—thinning hair..." Bree straightened in the easy chair because of Michael's suddenly intense questioning. She turned on a lamp and asked, "Michael, what is it? What does it matter?"

"Is he a threat to you? Did he threaten you last night?"

"No!" Tom Sutterfield hadn't threatened her. The black Mustang had. With everything that had happened today, she'd almost forgotten. Almost.

Michael caught the fleeting panic in Bree's eyes. "What is it? What happened last night?"

"I—"

"Humor me, Breez," he urged, a powerful echo of her fear ringing in him. "You're in trouble. We're all in trouble."

Chapter Four

Quite simply, Bree had lost the capacity to feel surprise. For eight years, she'd lived in fear of this moment, of *knowing* that she'd been discovered in spite of her careful lies. Intuitively, she knew now that it wasn't Michael who had found her first, or Michael that she had to fear.

Unable to sit still any longer, Bree got out of the chair and went to stand at the picture window, her arms wrapped tightly around herself. Michael's intensity scared her, but nothing like what she'd felt last night. *UFQ-9307...*

"I...last night, I was out on call at the hospital until late—eleven, maybe. I left the hospital and this car—a Mustang—started following me. I drove faster—*he* drove faster. I slowed down, and *he* slowed down." She told Michael about driving back toward town. She told him how, in spite of the fact that the Mustang hadn't followed her after that, it had pulled in behind her Eagle right in front of the police station. Bree left out how she'd felt stalked. Michael heard the effects of the ordeal in every word.

"Did you go in?"

Bree nodded. "I had the license number. UFQ-9307. I'll never forget it. According to the desk sergeant, the Mustang belongs to a county sheriff's deputy. He—the sergeant—wanted to know if I really wanted to stick with my story—if I was accusing an off-duty officer of the law of tailing me."

A sheriff's deputy? "Did you get a name?"

"No. I can't afford the kind of attention I was already getting, Michael! All I need now is the Sheriff's Department investigating me for being a flighty, paranoid woman. I haven't so much as jaywalked in this city since I came, and this afternoon, when Bill said he'd called the police, I—"

"I know. I saw what that did to you. But listen to me, Bree, and think very carefully. I heard your end of the telephone call earlier. You're in some kind of trouble at the hospital, too. Is there any possibility there's a connection?"

Bree shook her head. "None! I know Tom Sutterfield—I've known him since Eric entered preschool. Why do you think that one had anything to do with the other?"

Because in getting to know the territory as he'd been instructed by the taped message, Michael had seen Oral Jenner, the hospital administrator, on the pretext of a joint commission inspection of the lab Bree supervised. And while Michael sat in Jenner's office, he'd heard the guy set up a golf date with some deputy. If Bree was in any sort of trouble at the hospital now, Michael couldn't ignore the possibility of collusion.

"I'm going to call Carl Blessing, Bree. You can't even go to Public Records and look up that deputy's name now without drawing scrutiny. Blessing can run a computer check."

"Why would Blessing get involved?"

"He already is, Breez." Michael discovered he would rather have cut off an arm than put that fear back into her eyes, but he had to make her understand what she was up against—and that her only chance lay in trusting him—absolutely. He put aside Eric's skateboard and pulled out the sheaf of papers Kendall had brought in a security box along with Michael's fresh clothes.

The papers contained not only the dossiers Blessing had compiled on Bree and Patrick Marquet, but a transcription of the tape Michael had heard at the Buckhorn Bar, as well. Without a word, Michael handed them to Bree.

Hesitant, she took the papers from Michael, sat down and began to read. Form and substance engraved indelibly in his memory, Michael waited.

SUBJECT: Sabrina Jean Huntley Preston, a.k.a. Bree Gregory. One (1) dependent child known as Eric Jason Gregory, born July 1, 1983, presently enrolled in St. Stephen's Elementary School.

ADDRESS: 14 Thistle Ridge Road, The Ridges. Mesa County Filing #1, Block 4, Lot 3, Grand Junction, Colorado.

SUBJECT'S OCCUPATION: Chief Medical Technologist, Mesa County Memorial Hospital; tenure: seven years.

Michael watched as Bree scanned the report, which continued on for no more than another page. She had less actual identification than the average illegal alien. No bank accounts, hidden or otherwise. No charge accounts, no credit cards, no debts of record. No property-tax assessments, no car registration, no welfare applications or Social Security benefits for the dependent child. FICA and tax records documented an income of twenty-five thousand dollars a year, taxes withheld always in slight excess of those due.

A Colorado driver's license issued to subject listed the name and address of a Caucasian female, height five feet six inches, one hundred twenty-one pounds, eyes blue, hair blond. The report named the brand of her hair coloring.

Bree chewed in subconscious distress at her lips, but without pausing, she turned to the three pages on Patrick Llewellyn Marquet. Again, Michael knew exactly what Bree read.

Benefactor of subject Bree Gregory, Marquet owned the house she lived in and the car she drove. Deposits of cash to his account at the Mesa First National Bank coincided with the dates of her biweekly paychecks. On initial computer scans, there were found no prior connections between Sabrina J. H. Preston and Patrick L. Marquet. Further computer searches were in the works.

Bree smiled bitterly. Blessing knew with what product she bleached her hair and yet had not discovered that Patrick was Henry's nephew.

She'd known that Patrick was once a screenwriter; she learned now that Patrick had been blacklisted a dozen years before, run out of Hollywood on a rail for plagiarizing Goldman scripts.

"Was this necessary," she queried coldly. "Digging up all this old news about Patrick?"

Michael shoved his fingers through his hair. "Yeah, Bree. I kind of think it was. The man is a fourteen-carat fool—and your whole cover depends on him! He *owns* your house, your car, everything. Suppose he wanted to scare you badly enough that you'd have no choice left but to put yourself deeper into his clutches?

"Or suppose he's tired of covering for you, tired enough to be bought off. Damn it, Bree, someone blew your cover. Someone sent this stuff to Blessing. You tell me who blew your cover if Marquet didn't. Who else knew?"

"Maybe you've engineered all of this to get even with me for keeping Eric a secret from you! Maybe you compiled these dossiers to build a case for legal custody!"

Michael's jaw clamped shut. It bothered him, thinking Bree could truly believe that. He *had* hired an attorney to begin the process of gaining custody—partial custody, at the very least. But *he* hadn't started any of this or compiled those dossiers to use against her. He crammed his hands into the pockets of his jeans and let her think about it in silence.

Bree regretted her spiteful words the minute they were out. If he'd truly wanted to get even, Michael could have snatched Eric away from her so fast she'd never have guessed what had happened, or have ever seen Eric again. "I'm sorry I said that, Michael."

He shrugged. "Read the transcript, Bree."

Her uncertainty growing ever deeper, Bree read the first few lines of what was labeled a transcript of a tape recording. "Vengeance is mine. Preston is dead. Long live Preston." She read on in horror. The last two pages were a collage of photos, each marked by a skull and crossbones.

Bree's heart thudded painfully at all the threats, at the purely malicious game of cat-and-mouse described by Joe Preston's so-called avenger. But the photographs sent a chill through her for some reason beyond the obvious—a shadowy, elusive memory that no matter how she tried, she couldn't bring into focus.

The papers slid from her fingers, raining down on the floor one by one. It was simply not possible to feel any more fear.

She didn't know who or why, but at last she understood. The players in this deadly game were all in place—Michael, Eric and herself, Martha, Patrick—not to mention the others in the marked photographs. Even Sutterfield's ploy with the hospital administrator could not be taken at face value. And then there was UFQ-9307. And still, after all these years, she had Joe Preston to thank for it, one way or another.

"How could I have been so wrong about Joe?"

Her voice was nothing more than a ragged whisper, an expression of self-torment. Michael could tell her that Joe had duped them all, the best and the brightest in the nation included. He could tell her that people fall in love with the wrong one all the time. He respected her strength too much to offer trite excuses. He wanted to hold her.

She wanted to be held, comforted. But real comfort was out of the question, at least until this threat to them all was destroyed. The thought of facing this night alone was more than she could stand. "Will you stay the night?"

Both of them heard the echo—she'd asked him to stay once before, years ago.... The night Eric had been conceived.

Michael's chest tightened for no good reason. "Why?"

Embarrassed, Bree glanced away. "Eric..."

Michael wanted to suggest that they not blame this sudden tension between them on Eric. He did the kinder thing, reacting to the threats that had motivated her request. It wasn't that he feared an assault in the middle of the night— murder in their beds didn't fit the flamboyant, terrorist style of Preston's avenger. "Nothing will happen tonight, Breez."

Bree got up to lock the door. "I'd still feel better."

Michael agreed because, in spite of his assurances, he would feel better, as well.

FOR A WHILE AFTER BREE went to bed, Michael wandered her house looking for sandpaper to smooth off the splintered edges of Eric's skateboard—and wishing for a hot shower to ease the tension and kinks out of his muscles.

He made the phone call to Blessing, though it was after 2:00 a.m. on the East Coast, and asked for everything he could get on UFQ-9307—on the whole damned Mesa County force, for that matter. But he never found the sandpaper, and the shower in the main bath, Eric's bathroom, wasn't functioning. Which left him only the shower in the bath off Bree's room.

He couldn't possibly walk by her bed without noticing the gentle swells of her body beneath her sheets. But he'd craved a shower for nights on end, and spit baths at the ten-inch camper sink didn't compare. A man needed a shower. *He* needed a shower.

He just hadn't counted on seeing the vial of White Linen on her dresser or using shampoo that smelled like Bree.

But while he stood under the stream of hot water, Michael forgot the small things that tended to catch him defenseless and off guard where Bree was concerned. It'd been a long time since he'd had a woman, but the avenger's game was on now. Michael felt the certainty in his bones, and his bones overruled the longings he felt elsewhere in his body.

Patrick Marquet had his motives. The hospital administrator played golf with a sheriff's deputy. A sheriff's deputy had followed Bree in a vintage Mustang. And then there was Sutterfield, whom Bree was tempted to overlook. The question remained: which were the puppets and which the puppeteer?

Michael dried off in the dark, wondering if his memory had overrated the therapeutic merits of a shower.

THE FOLLOWING MORNING Bree arrived at the hospital in her Eagle by seven-thirty. Ordinarily she'd have been at her desk even earlier, but she wouldn't catch Oral Jenner in his office before eight, and this was the second of her three days off. She went to the nearly empty cafeteria for a cup of coffee, and there she spotted Jenner deep in conversation at the furthermost table with Tom Sutterfield. Foreboding churned in her stomach.

Bree chose a carton of milk over coffee, dropped her coins into the basket by the empty cashier's stool and headed toward the back corner. Determined not to see conspiracy in what might be a perfectly innocent meeting, Bree intended to treat the grapevine tales as just another amusing diversion for the staff.

Acting on impulse before either man noticed her approach, Bree greeted them. "Good morning, gentlemen." She pulled out the chair next to the administrator and sat down. "Dr. Sutterfield! I understand you want blood—mine." Though wariness hummed through her, Bree forced herself into a nonchalant, it's-your-turn kind of smile.

Sutterfield's lips compressed into a thin, tight line. Every nerve in Bree's body went alert. He would have been handsome if his complexion had been less leathery, but it gave him the look of an aging Western cattle baron. He regarded her now as if he had nothing to say to her, and Bree felt nothing but bad vibes.

Administrator Jenner, on the other hand, had a great deal to say. "Well, if it isn't Miz Gregory." Pasty-complexioned, Jenner had always reminded Bree of the junior-high-principal sort—given to tyranny and overblown self-importance. This morning, he did nothing to correct her impression. "I'll forgo any commentary on your interruption and lack of any manners in favor of getting straight to the point. I will not have my staff spouting off to the physicians who serve this hospital."

"I did *not* spout off," Bree objected. "At least, not with any offense intended. Tom—"

"You see there," Jenner interrupted, poking his fleshy finger at her, "that is precisely the attitude, presuming to refer to a doctor by his given name, that I find so deplorable."

For a moment, Bree just stared in disbelief at the two men. She'd been on a first-name basis with them both for years. "I have served pancakes at Little League breakfasts with *Tom* Sutterfield. I've helped *Gloria* Sutterfield put on fund-raisers for St. Stephen's, and I've—"

"Nevertheless, missy," Jenner interrupted with a currying favor glance toward the silently denouncing Sutterfield, "in this hospital, you will accord this man the respect due him as your superior. I'm telling you, Bree Gregory, I will not tolerate this kind of insubordination." Nodding at Sutterfield, the real object of his ingratiating tirade, Jenner concluded, "If he wants your blood, I'll personally serve it to him—in a silver chalice, if need be."

Bree laughed, more at Jenner's absurd statements than in humor. Even the slightest chance that both Jenner and Sutterfield were involved in treachery ruined her sense of humor. "Oh, Jenner, come on! Don't you see? That is the most godawful bloodbank pun I've ever heard. If this isn't a practical joke—"

"He's serious, miss. And so am I," Jenner snapped.

"Well, that's your opinion," Bree retorted. "Why don't we just let *Doctor* Sutterfield speak for himself? Tom? Tell him! We were wisecracking about blood in the O.R., letting off steam—relieving tension, and this is just more of the same..." Her voice trailed off in the face of Sutterfield's strangely ruthless silence. "Tom?"

She could have sworn a look of apology skittered across his eyes, but there was nothing even vaguely regretful in his icy tone of voice. "You were, and are, out of line. Period."

Bree swallowed and her chin lifted a bit in defiance of Sutterfield's accusation. Something in his manner and in Jenner's reminded her of Patrick's vindictiveness. Jenner might be simply groveling after Tom Sutterfield's good graces—and she could almost forgive him that. No hospital administration these days could afford to alienate its doctors. But Tom Sutterfield had no one to grovel to, no one to impress by turning on her this way. She'd fed his son supper after too many baseball practices to believe any of this. How dare he?

She stared straight at him with fire in her eyes. "Why are you doing this? Why?"

Sutterfield shook his head and traded meaningful glances with Jenner—looks that insinuated she'd gone over the edge with paranoid delusions to suggest that he was *doing* anything to her.

"Perhaps if you apologize," Jenner offered.

Bree ignored Oral Jenner and continued to address Sutterfield alone. "I won't apologize over this petty garbage, Tom."

His shrug had a suit-yourself attitude about it. "Jenner—"

Jenner snapped to—he might as well have saluted. "I'm afraid that you leave me with no alternative but to hit you with a three-day suspension, Bree. Does that seem appropriate?" he asked of his VIP surgeon.

"Appropriate!" Bree mocked the wrist-slapping suggestion. "When lab staffing is already critically low? That makes a lot of sense, Oral."

Sutterfield picked up his coffee, swirled the dregs and then drained them. And as though he knew how ridiculous the whole affair was but tired of her challenging him, Sutterfield slammed down his mug. "Tough."

Bree rose from her chair and shoved it under the table. "You may not be able to run this hospital without the goodwill of the doctors, Oral. But try keeping them happy for the next seventy-two hours while the lab reports take all damn day to get out."

She turned to leave the hospital, but Sutterfield's parting comment stopped her cold.

"Watch your back, Bree. Watch it real good, huh?"

But when she turned to get a measure of his words in his expression, Tom Sutterfield's face was an emotionless mask.

WATCH YOUR BACK, BREE. Watch it real good. What did that mean? Was it a threat? A warning? Both? Which? Or did it even matter?

Bree shoved everything but the road ahead of her and the cars following behind from her mind as she drove home. By the time she pulled the Eagle into her driveway, getting Eric out of harm's way—and innocent, elderly Martha, as well—seemed nothing less to her than imperative.

She found Eric and Michael cleaning up the kitchen mess from a blueberry-pancake breakfast.

"Hi, Mom!" Eric chirped. Bree had never seen him so happy wiping the kitchen table as he was now. "Where'd you go?"

"To the hospital.... I just negotiated another three days off. How about that?"

Standing at the sink, Michael let the pancake griddle slip from his grip back into the dishwater and turned to dry his hands. Bree exchanged glances with him. The misgivings in his eyes made the smile she'd put on for Eric's benefit fade.

"How'd you do that? Aren't you shorthanded and all, Mom?"

"They'll survive. I'll take over for you if you want to go feed Caruso, sweetheart."

"Can we go up to the cabin, Mom? Can Mike come, too?"

"Eric!" Bree glanced sharply at her son. Since he'd been old enough to talk, he'd known the cabin near Ouray in the San Juan Mountains to the south was their secret. Only one man knew of it, the old man who'd sold the place to Bree, agreeing to keep the property in his name for a while. No one else, not Martha, not Patrick...not even Carl Blessing knew of her one last haven on earth.

His whole life long, Eric had managed to keep this secret—until now. His chin quavered under Bree's silent, angry disapproval, and his eyes darted between her and Michael, who looked questioningly toward Bree.

"I only meant to the mountains, Mom."

Bree understood Eric's strongly conflicting emotions. He didn't want to feel bad about spilling the beans, but by now, he understood truthfulness and honesty were Bree's highest expectations of him. He didn't want to feel bad about telling Michael anything at all, it seemed.

Bree took a deep breath. Eric had unwittingly saved her the trouble of lying to Michael about the existence of her mountain haven. "It's all right, Eric. I'll think about it—I'll even speak to Mike about it—if you'll go get Caruso fed. Deal?"

Off the hook, Eric nodded and hustled outside. There came the familiar slap of the basset hound's plastic pork chop against the siding and the still-unfamiliar two-fingered whistle. Bree's shoulders drooped with weariness.

Michael didn't doubt Bree would tell him what this little encounter with Eric had been all about in time—but right now, he needed to know what had happened at the hospital. Nearly verbatim, with all the undercurrents of facial expressions, Bree relayed the conversation with Sutterfield and Jenner while Michael finished up with the griddle and stovetop.

His own expression never varied from one of intense attention to her words. "Sutterfield told you to watch your back?"

Nodding, Bree got up to pour herself a cup of the coffee Michael had made. "Yes. Michael, I've got to get Eric out of here. I just can't stand the thought of—"

"You can't do that, Bree."

"The tape said to build your house. Can you do that *and* protect Eric every hour, every minute? Of course, you can't! I can get him out of here, Michael, and I will. Today. This minute, in fact!"

Bree put down her mug and turned on her heel to go start packing. Michael caught her by the wrist before she got near the stairs. "Damn it, Bree, you can't go flying off the handle. You have to think, and you'd better think about what other 'rules' of the trumped-up game there are. If you leave, people will die. Your friends, Bree, will die."

Toe to toe with Michael, Bree jerked her wrist from his fingers. "In case you haven't noticed, Michael, I no longer have a clue as to who my so-called *friends* are! Aside from Martha, I don't give a single damn! Besides, I will come back—as soon as I know Eric and Martha are safely hidden."

"Hidden where?" he demanded, following her up the stairs and into Eric's room. "What if Joe's avenger gets to both of us? Will Martha know what do with Eric if we never come back?"

Bree dragged out Eric's suitcase and threw it open on his unmade bed. "I'll think of something." She threw Eric's little-boy briefs and jeans and shirts into the suitcase.

"What, Bree? What will you think of? Who will take care of him the rest of his life if not you?"

Michael watched her frenzy as she slammed the suitcase down and then pressed her clenched fist to her mouth. He hated himself for having to badger her into facing the reality of ugly consequences. In a more perfect world, he'd have mounted his steed and faced her dragons.

The world was a damn far cry from perfect.

Michael put his arms around her from behind and rested his cheek against her silky hair. "Shh, Bree. It'll be okay. *Is* there somewhere safe for them?"

The comfort of Michael's arms was almost more than she could bear. The solid warmth of him made her shivering worse, and he only held her tighter to the wall of his broad, muscled chest. "I have a cabin in the mountains a few hours south of here—that's what Eric was talking about."

"Where, Bree? And how do you know it's safe?"

She wiped her tears with her wrist and moved out of the comfort of Michael's arms to face him and explain. Somehow, the words that would betray her one last secret failed her.

The only thing that mattered, that had ever mattered, was Eric. She'd done everything she could to protect him, and now, everything she'd done seemed foolish and utterly naive.

Running was still an alternative. Thanks to the ambassador, her beloved godfather, Henry, she had a veritable fortune stashed in a numbered Swiss account—collecting interest all these years to bankroll another escape, if that ever became necessary. Her whereabouts discovered now, she had the cabin, paid for in cash from her numbered account, as a refuge.

Michael saw the wariness in her, ingrained after all her years alone, trusting no one but herself. The ache in his chest had a lot more to do with the selfish need to be trusted than with resentment. He reached out toward her and though a tiny reactive flinch passed through her, Bree didn't move away. He touched her cheek with his fingers and cupped them under her chin.

"I'd walk through hell in flames before I'd betray you, Breezy."

Her throat clogged with unspent tears, Bree nodded. Her hand went up to clasp Michael's outstretched wrist. "Will you drive up with us? We could spend the night and come back early in the morning. Maybe the Mad Hatter won't even know we've been gone."

Michael knew she'd make it, then, if she had the humor left in her to dub their enemy the Mad Hatter. He slid his hand beneath her silvery blond hair and pulled her to him. His lips ached with the anticipation of touching hers, and he felt a man's longings swelling in his body. When their lips touched, the longing for her became nearly unbearable.

Bree watched Michael's lips descending toward her, and saw them open ever so slightly as they took hers. An exquisite sensation shot through her. He tasted her and their kiss deepened. She pressed herself against him and their embrace tightened.

And then the screen door slammed in Eric's noisy wake. Bree jerked guiltily backward. Confusion and longing and denial rankled in her heart. Mostly denial.

She didn't need Michael or his heart-knocking kisses. She needed her world—the illusion she'd created—restored intact. She had no business putting a dram of faith in pleasure like that.

The ray of hope in Michael's eyes went out. What had he expected? That with one kiss, he could restore in her the faith he deserved? The one instinct she should have trusted and hadn't? *The world-class delusions of a fool,* he thought. His slow, artful smile took deadly aim at *her* delusions. "My mistake."

Bree wanted to shrink from Michael's bitter sarcasm. The survivor in her refused to let it happen.

SHERIFF'S DEPUTY ROY Danziger sat in the Larkspur Cantina eating his fajita platter to the company of reruns on the bar TV set. His leg ached, and his head throbbed with the onset of a blinding headache. The shots of tequila had failed to numb his pain, which made the appearance of Patrick Marquet doubly unwelcome.

Danziger watched Marquet searching the darkened bar with a twist of his lips. Marquet was no one he'd have given a moment's notice but for his connections with the Widow Preston. That intrigued Danziger, intrigued him very much. So much, in fact, that he'd actually cultivated Marquet's company. For a fool, Marquet could be unusually clever, even insightful. He'd once questioned why a Mesa County deputy would remember anything about Joseph Preston, for instance.

"She's gone!" Patrick sputtered without preamble. "Taken the brat and the old lady and Tallent with her."

"She'll be back," Danziger answered. *The whoring shrew.* "She knows you're her only salvation."

"Does she?" Patrick whined, wanting to believe. "You couldn't tell it by the way she's behaving."

Danziger washed down a bite of his fajita with a swallow of water, thinking quickly now, out of habit and absolute necessity. Where would she go? "Of course, she does. Maybe they've just gone off on a picnic. You must keep in mind your coup, my friend. Your screenplay is worth any amount of aggravation!"

His agitation wearing off, Patrick nodded thoughtfully. "Of course. And she promised to be back in the morning."

A surprising relief poured into Danziger's veins. "Well, there you are. She'll be back tomorrow."

She'd gone to her mountain cabin. He'd bet his niggardly county salary on it. Idly, he pushed grilled beef and peppers around on his plate—and smiled, if only to himself. By the most serendipitous coincidence, he'd discovered her ultimate hideaway. He'd been looking for a fishing stream in the San Juans, and happened across an old man so unsuspecting as to warn Danziger that the "widow lady" didn't much care for strangers hanging out "anywheres near" her property.

The very word *widow* set off all kind of fireworks in Danziger's head, and he'd taken a huge, wild chance. "Sabrina... Bree, you mean? With the youngster—what's his name—Eric?" he'd asked with a mere, masterful hint of credulity. What did he have to lose, after all?

By the shock of recognition in the old man's eyes, Danziger had known he'd hit pay dirt. He'd promised faithfully, on the spot, never to return. The old man had actually believed him.

"Well," Patrick snarled now, "I've a thing or two to show Tallent."

Nodding in feigned agreement, Danziger thought Marquet incapable of showing himself to the door. Beyond that, Danziger contemplated the way serendipity favored the open mind—his mind. Such incredible good fortune to have stumbled over the Widow Preston's hideaway! And just as he gave thought to the vagaries of fortune, chance favored him again.

The local television news team interrupted the program in progress for a bulletin. An armed and dangerous escaped prisoner was suspected to be in or around the Telluride area. Residents of Ouray, San Miguel, San Juan and Dolores counties were advised to be on the lookout and to keep their doors locked. Telluride was one short jaunt from Ouray, and Ouray, gem of the Rockies, was an even shorter jaunt to the widow's cabin.

Danziger smiled as his headache faded. The opportunity for a little anonymous terror was simply too keen to pass up.

"Take hope, my friend. Tonight marks the beginning of the end."

Chapter Five

Bree was determined for Eric's sake to make their trip to Ouray seem a spur-of-the-moment lark, but her glimpse of Michael's shoulder-holstered nine-millimeter automatic pistol left Bree with no illusions. Once, in her other shadowy, nightmarish existence, Joseph Preston had had a collection of weapons to supply an arsenal—in her home—and she'd thought nothing of it.

Much as she accepted that a rose had thorns, she accepted that such a knight had armor and weapons. Joseph Preston made the world a little safer in his service to his country. She just hadn't guessed that that country wasn't hers. Stupidly, on the night they'd arrested the traitor and hauled him off to ultramaximum security, she asked, "Why? Why didn't you tell me?"

He'd sneered at her naiveté, and the last words he ever spoke to her were honed with contempt. "You never asked, Sabrina."

Bree swallowed hard while Michael pulled the holster from his duffel bag. "Joe had one of those."

"I'm not Joe, Breez." Quietly, carefully, Michael removed the automatic, stripped off his shirt and flexed his T-shirted shoulders into the holster.

Bree's stomach knotted. "He could break it down to its smallest parts and put it back together in five minutes flat."

She knew, he'd done just that a hundred times on her kitchen table—a point of honor in a man with none.

"It'd take me a half hour to do that."

"Is that supposed to make me feel better?" Her eyes searched Michael's. He'd meant to reinforce his claim. He wasn't Joseph Preston or anything like the man who'd betrayed Michael as much as he'd betrayed Bree.

Bree couldn't forgive herself for failing to see evil written all over Joe Preston. Instinct was all anyone ever had to go on. Why was hers so spectacularly, ruthlessly deficient? Michael's gun wasn't Joe's; Michael wasn't Joe. But the automatic—Joe's weapon—seemed a perfect example of her inability to put two and two together and come up with four. Suppose she was wrong now, putting her scant faith in Michael?

"Do you have to wear it?"

Anchoring the weapon in the leather holster high up on his side, Michael nodded. "Won't do us much good in my duffel bag."

Her eyes darted around the cramped space of Michael's camper, more to avoid the intensely masculine tufts of hair beneath his arms than the gun itself, settling at last on the shirt he pulled out of a tiny closet—one too heavy for the heat, but one that would conceal the shape of the leather strap on his shoulder. He pulled on the shirt, and left it to hang unbuttoned.

Outside, her son played with geese, innocent of the automatic pistol and its sinister implications. "Eric—"

"Will never know about the gun. I swear, Bree, he'll never know—not unless it's the only thing that saves his life."

She believed him. Heaven help her truly meager instincts, she believed him.

Within the hour, Michael and Bree sat down with Martha and Eric, to explain their sudden trip to the mountains. With her usual aplomb, Martha accepted Bree's explanations—that she was the traitor Joseph Preston's widow. Bree could see that his name sent chills through the old lady. Joe had been no ordinary flash-in-the-pan mole in the news and as quickly forgotten. But Martha just patted Bree's hands, conveyed her unshakable faith in Bree's innocence and then prepared herself to stay in the mountains with Eric.

Though Eric would be protected from knowing about Michael's gun, he, too, had to understand the true purpose of this journey to Ouray—to hide away—and why. In his typically childish way, Eric didn't care why they were going. He only wanted to know about the very bad man his mom had once been married to.

"Was *he* my dad?"

Bree's heart wrenched painfully. Michael shook his head. "No, Eric. He wasn't."

Despite his current fixation on wanting a dad, Eric didn't ask who his real father was.

Her relief almost palpable, Bree turned away to help Martha. By eleven o'clock, they were all packed into the Eagle, including Caruso and Liliput, Martha's ancient gray tabby cat, and they left Grand Junction headed north to Fruita.

They took U.S. 70 east, then headed south. In the town of Delta, Michael turned off Highway 65, east onto Highway 92, and followed a roundabout to Montrose. Along the way Eric, Martha and the two pets fell asleep, but with the detour, Michael was able to satisfy himself that no one was tracking them.

For a while, he entertained fantasies of driving east until the Atlantic itself stopped them, and after the road bore south toward Blue Mesa Reservoir, he thought of quiet, white beaches in Mexico.

"Do you think we could just keep going and going?" Bree asked.

Michael let go of the steering wheel with his right hand, and stretched his arm along the seat rest. A few hours ago, he'd wanted to shake Bree for acting as though his kiss hadn't meant a thing to her. Now, he couldn't keep his fingers from toying with the ends of her hair.

"How about passage on a slow boat to China?"

Bree smiled pensively. The fantasy was nice. The touch of his fingers on her neck was nice. But there was no way she could even contemplate such fantasies now with no better instincts than those that had led her to be so deceived by a monster such as Joe Preston.

Eric deserved the chance at a normal, happy, unthreatened existence. Until the Mad Hatter was out of their lives forever, Eric had no future. Michael kept driving, but when he connected again with the route to Ouray, Bree gave up her useless fantasies of a better yesterday and a slow boat to China.

They reached Ouray and then the steep, graveled road that fed into the rutted turnoff below the cabin. The air temperature had cooled measurably. Surrounded on three sides by fourteen-thousand-foot mountains, Ouray's own elevation approached eight thousand feet above sea level. Bree's cabin was another five hundred feet higher. The scenery was spectacular.

Michael guided the four-wheel-drive Eagle up one final incline and emerged from the cramped space in the car to stand in awe of the cabin—calling the structure before him a "cabin" was an understatement if he'd ever heard one. He'd imagined a log-constructed one-room deal and an outhouse complete with a carved moon.

He noticed electric service and a camouflaged propane tank back down the hill, and he guessed that Bree had left her road deliberately unkempt so fewer strangers would be inclined to intrude. But this was a mountain *home,* and he liked what he saw very much.

Bree begrudged Michael his obvious pleasure. Couldn't he see that the massive stone chimney needed a lot of external repair? Wasn't it painfully obvious that the porch sagged? That the porch swing was weather-beaten beyond repair? That the cedar siding desperately needed a coat of water sealant, and that the windows—every one of them— needed replacing? What business did he have appreciating any of this? The place was *hers,* hers and Eric's and no one else's.

Michael noticed all the problems. But there were flowers—primrose and pansies planted in a profusion of clay pots, and wild rose bushes that Bree's hands had tended. Morning glories climbed trellises off the porch. There were even pretty curtains hanging in the windows. He suspected it was only her fear of strangers that kept Bree from hiring out the other work that needed to be done.

The sun was already blocked by massive blue spruce and ponderosa pine and a thick stand of aspen, but shafts of sunlight penetrated here and there. Michael inhaled the scent of pine and listened to the sounds of a rushing stream nearby. A mule deer doe appeared with her fawn. Michael could spend his whole life here and never want for more.

He could almost forget the desperate trouble they were in.

Bree helped Martha out of the car and walked with her up the flagstone path. Whatever charm Michael saw in the place escaped Martha's elderly eyes, and she fretted over how thin the air was at this altitude and the problem of getting even so simple a thing as groceries delivered. And how cold were the nights, anyway? she wanted to know.

Troubled by details she hadn't considered in her plan to hide Eric and Martha, Bree cast Michael an anxious glance. She sent Martha and Eric on in, then turned back to Michael.

"Suppose Martha's heart does fail in this oxygen-sparse air? Suppose Eric pulls some typical little daredevil stunt and winds up with a broken leg?"

"They're still better off here than in Grand Junction, Bree. No matter what happens up here, they'll be beyond the striking distance of Joe's avenger." Besides, he hadn't told Bree yet, but she'd be staying on with them, which made those concerns manageable. "Come on. Let's get settled in."

"Michael, I—"

But he'd already called for Eric and stepped off the porch to help his son carry in the supplies and clothing they'd brought. Suddenly, Bree's plan seemed foolish to her beyond words. How could Michael simply ignore the troublesome holes in her plan to stash Eric and Martha out of harm's way? Left with nothing else to do, she gathered fresh linens from a cedar chest to make up the beds.

Michael caught her taking her frustration out on the sheets. "Suppose you quit second-guessing yourself?"

Bree jerked the gathered corner of a bottom sheet over the mattress. She resented the way he filled the doorway with his broad shoulders and his cocky masculine stance—but those things were about bringing this man—any man—to her hideaway. Hers and Eric's.

"Suppose you tell me why you're acting like you don't realize how hopeless it is, expecting Martha and Eric to manage up here by themselves?"

He watched her stuff a goosedown pillow into a pillowcase. "Bree—"

"Why did you change your mind?" she demanded.

"About what, Breez?" he answered.

"About coming here! About getting Martha and Eric out of Grand Junction when we know it will trigger the Mad Hatter—"

"That's why. That's exactly why."

Sudden understanding hit Bree and she sank down onto the unmade bed across from the one she'd just made up for Martha. "To provoke him?"

Michael nodded. "He's insidious, Breez. He drew me in, knowing that I'd come for my son—I'd bet he also knew the size of the wedge that would drive between *us*—not to mention raising Marquet's hackles. Jenner is breathing down your neck, and Sutterfield...who knows? Maybe he's just jumping on the bandwagon, getting off on his intimidation tactics. Everything you've come to take the slightest bit for granted is being jerked out from under you, and you can't even drive home without being followed. And we still don't know which of them—if any—is orchestrating this little campaign."

"I know all of that, Michael. But I'm getting a pretty strong feeling that none of it tells me *why* you changed your mind—that you have some hidden agenda here—"

"We've broken the rules," he said, interrupting, "and he's got to move now—to respond. He won't like it, but that's tough." The gray in Michael's eyes took on the shade of steel. "The three of you are out of his clutches, and I'll be waiting for him."

Bree stiffened. Michael hadn't been concerned about Martha and Eric being alone up here because, all along, he'd planned for her to stay with them! "*We'll* be waiting, Michael. I'm through with running and hiding."

"Don't be an idiot, Bree," he grated out harshly. He shoved away from the door and sat across from her on the bed she'd just made. He had to handle this right because there was no way he'd let her set herself up as a target. His forearms rested on his knees, and his fingers steepled down between his legs.

He let his gaze wander to the signs of Bree's existence here. An intricately patterned quilt hung on the wall behind her. Beneath the lamp on the bedside table next to him lay one of her precious linen mats—they were all over the place, and in their flaxen silence, spoke volumes on the importance of the cabin in her life, in his son's life. This was a place of safety, her haven, and the place where his son might yet grow up under her gentle touch if events in Grand Junction blew sky-high. He told himself if she were any other woman than his son's mother, he'd walk away and let her fend for herself. He almost believed it.

He could feel Bree's resistance to staying. "Breez, you need to understand—"

"If you leave me up here, Michael, I swear I'll hike down this mountain and thumb my way home."

"Eric needs one of us—"

"Eric needs a lot of things, Michael. Eric needs his father. I've never denied that, even when I chose differently."

Michael's fingers came apart. His soul was coming apart at the thought of getting himself killed protecting them when he'd only just discovered any real warmth, and he shoved one hand through his hair. If she'd only trusted him in the first place, long before she knew her body carried Eric.... Now, stubbornly, she again refused to trust his instincts. "You're staying, Bree—"

But the argument wouldn't get resolved now, nor the tension between them, for Eric was at the door, holding Liliput and trailed by Caruso, with his fishing pole in hand. "C'mon, Mike! Can't we go fishing now?"

Briefly, but with fathoms-deep emotion, Michael's eyes met Bree's cornflower blue ones. He was prepared, because she was the mother of his son, to climb onto the proverbial horse and vanquish her enemies—even if he died in the attempt. But for these few, precious hours, the only thing in the world he wanted was to go fishing with his son.

After they'd gone, Bree left Martha to nap, then went to her loft bedroom to make up her own queen-sized bed. Ridiculous thoughts crossed her mind as she smoothed the down comforter over the wide expanse of her bed. What would it be like to wake up with Michael there in the morning? Every morning? He was the father of her son, and she'd never forgotten what it was to be loved by him. The night Eric was conceived, Bree knew she'd never been loved before. Used, yes. Never so... loved.

Impatient, even angry with the direction of her thoughts, Bree fluffed the pillows. She had to remember that Michael was in this for Eric's sake.

ROY DANZIGER PICTURED the town a mile or so down the mountain from the whore's cabin. He dialed the county courthouse, one block off Main at the intersection of Fourth Street and Sixth Avenue, and listened to the ringing tone. There was no impatience in him. If it took them a dozen rings to answer, what difference did it make?

Danziger was a patient man.

A woman's voice came on the line. "Sheriff's Office. How may I help you?"

Let me count the ways. In his throaty, harsh-as-lye voice, Danziger laughed in what he hoped was a suitably demonic manner and assumed an illiterate-sounding accent. "Get me the boss, ma'am. This here's Lem Croker, and I'm holdin' hostages I ain't afraid to bump off."

With no small pleasure, Danziger imagined the frenzy his call was creating. How many fools did they think could get on the line without giving themselves away? He looked at his watch, aware of exactly how much time he had before even the fastest trace could be managed.

At last, the sheriff answered. "Croker?"

"Ain't you the clever one?" Danziger taunted. "Clyde Easterday's cabin. You know it?"

"I know it. Croker—"

"Look, man," Danziger interrupted in his rough accent, "I wanna chopper up here with a pilot. I want a million bucks an' I want it now or the woman and kid're dead! You got that, man? You appreciate how I'm gonna hurt this woman an' kid?"

"Let me talk to the woman, Croker," the sheriff said. "I've got to speak to a live hostage or there'll be no deals."

Danziger laughed harshly—as much due to his own amusement as because he thought the real Croker would do so. "You watch too much television, man. I'm for real. You got one hour." Danziger let that sink in for a moment, then gave the sheriff all the motive he'd need to authorize a full-scale assault on the whore's mountain hideaway. "Oh, an' Mr. Sheriff? I got myself a sawed-off shotgun, and I'll blow away any uniform I catch sight of."

Danziger broke the connection before a trace could be completed, then monitored police radio bands. Within three minutes, a sharpshooting team had been called in—with every expectation of shooting to kill before the psychotic Croker could harm the woman and child.

Danziger smiled. Satisfaction twisted through him. The fools hadn't even thought to check. There were no phone lines to the cabin.

HIS ARMS SURROUNDING ERIC from behind, Michael guided his son through the intricacies of fillcting their catch of a half dozen rainbow trout. Bree had no trouble imagining that he'd had his arms just like that all afternoon, guiding, encouraging, teaching. Loving. Imparting masculine lore that Eric might never have gotten. The moment seemed to swell in time, excluding her from all but an occasional smile at Eric's delight.

For Michael, every moment raced by, shrinking away into a past he might not live long enough to appreciate, so that by the time dinner was over and Martha and Eric were tucked into bed for the night, the tension in him was thicker than the tiny swooping bats in the night.

He stoked the fire he'd taught Eric to build in the stone hearth while Bree sat sipping a mug of coffee at the end of the sofa. There were a hundred questions he wanted the answers to, experiences he wished he'd had. Tomorrow he might be dead—or the next day or the day after that.

Tonight, he granted himself the small surcease of wondering how Bree's slight figure had looked, thick with his baby. Or if she'd breast-fed his son. His eyes were drawn again and again to those places on her body. He forced his thoughts elsewhere.

"How can you afford a place like this?" he asked finally.

Bree set aside her mug. "Thanks to Henry. Before I left the embassy for good, he set up numbered Swiss bank accounts—one for me, one for Patrick in exchange for looking after me. I'd have done as well without Patrick's help, but Eric was just an infant and—"

"How much money are we talking, Bree?" In his heart, he wanted to know about Eric as an infant.

"Three million."

Michael whistled softly.

"For most people," she continued, "that kind of money would be a staggering boon, I know. For me...it's... security."

"To bankroll another escape if it ever came to that?" Michael guessed.

"Yes. And now, if it really has come to that, fine. But what happens the next time, when the money is all gone?"

"How much of it is left?"

"All of it, except the three hundred thousand I paid for the cabin. Is it important?"

"Money is a powerful motivator, Breez. Blackmail, extortion. Who else knows about the money?"

"Only Patrick."

"What about the real-estate company?"

Bree shook her head. "I found this place on my own, looked up the owner at the county courthouse and approached him myself. A man named Clyde Easterday. The money was simply transferred from my numbered account to another one to which only he has the numbers. I don't know what Clyde's done with it now, but I paid a hundred thousand over his asking price for his silence in our agreement. At his death, or when Eric turns twenty-one, title to the property will pass to my numbered account. He's just a nice, sort of eccentric old man, Michael, and he only knows us by our first names. If he's involved in any of this I'd be very . . . surprised."

All very professional, very slickly done. "You always did learn well, Bree. Henry Reinhardt's tutelage—"

"Don't blame Henry, Michael. I made my own decisions, and he didn't approve of them all." The intensity of Michael's gaze felt hotter to her than the fire crackling behind him, and she remembered how vehemently her godfather had argued on Michael's behalf. "You are named on Eric's birth certificate as his father, but I chose to sever all my ties to the past, even it it meant that you would never know of Eric's existence, unless he sought you out. Henry thought that part was a—" Bree hesitated for a moment, unable to meet Michael's eyes or voice Henry's opinion "—a monumental—"

"Mistake" was lost in the shot of a rifle, and the lamp at the end of the sofa exploded. The cabin was pitched into blackness, save only for the meager firelight. Bree's scream split the silence afterward. She heard Michael reaching for his shoulder holster as he pulled her to the floor.

"This is the law. You're surrounded and covered, Croker. Come on out with your hands over your head!"

Michael swore. "Who the hell is Croker?"

Bree had never heard the name, either. Eric came running out of his bedroom in tears. Bree rose to go to him, but Michael shoved her back against the couch.

"*Damn it,* Bree, stay put!" In three lunging strides, Michael picked Eric up under his arm and carried him back to his room.

"Come on out, Croker," the voice on the other end of the bullhorn blared. "You haven't got a chance in hell. Don't make it worse with a couple of murder raps!"

From around the corner of the sofa, Bree could just make out Eric's pajama-covered legs straddling one of Michael's where he sat on Eric's bed. She heard him soothing Eric.

More shouting, more gunshots went off outside, into the air, warning shots. An owl shrieked. Caruso leapt at the door, baying and snarling, and the tabby cat, Liliput, dashed under the sofa. Despite the crushing outrage in her and the frenzy of noise, Bree heard Michael taking precious moments to explain that it was all just a terrible mistake. Eric responded to Michael's gentle urgency well, agreeing to keep Martha safe. Bree heard her son coaxing Martha to hide with him on the floor between their twin beds.

Crouched low, Michael made his way to the kitchen windows. The men outside ignited flares of some sort that lit up the night. Michael plastered himself against the cabinets and peered outside at a dozen uniformed men in a kneeling stance, a dozen rifles aimed at the door.

One, bullhorn in hand, shouted again. "I'm warning you, Croker. Send out the woman and the boy, now. Now!" The words were punctuated by more shots into the air.

"Hold your fire!" Michael shouted, his own automatic pistol pointed toward the ceiling. A dozen excuses for these Rambo tactics raced through his mind, and the first was that this middle-of-the-night assault was just one more deadly ploy of Joe Preston's avenger. Who in the *hell* was this

Croker? Michael knew little about local police procedure in hostage situations, but firing into a house in which a woman and boy were known to be held showed ignorance. "Hold your fire," he called out again. "I'm not Croker!"

The window beside him exploded, blowing shards of glass in all directions.

Michael ducked beneath the counter, but in the light of the flares outside, Bree saw a thin stream of blood running from Michael's temple. Caruso snapped and snarled at the door.

"Now, Croker!"

Her heart pounding, rage surging through her body, Bree tried to get Michael's attention. There was a trap door beneath the rug in the kitchen, leading to the root cellar—he could get out that way. Wiping blood from his right eye with his sleeve, temporarily deafened by the shot so close to his head, Michael neither heard Bree's cries nor saw Eric darting from his room—until Eric swept aside the small rug and tugged at the trap.

"Here, Mike! It's a root cellar—you can get out here!"

Kneeling, for a split second Michael stared at his son, and pride obliterated even the horror of the moment. He jammed the automatic pistol back into its holster and hugged Eric tightly to him. Still holding the boy, Michael jerked at the trap, which opened with a protesting groan.

Michael released Eric and took the narrow stairs until his shoulders were level with the kitchen floor. Reaching for Eric, he motioned to Bree to follow. She scrambled on all fours to the trap door and sat on one of the steps, cradling Eric between her legs while Michael disappeared into the inky black cavity beneath the house.

She had no intention of waiting for them to attack. If Michael was to have a chance of getting free through the outer cellar door, she'd have to distract the gunmen with their high-powered rifles and their idiotic assumption that she was being held hostage by someone named Croker. She eased from behind Eric and climbed out of the dank stairwell.

Eric panicked and grabbed for her. "Mom?"

She touched his hair and smiled for him, taking precious moments herself now to ease Eric's ordeal. "I've got to go help, Eric. They won't shoot at a woman, but they might at Michael. Stay right here, sweetheart. Do you hear me? *Right here.*"

Tears streamed down his face and his nose ran, but Eric promised. "I w-w-w-ill, Mom. Right here."

Touching her fingers to her lips, Bree blew Eric a kiss and turned away. Her heart knocked painfully beneath her breast and her breathing was tortured, but she focused on the door, stood and walked toward it. She started to scream that she was coming out, that they should hold their fire, but her throat seemed to freeze and it took her invaluable seconds to regain her voice. She stood to the side of the door and opened it a crack. She heard the mechanisms of a half dozen firing arms pulled back to spring-load shells into the rifle chambers. The ominous, clicking sounds sent fury roiling through her.

"Stop it!" she screamed, flinging the door wide open. "Just stop it! I'm coming out, okay?" She stepped into the firelike light of the flares and put up a hand to shield her eyes from the intense light. "Are you all *crazy?* Has the whole world gone mad? There's no one here named Croker!"

Gradually her eyes adjusted to the glare of the flares and she saw doubt crossing the feeble minds of the men facing her—even confusion—but they were a little late in coming to that conclusion.

The man in charge, the one with the bullhorn still in his hand, stepped back from her fury. "Ma'am, there's someone in there with a gun—"

Michael came up from behind the sheriff and stuck the cold steel barrel of his pistol at the bottom of his skull. "Call off your men," Michael threatened softly, "and disarm, or I swear I'll blow what few brains you have to kingdom come."

The sheriff swallowed, clenched his fingers and reached for his own pistol with only his thumb. He tossed it onto the pine needle-covered ground. The look he cast Bree was pure murder. "You're threatening an officer of the law, boy—"

"Your men, sheriff. Now!"

"Disarm!" he snarled. Hesitantly, carefully, each man put down his rifle, followed by whatever handguns each wore.

His pistol held firmly in place, Michael reached for his wallet, snapped it open to his military-intelligence ID and shoved it in the cop's face. "It says Tallent, not Croker. Michael Tallent, and if you so much as draw a shaky breath, I'll sue you for everything from harassment to criminal endangerment."

Bree watched Michael holster his gun and shove the sheriff in the direction of the cabin door as the deputies eased off and disappeared on foot down the hill. Every vestige of her emotional energy spent, she sank against the badly weathered cedar siding behind her. The horror was over.

Or just truly begun.

Chapter Six

Pale and trembling like an aspen leaf in a strong wind, Martha emerged from the bedroom she shared with Eric as Bree followed Michael and the sheriff into the cabin. Eric didn't move from the dark stairwell until Bree held her arms out to him.

He flew into her kneeling embrace. This was the second time he'd endured a nasty, difficult ordeal, and the second time he'd clung to her neck as though he'd never let go.

Wordlessly, Bree met Martha's teary-eyed, disbelieving gaze. Loosening Eric's arms, she pointed him toward Martha. "Gramma needs a hug, too, sweetheart."

Eric ran first to Michael, whom he clung to for long seconds, and then to Gramma Martha. The sheriff shifted uncomfortably from one foot to the other and cleared his throat as if to apologize. Martha's scathing glance warned him off idle words, and he apparently thought better of it. She gave him one last withering glance and then guided her small charge into the bedroom and closed the door.

It took Bree longer to clean up the shattered glass all over her kitchen than it took the sheriff to explain himself. His office had taken a call from a man claiming to be the escaped convict Croker, claiming to have taken a woman and child hostage. He'd even named Easterday's cabin as the location.

Disgusted and deeply shaken, the glass cuts on his temple barely dried, Michael traded rapid-fire questions with the sheriff, who claimed he hadn't been able to trace the call.

No, Michael had neither seen nor heard of Croker. Yes, the sheriff understood *clearly* that Bree was under federal protection, that no questions would be answered as to her identity, the use of this cabin or its ownership, and that not one word of this travesty had better see print. Yes, Michael granted, his military ID photo was poor. No, the sheriff hadn't thought to bring with him a photo of the escaped, armed and dangerous criminal he'd been after in the first place.

Photos. *Altered* photographs. Immobilized by the images the phrase suddenly dredged up in her, Bree left off sweeping the ceramic fragments of shattered lamp into her dustpan. "Michael, I—the photos..."

Instantly, Michael was aware of her new dismay. "What?"

Bree looked as if she'd seen a ghost, but then shook her head as if to deny it. Abruptly, Michael rose from the kitchen table and escorted the sheriff out of doors. They exchanged no more than a few words before Michael returned, alone.

"Breez? What is it?"

Sweeping again now, Bree fought off the sensation of being dragged into some dark chasm straight out of her past, her nightmares. "Nothing. It's probably nothing."

Michael brought the trash bucket and let her finish the job as an outlet for her tension, but he had no intention of letting the matter drop. The photos were their only real lead, and if Bree had any recollection connected to them, he had to know what it was.

At last, she finished cleaning up the debris left by the gunshots, and she stood staring into the fire with her arms crossed over her chest. "What was that all about, Michael? How *could* it have happened the way he said?"

Wanting to go to her, to hold her, Michael felt forever caught up in conflicting roles where Bree was concerned. He needed, as a man, to comfort her. But as the one bent on vanquishing her foes, he needed to stay dispassionate, able to assess and to act.

He cursed himself for allowing these past few unguarded hours. "Our Mad Hatter's brilliant, Bree, I have to give him credit. He's had to do absolutely nothing except stand back and watch the fur fly. But anyone could have made that call to the sheriff's office. Croker's name must have been plastered all over the news. Anyone with two brain cells to rub together could simply pick up the phone and claim to *be* Croker. All the Hatter had to do was be alert to the situation to exploit the hell out of it."

"None of which explains the most frightening thing of all! Whoever he is, he knows about this place, Michael. He *knows!* How can he know that?"

Hell, Michael thought. The catch in her voice made him want to take her in his arms. "We won't know that until we discover who the Hatter is. More than likely, old Easterday said just one wrong word to the wrong person.... The sheriff agreed to see the old man—"

"Michael, no! Poor Clyde will have a heart attack if he thinks something happened to me or Eric because of him— and that sheriff has all the finesse of a mad dog!"

"He agreed to go easy," Michael said, trying to appease her, aware for the first time that Bree somehow trusted Easterday, "to approach the old man only about whether he's been to the cabin or seen *any* strangers around. And he'll be able to do it without an uproar while they're still looking for the real Croker. The sheriff's just a local yokel, Breez, and he thinks he's dealing with the feds here. He'll play it exactly like I told him."

"Have you still got the authority to throw the feds in his face like that?"

Michael grinned. "Nope."

Bree smiled shakily. The absurdity of the whole incident was too much. Twice now, the sheriff had been hood-winked—once by someone claiming to be Croker, and then by Michael's name-dropping, nonexistent clout. In the end, people believed what they wanted to believe or were told to believe. Just as so many had accepted that she must have been an accomplice to Joseph Preston.

Even she had believed what she wanted to believe—that Joe was one of the heroes. Everyone had been conned by Joe, true. But Bree couldn't forgive herself. She'd lived with him. *She* should have known.

Somehow, she should have known.

The sheriff was just one more dupe in a long, long line. And so she laughed, and the strain of the past forty-eight hours turned her laughter to tears.

Michael fought the nearly overpowering urge to take her into his arms and carry her far away from this deadly game of cat-and-mouse. But to protect her, he had to know what she'd remembered. "Breez, sweetheart, you've got to tell me what you were thinking about the photographs. Do you know where they were taken, who took them?"

"No!" Bree's hands fluttered for a moment and then crossed her body. Her arms folded beneath her breasts. Wary as a doe, her eyes flew to him.

"The pictures have nothing to do with anything, Michael. When you showed me the photos Blessing received, I was upset because it was obvious what the markings meant, but I was...I was alarmed for some other reason I couldn't seem to grasp. But when the sheriff said something about your ID photo being poor, it came back to me."

"What came back to you, Breez?" Michael prodded gently.

"I—well, it was when I was working at the FBI forensic labs, right after Joe and I—"

Her voice faltered, and Michael thought she must be unwilling even now to acknowledge her marriage to Joe Preston.

"Anyway," she continued, "I worked horrendous hours—middle of the night, weekends, holidays. One night, I came home and Joe was watching some reruns of *Twilight Zone*—not just watching, Michael. He was glued to this show, and I swear he didn't even know I was in the same room with him—or on the same planet.

"I came in at the middle of the show, so I don't remember that clearly what it was about, but I know the...the main character had developed a way to alter a person's appearance by altering the photograph as it developed. Joe was so hooked on that premise—and now we get those pictures marked up like that—I—oh, God. How could I have been so wrong about him?"

Michael had stood there watching her control disintegrating and he couldn't stand it anymore. Somewhere between the tightness of his chest and the ache in him that was purely masculine, Michael gave up the struggle. Her strength awed him. Even now, even while she relived one more moment that she believed should have tipped her off to the monster she'd married, Michael knew that she'd done what she had to do.

"I'm tired, Michael. So tired," she murmured distractedly. "The consequences only go on and on." Oh, God, she was so very tired of living with unforgiving consequences, of carrying on anyway, of being the strong one. Then Michael's arms went around her and the part of her that was so dreadfully tired yielded.

Michael gloried in feeling anything positive and powerful and promising because for so many years, he hadn't allowed himself such simple, uncomplicated joy. He'd had small satisfactions—getting himself through one day after another—but he hadn't known this aching, bittersweet pleasure since the last time he'd set himself the task of easing Bree's heart.

"Bree." He brought her closer still and caressed her hair and beneath it, her slender, womanly neck. Desires consumed him like fire consumes brittle hardwood. He wanted her. But more, he needed to reassure her. On a basic human level, the fear of someone as evil and deceptive as Joseph Preston was very, very real.

"I met Blessing," he said, "at a bar in Laramie back in May. He told me you'd been found, where you were. But there was a jukebox in the bar and this kid started plugging it with quarters. I think I only half heard what Blessing had to say because every move that kid made reminded me of Joe."

Michael threaded his fingers through her hair, over and over again. The feeling was just so damned...pleasing. Bree sighed with what Michael took for pleasure. A heaviness descended on him, in him. "Joe was what he was, Breez, and if it weren't for him, none of this would be happening. Everything is bound to remind us of him."

Bree reveled at the exquisite sensations of Michael's body so close to hers, in his fascination for her hair. She swallowed hard and concentrated for a moment. "Tom Sutterfield has a jukebox. He had a fifties party this spring—right after he bought it—to celebrate."

Michael's throat tightened and his hand splayed possessively on her back. "Did you go?"

"No. His wife, Gloria, mentioned the juke when she called with the invitation, but I... It reminded me of Joe, too."

Hating himself for the question, Michael couldn't keep his rusty voice from asking it. "Anything ever remind you of me, Breez?"

Bree pulled away enough to meet his gaze. "Everything, Michael. Every time I looked at Eric, every time he passed some minor milestone—first tooth, first steps, first Band-Aid—I'd tell you. There was this memory Michael in my head, you see, and I... and even this afternoon when you went off with Eric, I was telling the memory Michael how— how jealous I was of you, and it was you I was telling, see? Isn't that... isn't that just too ironic—"

His mouth smoothed her lips to cut short her precious, agonized confession. He hadn't known, hadn't heard her telling the memory Michael all those things, and it killed him that he'd missed them. But he knew now that in her heart, she'd wanted to share those moments with him. It wasn't so much that she hadn't trusted him as that she hadn't trusted herself and the unalterable truth that she'd once fallen for Joe Preston's line. He guided her head to his shoulder. His other hand clamped tightly to her bottom, fitting her closer to him.

Bree reacted to the fire in him, curling recklessly into his embrace. She was beyond thought and she simply reacted as a woman. She brought her hands to his chest beneath his torn shirt and stroked him. She brought her lips to his and opened her mouth to his tongue.

He mouthed her name, *Breezy*, against her lips, and she was lost. This heart glimpse of something exquisite overwhelmed her. She wanted that encompassing kiss more than she had ever wanted anything in her life. And even the encounter of her fingers with his shoulder holster, the leather warm and pliant in the slight hollow beside his pectorals inflamed her. Her fingers slid beneath the leather. She used her grip for leverage to pull him closer to her.

Michael broke off their kiss. It was her blatant, reckless disregard of his gun holster, so symbolic of everything she hated, that brought Michael crashing back to reality. If he ever saw regret in her eyes for what happened between them, it'd kill him. And he knew that he'd see that regret if he made love to her now when she was more vulnerable than she'd ever been.

He lifted her, as easily as if she weighed no more than their small son, and carried her to the loft ladder, where he helped her up. He pulled aside the comforter on her bed and then the sheet, and lay down next to her. For an hour, maybe two, he would hold her, nothing more. Even as her body stilled against him, he knew that she understood; terror and ugliness would confront them again.

Tonight, for the few hours that remained of it, he would hold her, keeping her demons at bay as if there were no tomorrow.

ONE DIDN'T ACTUALLY SEE the sun rise in Ouray, blocked as it was by the thirteen-thousand-foot Wild Horse Peak to the east. But the indirect daylight was sufficient for Michael to scavenge around for spent rifle shells. Even now, it enraged him that sharpshooters could have considered Croker so dangerous, they would shoot first and ask questions later.

He resented the intrusion, the Rambo mentality, the torn-up appearance of the alpine grasses and pine needles. It reminded him once again of the intimidation tactics that had coerced Bree into disappearing eight years ago.

He picked up a fallen branch and made an effort to restore the floor of the forest to its former state, then headed inside to toss out the spent shells. Bree sat at the kitchen table, poring over the pictures Blessing had been sent, the skulls and crossbones and the underlying photos.

Bree glanced up as Michael entered, instantly aware of his presence. He came close, looked over her shoulder at the photos, then turned away to discard a handful of shell casings.

He poured himself a cup of the coffee she'd brewed and sat down opposite her. "What do you see, Breez?"

He wasn't wearing his holster, just an undershirt and a pair of low-slung jeans, and for a distracted moment, she saw only his chest, only the swirls of silver-threaded black hair. Martha's cat, Liliput, jumped into his lap, and then it was Michael's hands, absently stroking the cat, that she saw.

Bree forced her attention from his lean, strong fingers back to the photos. "Did you ever notice the background?" she asked. "I didn't study these very closely the first time you showed them to me. Look," she said, pointing. "These four are all outside shots—Lincoln Park, maybe, from the looks of the trees in the background."

Bree's face was scrubbed clean and left bare this morning, and the bruise-colored shadows under her blue eyes stirred Michael's protective instincts anew. He unlocked his tongue from the pit of his mouth and paid attention instead to Bree's point.

"Lincoln Park?" he asked. "How can you tell that? They're all closeups, taken with a thirty-five millimeter camera and a telephoto lens. The backgrounds aren't even in focus."

"No, they aren't," she murmured. "I can't tell you why I think that, why the park even came to mind...but—"

"Okay, go with it, Breez. When were these four people at the park at the same time? Blessing got the photos in late April, so it would have had to be—"

"April! The preseason Little League picnic! Michael, that's it! These three—" Bree broke off when Martha came out of the bedroom.

Her expression weary and worried, Martha helped herself to the coffee. "Eric's still asleep. Don't mind me. I think I'll just go out and sit in the porch swing."

"Sure, Martha. Thank you."

After she'd gone, taking the cat with her, Michael gestured at the photos Bree had been studying and pointed at the women she had identified as the secretary at St. Stephen's and photos of two of Eric's preschool teachers. "Did he pick the people you would count as your closest friends?"

Bree nodded, sick at heart over the things the Hatter seemed to know. "We all belong to the same mothers' group at church. They all have families, Michael, children who depend on them. And, of course, Martha. These other two are at St. Stephen's now. This is Anne Benedict, the director, and Sister Marguerite," Bree pointed out, "will be Eric's teacher this fall."

Michael studied the photos again. "Don't you think it's weird that there are no men in the photos—not even Patrick?"

Bree shrugged and met Michael's gaze directly. "Not so curious. There hasn't been a parade of men in my life, Michael."

"What about Sutterfield?"

"Well, he's—oh, my God... Michael, he could have taken these pictures! He's a terrible shutterbug. He drives Gloria to distraction because she hates her picture to be taken... His camera is a thirty-five millimeter, I'm sure."

"That doesn't necessarily make him the one who took these, Bree. Does he develop and print them himself?"

"No, I don't think so. Whenever he's given me a batch, they've come in a Fotomat envelope."

"Then the skulls and crossbones had to go on during the printing—or on the negatives. Even if Sutterfield took them, someone else did that." Idly, Michael's fingers traced the eerie, threatening marks.

But soon, Bree gathered the photos from beneath his fingers, batched them into a neat little pile and replaced them in his duffel bag. He thought she probably couldn't tolerate looking at them anymore.

"Well, it's worth confronting Sutterfield, don't you think?"

"Could you do that, Breez?" Michael scoffed. "Could you really go to him and ask whether or not he took *these* pictures?"

"As well as you could," she snapped. "I haven't survived this long on shrinking-violet instincts, Tallent."

"I could take the creep apart with my bare hands for what he's already done," Michael retorted angrily. "I'm not going to apologize for warning you over what you could be getting into."

"Oh, gee! And I thought it would all be just a simple little parlor game!"

She left the table again, opened the ancient refrigerator, dug out a dozen eggs and began breaking them into a bowl. "Don't underestimate me, Michael. I'm a survivor, in case you haven't figured that out yet. And if I had to, I'd take on Satan himself. I wouldn't show Sutterfield *these* pictures, anyway. I'd just ask him for the negatives of whatever he took at that picnic."

He shouldn't have been surprised, Michael thought. She *was* a woman with powerful survival instincts, and he had to admit that her approach was basically sound. It gave away nothing to ask Sutterfield for those negatives, whereas showing him the marred photos would. If he were truly guiltless, Sutterfield might question the request, but he'd have no reason to refuse. If not, if he had some real role in this whole setup or if he'd hatched the whole scam, well... things would come to a head fast.

"What if it's Sutterfield behind this whole thing, Breez?"

"That's crazy. Why would he do that after all this time?"

"To quote Blessing, '*Why* almost never matters.'"

Bree tossed the egg shells into the trash. "Sutterfield doesn't have the moxie for this, Michael. You know, Joe had an ego that wouldn't quit, but there was something about him, some... force of personality, I guess you'd call it. Whatever else he was, Joe was never unsure of himself or a coward. Sutterfield is.''

Once again, Michael was impressed, even awed by Bree's perceptions. She trusted old Clyde Easterday. She had Sutterfield's number down to the last digit. Michael only wished she could give her fourteen-carat intuition more credence where he was concerned.

She'd never trusted him, and it galled Michael to no end. There wasn't any way he could keep the bitter edge off his words. "What if he was one of Joe's cronies? What if you're wrong now...?''

"Like I was with Joe?'' Bree finished his unspoken challenge. She couldn't stifle her own bitterness. "You wanted me to trust you, Michael, I know that. And I know you'll never forgive my faithlessness, but I can't change any of that now.''

Her heart twisted because it hurt to admit that nothing would ever be the same again between them because she hadn't trusted him when it mattered most.

"I trust you now, Michael. And if I'm wrong about Tom Sutterfield, then this will all be over sooner than we expected, won't it?''

THE TENSION BETWEEN THEM went unresolved all the way back to Grand Junction. Bree's mind kept coming back to Michael's reluctant observation.... *Our Mad Hatter's brilliant, Bree, I have to give him credit. He's had to do absolutely nothing except stand back and watch the fur fly.* Whoever the Hatter was, he'd managed just as effortlessly to set them at each other's throats.

Nothing could be more pointless—or harmful. They had to confront Sutterfield tonight, and they had to do it with a united front.

Michael called Bill Kendall as soon as they arrived home. From Bill's resolute expression when he arrived moments later, Bree assumed Michael had told him exactly why he'd been asked to stay with Martha and Eric. They needed a bodyguard—it was as simple and as dangerous as that—while she and Michael were gone. Though she'd never before seen this side of Bill, Bree pitied the man fool enough to tangle with him.

Back in her car on the way to Sutterfield's home, Bree asked, "How far do you trust Bill Kendall?"

"It's a little late to be asking that, isn't it?"

"Tell me *why* you trust him, then—and turn left at the second corner."

"He brought Billy along when he offered a bid to do the foundation on my house. Eric was with Billy. It never occurred to me that Eric would be with someone you didn't trust." Michael shrugged. "I have faith in you, Bree, and in your instincts, even if you don't. There are other things, of course. Blessing came up with a clean report on Kendall. He has plenty of money stashed away from his football days, but he works as if he didn't. He's humble as apple pie around the job, and he's happily married—and conceited about that. If he had a mean bone in his body, he busted it linebacking.... I guess you could say I trust him."

Bree nodded, but the closer they came to Sutterfield's place, the greater the tension rose in her.

Michael seemed attuned to her rising dismay. "Breez," he offered quietly, "I can do this alone."

She shook her head. "Together, Michael, or not at all. Next left, second house on the right."

Michael pulled into the circular drive in front of a brick Tudor-style home. He got out and came around to help her out before she could open her door. He held her hand as she got out of the car, then pulled her right into his arms—and kissed her, long and solidly.

Desire raced through her, right there on Sutterfield's drive. Her fingers touched her lips in bewilderment. "Why did you do that?" she whispered.

"You needed it," he retorted. "Lighten up, Breez, or you won't last the first round. Besides, we're taking every opportunity to show these bastards a united front." His gaze darted upward to indicate a figure watching them from an upstairs window. He smiled at her as if she belonged to him, and cuffed her chin with a knuckle. "Smile, sweetheart, or it won't work."

She smiled over clenched teeth. "Wipe that look off your face, Tallent. I don't like the implications." But her heart warmed. If he'd meant to distract her, he'd succeeded.

He grinned, and his fingers did wicked things to her nerves, trailing up her bare arms, closer to her breasts. "Suffer with it, Breez."

Her eyes fluttered shut in pleasure from her suffering at his hands. "Shouldn't we go—"

"No," he murmured, his voice low. The slightest pressure of his hand to the backs of her arms brought her closer and he touched his lips to her cheeks, her temple, her jaw. "The longer we stand out here, the more worried Sutterfield gets.... Smile, Breez. We're having fun. Tell me why *you* trust Kendall."

Bree smiled, flirting. "*Because* he's conceited about his love life," she answered, remembering Michael's comments about Bill's happy marriage. "He's got a right to be conceited."

Michael caught her chin and looked her square in the eyes. "How would you know?"

"Cindy told me. Did you think only men talk, Tallent?"

Lord, Michael thought, the woman would drive him crazy! When she chose to turn on the charm, Bree turned it on all the way. His voice grew more gravelly. "Why are you on this 'Tallent' kick, Bree?"

He watched the siren smile edge out of her eyes.

"It helps me keep you separate from the memory Michael in my head."

Oh, God. He wanted nothing more than to *be* separate from that unreal image in her memory, to be a real man to her and do to her what a real man does with a woman. With her. Michael cursed. Grabbing her wrist, he led the way to the entry.

Sutterfield opened the door almost before the chimes rang out. Taking one measured, unbending look at Michael, he spoke to her. "You've wasted your time coming here. I have nothing to say to you, Bree." He gave the door a push trying to shut it in their faces. Michael stuck his foot out and jammed it open.

"I'd as soon shove my fist down your throat as look at you, *Doctor* Sutterfield, but the lady would like to talk."

Sutterfield shrugged, cast Bree a scathing look that made Michael still angrier, then opened the door. They walked into the air-conditioned house and followed Sutterfield to the family room.

The first thing that struck Michael after its size was the quality of the house's construction. This house had to be in the half-million-dollar range, even in the depressed Grand Junction market.

The second of Michael's observations was that despite Bree's having characterized the man as an inveterate shutterbug, there were next to no photographs around.

The third was Sutterfield's jukebox.

The juke wasn't one Joe Preston would have coveted. Its dome was scratched in several places, and a few selection keys had been replaced. But Michael's reaction to the juke must have looked like keen interest to Sutterfield. He plugged the juke in and watched the domed area light up. His hostile attitude seemed to vaporize into thin air. Michael exchanged glances with Bree while she sat on the sofa.

"It's a beauty, isn't it?" Sutterfield asked.

"Yeah," Michael nodded, his sarcasm veiled. "A real piece of work."

"Watch the mechanism—works like a dream." Sutterfield jabbed at one of the keys and watched as a disc was plucked out and carried into place on the turntable. The needle arm descended on the Beatles' "Octopus's Garden."

Grinning, Sutterfield stood listening with one proprietary hand on the jukebox's dome and the other resting on his hip. Michael folded his arms across his chest. Something about the way Sutterfield looked at Michael made alarms go off in his head.

His smile turning cunning, Sutterfield pointed at Michael. "I remember you now—you were with Bree the day Eric pulled his disappearing act."

Two thoughts went through Michael's head. One was that he didn't much care for Eric's name coming out of Sutterfield's mouth. The other was that Sutterfield was lying—he hadn't just now remembered at all. He'd recognized Michael even before he opened the door. He'd almost certainly seen them together when Bree had checked with him after Eric ran away.

"Bree!" Sutterfield exhorted, his expression guileless. "You are remiss in your social graces! Shouldn't you introduce me to Eric's father?"

Bree's flesh crawled with shock, but if he'd expected a reaction from her, he got none. She stared at him blankly, and disappointment flitted across his eyes.

"The name's Tallent, Michael Tallent."

"Quite a family resemblance," Sutterfield commented, his piercing gaze trained on Bree, searching out the lie. "I often thought, in my med-school days, of taking up plastic surgery. Likenesses intrigue me—facial bone structure, for instance. Yours, Bree, has always fascinated me. Now that I see Tallent, I must say I see very little of you in Eric."

Bree struggled to keep control despite Sutterfield's taunting. The fear of being recognized everywhere as Joe Preston's widow had risen sharply in her, and she had to give over everything in herself to keep going.

"Tom, I've misplaced some pictures you took last spring at the Little League preseason picnic. Michael would like to see them. I'll pay you for the negatives, or return them after getting copies—whatever you like."

It was Sutterfield's turn now to be surprised. His glance darted to Michael, then away, as if thinking where the negatives might be. But the record ended and Sutterfield had an excuse for turning aside. He selected another song and stood smiling until "Eleanor Rigby" began.

"Poor Eleanor Rigby..." Images assailed Bree and she shivered. Sutterfield's smug, self-satisfied smile reminded her viscerally of Joe Preston.

Michael began wandering about the room while Bree described what pictures she wanted. He noted the thick slate-colored carpeting, the stacks of walnut shelving, a built-in sound system cabinet with beveled glass doors. A Mickey Mouse designer telephone sat on an antique roll-top desk. At last, he paused, picked a pencil from a brass holder on the desk and leaned indolently against the desktop. He'd seen enough, and with the jukebox, heard enough. "The negatives, Sutterfield."

Clearly puzzled as to the measure of Michael's quiet, almost threatening insistence, Sutterfield reached for a photo album. "What's the big deal with those pictures?—hell, I'll give you mine."

Michael worked the pencil over and under each finger of his hand. Bree exchanged glances with him again, then spoke to Sutterfield. "I just want prints. There's no need for you to give me yours—"

"Well...I don't have them."

The pencil snapped between Michael's fingers in the sudden silence, evoking the sound of breaking bones. "Where are they?"

Sutterfield strode angrily around the jukebox and pulled the plug. "The Sheriff's Department borrowed them—months ago."

Chapter Seven

"Why?" Bree asked, fresh dismay eroding her careful control. "Why would the Sheriff's Department want those particular negatives?"

Sutterfield shrugged insolently. "They said there was some possibility I caught a local con artist in the background—and that the negatives might aid in their identification process."

Reminded of Bree's assessment of the man as a coward, Michael shot a warning glance at her, and then threw Sutterfield the one curve that might expose him. "Blessing said you'd say that."

"Who's Blessing?" the doctor snapped, his arm resting on the jukebox dome.

If Sutterfield recognized Blessing's name, he was very clever at concealing the fact. Though it proved nothing, Bree saw in Michael's body language a small measure of relief. She felt none. UFQ-9307 belonged to a sheriff's deputy, and Sutterfield claimed the Sheriff's Department had the negatives. The connection was ominous enough—the alternative, that Sutterfield had etched those photos himself with the skulls and crossbones—was worse. "Tom, was it a deputy who took the negatives?"

"I suppose. It wasn't Ballard himself."

"And the negatives were never returned?"

Before he could answer, the Trimline phone next to the Mickey Mouse phone on the desk rang. Sutterfield shoved away from the dome of his juke and moved to answer the summons. "I don't know if I'll ever see those negatives again, social graces being what they are among the county cops." He lifted the receiver. "Sutterfield!" he snapped into the phone receiver.

He listened for a moment, then grunted an assent and hung up. "You'll have to leave now. I've got a hot appendix to ice at the hospital."

"Don't bother showing us out," Michael said with heavy sarcasm. "I know the territory."

Bree recognized Michael's reference to the taped directives Blessing had given him and the line that advised that he "learn the territory." Sutterfield looked blankly at them both for a second, his smile evasive. "Bully for you, Tallent. Bully for you."

MICHAEL AND BREE LET themselves out the front door with its leaded glass windows. When the bolt slid quietly into place behind them, her knees buckling as though every sinew and tendon had been severed, Bree reached out to Michael.

"Easy, Breez. Take it easy. You handled everything fine."

The air outside Sutterfield's air-conditioned house felt like a blast furnace to her, sapping even the dregs of her energy, but Bree nodded and let go of Michael. "Just get me out of here."

"He's probably still watching."

Again she nodded. Now was the worst time to let Sutterfield imagine he'd gotten to her. She laced her fingers through Michael's and they headed for the car.

Two blocked from Sutterfield's house, Bree closed her eyes, and she shivered violently, despite the heat. "I was wrong about him. He knows—"

"You weren't wrong—"

"Michael, he *smiles* like Joe, he has a jukebox like Joe, he plays all Joe's old favorites. He knew you're Eric's father. *He knows who I am!*"

"C'mon, Breez! His know-it-all smile is only *like* Joe's—and, yeah, he has a jukebox, but Joe wouldn't have one that wasn't in mint condition. There are only a hundred million of us who listen to the Beatles, and there's no great revelation in his seeing Eric's resemblance to me—"

"None of which explains his comment about my bone structure! He might as well have said, 'You must be Sabrina Preston, the mole's widow! No way your bleached hair buffaloed me—*I know who you are!*'"

"If he knows and if he's trying to intimidate you with knowing, it has to be because someone else told him."

"But who? Why? What's in it for anyone?"

"We can't rule out the possibility that someone besides the Hatter knows who you are or that you were married to Joe. As to why, there are several possibilities. The ambassador's money, revenge—who knows how many people Joe burned one way or another? Blessing sent me because even he is threatened. Sutterfield could be collecting payola just keeping someone else apprised of your activities."

"Suppose Sutterfield altered the negatives himself by putting those skulls and crossbones on them," Bree argued. "The fact that the negatives had to be marked up like that is a compelling enough reason for refusing by itself."

"But would he know how to get them to Blessing—where Blessing lives? The man we're after not only knows Blessing, he knew exactly how to get those photos through him to me."

Automatically checking his rearview mirror, Michael drove across Hedlands Parkway and swung west, following the highway in the direction of the town of Fruita. "Frankly, I'm more spooked with the claim that the Sheriff's Department borrowed the negatives. Suppose the deputy who followed you is the same one who got them from Sutterfield?''

UFQ-9307. Bree sighed and for several moments, stared out into the deepening twilight. There were simply too many unanswerable questions, and the dark, ugly feelings UFQ-9307 inspired made her prefer to think Sutterfield *was* the Mad Hatter—a simple case of better the devil you know than the one you don't. ''Either way—'' Abruptly, Bree sat straighter, intent on the car in front of them. ''Michael, that's Patrick's Mercedes. But . . . he's driving into that parking lot!''

''Yeah, so?''

''It's a topless bar, Michael! Patrick would never, ever willingly frequent such a seedy kind of place. What . . . Do you think he could be meeting someone?''

Michael slowed the Eagle and put on the turn signal, watching as the Mercedes's headlights were doused. Marquet got out. Casting anxious glances over his shoulder in every direction as he checked and rechecked the lock on his door, Patrick hurried toward the bar. ''Bingo,'' Michael murmured. ''We'll wait over at the far edge of the lot and see who comes out with him.''

''What if he or whomever he's meeting spots us—they know my car.''

Michael parked the Eagle where there would be no chance of missing Marquet's exit and took Bree's hand. ''We'll know something we didn't before. They won't.''

PATRICK ENTERED THE smoke-filled den of iniquity with an aversion bordering the point of nausea. In all the months he'd known Roy Danziger, he'd never suspected his friend of harboring such squalid tastes. Patrick simply preferred naked women in a more exclusive, refined setting. His eyes burned as he sought out Danziger.

He discovered him in the back booth, tucking a bill into a waitress's G-string. Patrick couldn't prevent staring in fascination, but he felt pea green and hoped it dark enough that Roy wouldn't notice.

"Patrick. Good of you to come on such short notice!"

Clearing his throat for the first of many times, Patrick endeavored to come up with a civilized response. "I would have preferred the country club, Roy."

"I'm sure you would, Patrick. *I* would. But then, you have little Bree to lust after, and I, alas have no one. Forgive me my baser instincts, my friend."

Patrick struggled to keep the shock from his expression. *Lust* was the very last word he'd assign his feelings for Bree. But his outrage was a powerful counterpoint to his need for Roy and Roy's friendship, and Patrick didn't know what to do. "I have certain standards, Roy, which I understood you to share."

Danziger sat back in the booth and lit a cigarette. Sometimes he had to wonder. For a man once capable of creating an Oscar-winning script, Marquet could be unbearably dense. If Marquet had the sense God gave a sewer rat, he'd surely understand that he was being dragged through the muck right along with sweet Breez.

"Perhaps our association is wearing a little thin on you, Patrick. I am a man of very... eclectic appetites. But then, I'm not sure you're finding the manner in which Bree seems to be cleaving to Michael Tallent especially... auspicious. Of course, there are further steps to be taken in disassembling that relationship. Do *you* know what they are?"

Patrick's stomach plunged still further with the very thought of giving up his ally. Though he was choking on the haze of smoke, Patrick hurried to reassure Roy. "In whatever surroundings I find myself with you, I leave inevitably enlightened. Tell me—" Patrick coughed "—what must I do to end this entanglement Bree has developed?"

Crushing out his imported cigarette, Roy sat forward. "Did you know that Michael Tallent fathered Bree's child?"

As if struck in the face, Patrick recoiled. "No!"

"I'm surprised the resemblance has escaped you. The boy is a veritable pastiche of Tallent's features!"

"But this is awful! Bree will find it impossible to drive him away!"

"Patrick, can you be so easily dissuaded from your purpose, from seeing this magnificent story to its denouement? The man is no match for your wit. He has solved the problem for you. He has already approached an attorney about filing a custody suit." That much, Danziger thought, was true.

"Occasionally," he continued, "I play golf with Oral Jenner. He tells me Tallent is pressuring the Mesa Memorial Hospital directors for an immediate and permanent suspension of Bree Gregory." He knew Tallent's attorney had merely asked in writing for Bree Gregory's employment records, but Marquet swallowed lies as easily as the truth.

"Tallent's strategy must have been to force the dismissal. If she were left penniless, his suit for the brat's custody becomes unimpeachable."

Patrick shook his head. "She has my uncle's money!"

"Of course! But whether Tallent knows that or not, he's no fool, my friend. Why do you think he courts her while plotting behind her back to steal the boy from her? He wants her under his thumb, that's why. If she took a notion to run again, all would be lost. *Your* strategy lies in revealing Tallent's treachery—now. He wants the boy and he'll stop at nothing."

Roy withdrew a piece of paper from his wallet and handed it to Patrick. "This is the name of Tallent's attorney. Give her this name. Let her discover for herself that she's consorting with a viper. I should think her subsequent behavior far more to your fancy.''

Overwhelmed with the insight and evidence his friend delivered time after time, Patrick's gratitude knew no bounds. Clogged lungs, irritated throat be damned. He'd been right to forgive Roy his baser nature. For several long moments, Patrick sat deeply in thought.

Then Roy lit another cigarette. The matchstick flamed until the acrid scent of Danziger's burning flesh bit at Patrick's nose. Danziger seemed not to notice at all! But then, he blew out the flame, considered his thumb and smiled.

Patrick had never seen such a smile. Danziger had deliberately inflicted the burn of his flesh. And then, smiled.

Unnerved as he had never in his entire life been, Patrick fought the reflexive urge to vomit. Danziger's gesture had triggered in Patrick's zealous imagination a metaphor more elegant than words. He saw that with Roy Danziger, he was himself playing with fire.

MICHAEL AND BREE SAT IN the dark with the car windows rolled down, listening to the pounding, exotic beat coming from the topless bar. Bree leaned her head against the seat back and sighed. ''At least it's not the Beatles.''

Michael smiled sadly. ''Too bad Joe didn't go for the Rolling Stones. I could go a lifetime without listening to them. I'm not sure I want to give up listening to the Beatles.''

Something in Michael's wistful tone of voice made Bree think he planned to be listening to the same music with her for a long, long time. Tears clogged her throat, and the best she could do was shake her head. ''Me, either.''

Michael's jaw tightened until it cramped. It was easier to watch the door for Marquet than to sit there wishing things had been different between them.

''How long has Sutterfield been here?'' he asked.

"In town? He was in practice when I started at Memorial. Why?"

"How eager did he seem about getting to know you?"

"Not very... I met him and Gloria when I started going to church at St. Stephen's. Are you thinking—"

"He doesn't have any pictures on the wall or his desk—even the bookcase—but you told me he took half your pictures of Eric. What about his own kid?"

"Scott... Are you saying Sutterfield is truly only interested in the pictures of Eric?"

"And of you, maybe."

"Then what you're really suggesting is that he's been spying on me all these years?"

Michael shook his head absently as he watched the bar door, his thoughts racing far ahead. "It's a possibility. It seems pretty far-fetched. Still... Eric has to be told I'm his father, Breez. Now, before he hears it from Sutterfield's kid."

"He won't... that won't happen!"

"None of this should be happening, Bree," Michael warned her gently. "I'm just trying to think ahead—"

"But... I don't know how to tell him."

"Then I will."

"Michael—"

"Use Tallent, Bree, if it helps you keep things straight in your head. I'm not the memory Michael you can summon up when it's convenient. I'm here, I'm real and I'm not going away."

"Michael, for God's sake, I'm not fighting you! Of course, Eric should know. But don't you think we could get out of this mess first?"

"No." The longer Michael sat here waiting for Marquet to show, the shorter his fuse got, and it was getting dangerously close to lighting up the night. "As long as anyone knew who you were, you made an easy mark, Bree. Getting me here was the trick, and I may get killed because, bottom line, I'm the one who blew open Joe's cover. If I'm going to die, Bree, I'm first going to see Eric look at me and know I'm his father. Can you understand that?''

She could. She did. Staring at the flickering pink neon sign above the bar door, Bree recalled with total, bitter-sweet clarity the look on Eric's face this very morning. He'd volunteered to dry the breakfast dishes just so he could tell her privately that *if* he had a dad, he'd want the man to be Mike.

In his own childish way, Eric had set out all the arguments, carefully phrased so Bree wouldn't think he didn't love her anymore. *Mike doesn't have any kids of his own. Mike's house is gonna have a playroom that takes up the whole attic*... Mike knew how to do this, build that, catch fish and make the bad guys go away. And more than anything, Mike paid attention to her son like no *man* ever, *ever* had....

No one knew better than she, not even Eric, the exquisite quality of Michael's attention. When you spoke, Michael listened—a child knew those things. Eric knew. And when Michael kissed, that kiss was all—a woman knew. Bree knew...just as she knew the stars in her son's eyes, the glow, the grin that Michael wanted to see when Eric learned the truth about his father.

Bree closed her eyes against the lurid pink, flashing neon and knew that what Michael said was true. Eric had to know. It just wasn't that simple.

''A seven-year-old's logic will tell Eric that your dad is your dad, and a mom doesn't hide things like that. I'll lose him, Michael.''

If she'd said that a few weeks ago, Michael would have come down hard on her. *Life's hell, lady, and then you die. You've had him for seven, almost eight, years, and now it's my turn.* Even three days ago...

The simple truth of the matter was, without Bree, he'd have no son at all. But she'd raised Eric to honor truth above all things because the cold, calculating lies Preston perpetrated had destroyed her. Now, the lies she'd been forced to live could destroy Eric in the same way.

Michael watched men come and go in a steady stream, but none, so far, had been Patrick Marquet, and his patience was wearing thin. But he understood Bree's concern. How did one go about casually destroying a child's tender faith?

"Eric isn't going to be happy with either one of us, Breez, for having kept this a secret from him. But he's smart and resilient. It won't take him long to figure out that later was better than never."

Michael turned sideways in the seat to better watch the exit for Marquet. Leaning against the door, he pulled Bree to him, and his arms closed around her.

For a moment, Bree savored the sensation. She wanted to believe that she wouldn't lose Eric, but in so many ways, she already had. His need for a father was beginning to outweigh his need of her. But in Michael's arms, she knew more comfort and tenderness than Joe Preston had ever shown her, and she knew Eric's needs would nowhere be better met than with this man. Which made believing him about Eric's resilience easier still. Easier, and that much more a perilous trap.

His pleasure in holding Bree unfurled slowly, then faster. Too fast and unexpectedly to deny. His hand tightened on her hip, and the other sought the soft, womanly curve of her breast. Compassion and untempered desire flared up in him.

A small cry escaped her throat. Their kiss began and lingered, intensifying, and if Bree thought at all, it wasn't about the perils they fought or that Patrick might emerge at any moment from the bar. She didn't want to think, only to feel, if only for this one moment out of time.

Seeking only to get closer, she moved. Or he moved. Neither could tell which. His thigh grazed hers and her hand splayed against his chest. Nothing they could do seemed enough toward getting closer.

The throbbing music blared suddenly louder, as it did every time the door of the bar opened. Through the fog in his head and the heat in his body, Michael forced his eyes open. This time, the departing customer was Patrick Marquet.

Bree felt the tension reclaim Michael's body and she straightened to follow his gaze. Patrick was just coming through the door, followed by another man neither she nor Michael could see until Patrick began jogging toward his Mercedes. Even then, the other man, his gait somehow strained or stiff, was nothing more than a dark, ordinary shadow against the darker night.

The car he drove away in, however, was vintage. A gleaming black '65 Mustang.

"That's the one that followed you?"

Tongue-tied with shock, Bree could only nod.

Michael straightened and took his right arm from around Bree, who resumed her place by the passenger window. For long moments after both the Mustang and the Mercedes disappeared, they sat in silence.

Patrick Marquet was in collusion with the deputy who owned the vintage black Mustang, UFQ-9307.

Stamping down on the clutch, Michael started the Eagle, down-shifted and quickly pulled out of the parking lot, this time headed back to Grand Junction. "Marquet is your Judas, Breez. He's selling you down the river."

Where tenderness and desire had been only moments before, anger filled her. Patrick! Patrick, whose loyalty and protection Henry Reinhardt had purchased outright with half his fortune. Patrick, who claimed to love her. Patrick.

If all the ambassador's millions weren't enough to ensure his nephew's silence, what had anyone else to offer him?

"Blessing was right," she said. "*Why* simply doesn't matter. No reason on earth could come close to justifying Patrick's treachery."

Although Michael agreed, his thoughts were elsewhere. He understood Bree's preoccupation with Marquet—she'd counted on his silence and goodwill for too many years not to be caught up in his betrayal. But she needed to get past that, to look beyond Marquet for the real threat.

"Patrick is just a world-class fool, Breez, a patsy. It's beginning to look like the deputy is the mastermind pulling all the puppet strings—at the very least, he's the one common factor. I'll call Blessing when we get home. He should have something on the sheriff's staff by now—or at least the Mustang."

"And then what?" Bree asked, her anger at Patrick unabated. "Even if Blessing has a name, what good will that do us?"

"Depending on the name, a lot. There's always information to go with a name, you know."

"But how will information change anything? We'll still be sitting ducks, waiting for the Hatter to jerk some other chain!"

"Bree," Michael responded, his voice lethal as a razor's stropped edge, "remember, this is no parlor game. Did you think I'd sit politely waiting, or maybe say, 'Gee, pretty please, Mr. Mad Hatter, will you lay off the intimidation tactics?'"

"No, but—"

"When I know who the bastard is, he's dead, Bree. Nothing pretty, no euphemisms, not *as good* as dead, and not pushing-up-the-daisies. *Dead,* Bree, before he kills us off one by one."

"Oh, that's just charming, Tallent! Then they can throw you in prison for the rest of your life and Eric can visit you there!"

His anger abating—at least his anger toward her—Michael flicked the turn signal on at Thistle Ridge Road. "Self-defense is not a crime, Bree. And if a man's family is threatened, it's all the same." He pulled into her driveway, shut off the engine and then ran his fingers up her neck to her cheek. "I don't want to die, sweet Breez. I want to live long enough to see if I'm really falling in love with my son's mother all over again."

BILL KENDALL WAS NERVOUS. He didn't like it, wasn't used to it and didn't want to get that way. Mike and Bree had been gone far longer than any of them had anticipated, and though Michael had filled him in on what had happened in Ouray, Kendall still couldn't quite believe it. When he heard the car pull into the drive, he shot out of Bree's only easy chair and turned off the latest Clint Eastwood flick. Murdering villains were supposed to stay in the movies.

Bill stepped out onto the porch as Michael and Bree got out of the car. "You two been out necking?" he cracked, mostly to relieve his own edginess.

Grateful for Bill's easy humor, Michael grinned and pulled Bree closer. "Eat your heart out, buddy."

"I get more lovin' at home than you two'll ever catch up with," Bill retorted. "Eric and Martha are fine—asleep. You need anything else?"

Lighthearted banter abandoned, Michael asked Kendall to come in for one more minute and headed for his duffel bag. He pulled out his wallet and handed Kendall three bills. Kendall started to hand them back, then noticed the thousand-dollar denomination. "What is this? You carry this kind of money all the time?"

"Only on alternate Fridays," Michael wisecracked. "Three grand is only what I owe you, Bill. Things have a way of exploding around my ears lately, and I don't think it's healthy for you or Billy to be hanging out anywhere near me. Take the bucks and lay low for a while. Please."

Bill's ruddy complexion went flour-paste pale. "I never saw trouble like this. Can it really be that bad?"

"Could be. I wasn't exactly expecting that assault at Bree's cabin last night."

"Man, this is enough bucks to get the three of you halfway around the world. Why don't you all take it and get the hell outta here?"

"We can't, Bill," Bree murmured. "Michael is right—the less you know, the safer you are. Please. Take the money and...stay away."

More confused than ever, Kendall jammed his fingers through his hair. "Well... Suppose I take Eric and my family on a little vacation? He'd be out of danger and great company for Billy...." But Kendall's voice trailed off when by their expressions he knew that wouldn't work, either. Nothing was likely to work, he finally understood. He gave Michael a great bear hug and Bree a kiss on each cheek, and begged them to be careful as he left.

Michael went straight to the phone and placed his call to Blessing—which was transferred by the answering service to the computer complex. One of Blessing's technician's advised Michael that unless they were in trouble, Blessing would return the call in the morning.

Which told Michael they'd found nothing on the sheriff's deputy. Nothing at all.

THE EXQUISITELY tonal gong in the grandfather clock standing sentinel over his living room sounded twice. He poured himself another shot of Glenfiddich, inhaled its single-malt aroma and drank just as deeply.

He'd botched the appendix, botched it bad. It had taken him four hours to cut out the poisoned tissue, sop up the blood and suture off the bleeder. Years had passed since an operation had gone quite this badly, and it only served to remind him how he'd survived so long on so little native talent.

Sitting in the dark, he had no trouble visualizing every aspect of his...success. Humorlessly, he laughed, recalling old med school bromides. *What do you call the guy who graduates last in his class? Doctor, of course.* Hell's bells, somebody had to be last.

He was it. Last. Nothing much had changed over the years, either. You couldn't tell it from his possessions, though. He had four thousand square feet of house decorated and furnished by the best interior design team in all of Colorado, a Beemer—his '89 BMW 325i convertible—and an '85 Jeep Cherokee.

Bree Gregory was the reason for all this. Someone wanted her watched. Someone wanted monthly pictures and reports. And in return, that someone was willing to persuade the powers that be to look the other way when he botched some penny-ante surgical procedure—which meant that, despite the impoverished community in which he found himself, he'd done very well, indeed.

He listened to the grandfather clock sound the half hour, and lit a cigarette. For three years—since the time her kid had entered St. Stephen's preschool—his responsibilities had been a simple matter of taking a few pictures and reporting every word of his every conversation with Bree Gregory to the bland little man who'd first recruited him. Suddenly, nothing was even that simple.

He'd couldn't begin to fathom why anyone was willing to go to such lengths to know exactly what she said, where she went, with whom and why. He'd never asked—it was understood that questions were not entertained. But he'd never expected to be asked for anything more, either. The funny thing was, he liked Bree and Eric.

Things were happening around her now that he didn't understand at all—least of all why one night he'd been joking with her and the next, ordered to make of it an instance of insubordination. Unless... unless Michael Tallent's appearance was what his recruiter had been waiting for all along.

Despite the long hours and most of a fifth of Scotch, his hands were shaking when the Mickey Mouse phone he loved rang. Gloria and Scott were asleep—they'd never hear it ringing, and so he was tempted to let Mickey ring until he quit.

In the end, Sutterfield answered. Wanting nothing to do with Bree's trouble, he wanted more to continue in the lifestyle to which he'd become so thoroughly accustomed.

Chapter Eight

At 3:00 a.m., Bree's telephone rang. Michael came awake on the sofa and slammed the ammunition clip tightly into the butt of his pistol. He let the answering machine intercept the call and heard his own curt message: "Tallent—leave a number. I'll get back to you." In response, after the tone, Blessing's voice snapped back. "If you're there, pick up the phone."

Michael pulled the clip loose again, plucked the receiver off the wall phone and returned to sit on the sofa. He stuck the gun back into his shoulder holster and shoved the holster beneath his shirt on the floor.

"Blessing... What have you got?"

"Nothing—a list of names, hard copy of State of Colorado faxed to me. Nothing else. My computers fall into this unrecoverable loop every time we tap into a database containing the name of any member of the Mesa County Sheriff's Department. We've been anticipated, Michael, and worse. The son of a bitch has penetrated my computers. If he can do that, he could conceivably tap in at State, Joint Chiefs and NSA. God only knows where else...."

Michael rose slowly from the sofa, the phone receiver tucked between his ear and shoulder. "Are you saying the jerk threatening *us* has programmed naval intelligence computers into an irretrievable loop just because you call up the *Mesa County Deputies?*''

''That's exactly what I'm telling you. I've never seen infiltration like this—it's like a kid taking a joy ride. No real damage, just harassment. But, my God, Michael. Think about it! Whoever he is, he's got us cold.''

The scenario took no thought at all. This was every psycho hacker's dream and every government official's worst nightmare. But this psycho was one and the same man who amused himself toying with Joe Preston's widow. Michael caught sight of Bree, clad in a long robe, descending the stairs. ''Any way to know if he's pulled out any national security data?''

''By all indications thus far, no.... Michael, I've got to send in a strike force—''

''You do that and he'll blow your whole system to hell and back.''

Blessing's silence indicated he suspected that was true. ''Then you've got to find him, Michael. He's become an intolerable security risk!''

Pacing, his eyes on Bree, Michael dragged a hand through his hair. ''This can't come as much of a surprise to you, Carl—you knew he was a security risk by the fact that he'd sent a public courier to your home. So now it's a safe bet he's covering as a county deputy. Which one would you suggest I start with?''

''Michael,'' Bree interrupted softly, pulling a pencil and paper from the telephone drawer, ''if he's got names and we check the county records for the owner of the Mustang...''

Michael took the pad and pencil. ''Give me the names you have,'' he directed Blessing.

Bree switched on the lamp, drew the living room drapes closed and watched as Michael recorded names. Abeyta, Franklin J.; Anderville, Mark C.; Cerner, Gary W.; Danziger, Roy F.; Mouser, Charles R.; Mouser, Richard L; Tschetter, Philip Z., Jr.

It took Michael no longer than thirty seconds to ask if the list contained personal addresses and to get off the phone with Blessing once he'd learned that it didn't. He didn't need or want the old man's advice, either.

"We could try to get a name out of Patrick," Bree suggested.

"We could," Michael agreed, studying the names on the list. "But . . . Marquet is the weak link, Breez. He's already betrayed you. I'd just as soon he didn't know we've got even this much. It'll keep till morning."

"I'm going in to work tomorrow—"

"After the suspension Jenner socked you with when Sutterfield made such a stink? Why, for God's sake?"

Bree sank down onto the second stair riser and hugged her knees to her chest. "It's not Jenner who will be hurt if I don't go back tomorrow, Michael. My technologists have to be exhausted," she explained earnestly, "and when you're exhausted, you make mistakes, and then innocent people suffer, or worse, wind up dead."

Michael drew a frustrated breath, switched off the lamp and pulled the draperies open. Illuminated again by the scant light of a warning quarter moon, the eeriness only underscored Michael's doubts. He understood Bree's reasoning and had to respect the decision—but he didn't have to like it. These were no ordinary times, and he didn't want Bree alone any more than he wanted Eric left unguarded with Martha.

"*You* could wind up dead, Breez, if I'm not around."

"I could wind up dead if you are," she rejoined, her voice cracking, "but I have to go in to work, at least for a while. Besides, I don't think the Hatter is quite done terrorizing us yet. Do you?"

Her cynicism bothered Michael on a couple of levels, but mostly for the implication that even with him, she wasn't safe. Was she beginning to think there was no way to survive, no way out? "Have you given up, Bree?" he asked, his own voice low and disturbed.

Chin raised and lips pursed, Bree clamped down on the fear, just as she had for most of her adult life, and the look she sent Michael told him his question didn't deserve an answer. "I'll go to the Department of Motor Vehicles on my way in to work. The Mustang belongs to one of those men, Michael, and I'm going to find out which one of those deputies it is."

"What's changed, Bree? Three days ago—"

"I had no idea I'd already been discovered," she finished for him. "Three days ago, I thought I was still safe, still anonymous, still just Bree Gregory. None of that was true, even then, and we didn't have any reason to connect the creep following me with the rest of this. Now we know there must be a connection, and . . . I have nothing more to lose, Michael."

Despite her determined words, Michael heard the tremor in her voice and saw the sheen of moisture glittering in her eyes. The scent of White Linen reminded him again of her strength, which only reminded him it was her strength that had enabled her to live her fugitive existence without him.

He understood her reasoning. He respected her judgment. He acknowledged her strength. Still in all, he gestured for her to join him on the sofa, and wished to hell there was one small corner of her existence in which she truly needed him.

Wearily, wanting nothing more than to surrender her constant control for an hour or two, Bree got up from the stair riser on which she'd been sitting and went to stand beside him. "Don't think I'll sit quietly by and let you rescue us, Michael," she whispered fiercely.

Pulling her onto the couch beside him, Michael kissed her just as fiercely. It wasn't a gentle kiss or a short one meant to shut her up. It was heated and intemperate and bruising, and Bree only wanted more of it, this proof of Michael's caring and endurance. And when he broke off his kiss, his words confirmed what his lips had so thoroughly already conveyed. "Don't think you're in this alone, either, Breez. You're not."

He put his arm around her, and when she'd recovered a little from his kiss, Bree became aware of a profound relief that she wasn't in this alone. Curling up next to Michael, she allowed the blessed, all-too-temporary relief to consume her. Long moments later, she asked, "What shall we do about Martha and Eric?"

"As long as things go the Hatter's way," Michael answered musingly, "it's unlikely he'll bother with Martha. She agreed to stay tonight. Will she stay until this is over? Stay inside and keep away from the doors and windows?"

Bree nodded. "She's really terribly frightened, but she thinks you're the greatest thing since sliced bread. She'll agree to whatever you ask of her. Will you keep Eric with you, or should we take him to St. Stephen's day care?"

"I'll keep him—until I can't anymore."

Michael didn't need to tell her under what conditions he'd have to leave Eric at the parish basement day-care center, or why Eric shouldn't be around him once she had supplied Michael with the name of the deputy who owned the Mustang.

"Eric will want to be with you as much as possible, but St. Stephen's will take him anytime—or you could bring him to me at the hospital. I used to let him play with the stamps at the desk when I was called in and couldn't find anyone to watch him."

Michael nodded his assent. He meant to suggest that if she had no choice but to go in to work in a few hours, she'd better go back upstairs to her bedroom, which Martha was now sharing, and get some sleep. But he kept quiet and shifted positions until Bree rested against his chest. He reached to the floor to make sure his pistol was well within reach, then crossed both arms over her.

Bree fell asleep before he'd done with arranging their limbs, and Michael wondered if she understood the extent of her own exhaustion. He focused on the soft rhythm of her breathing, and despite the heat of the night and the heat of Bree's body fashioned so close to his, he fell into his first moments of a truly relaxed sleep in days.

IN A COMMERCIAL-DISTRICT warehouse nowhere near the apartment listed as his residence in the Mesa County personnel records, Danziger sat at the computer he'd assembled and modified himself, watching his terminal transcribe the conversation between Carl Blessing and Michael Tallent.

Danziger had taken considerable care and expense in the specifications and assembly. The computer served a variety of purposes, the least of which was tapping into local phone lines, the highest and best use in his ability to breach security measures on intelligence computers around the globe.

Blessing's frenzy amused Danziger—or would have had he been able to see past his violent headache. Certain that, could he focus his attention at all, his leg would be similarly cramping, he swallowed black-market morphine with an ice-water chaser.

Despite the massive doses of painkiller, sleep would elude him again tonight. Sometimes, he went for months without a headache. His leg bothered him continually. But he was no simpering weakling. Ordinary mortal frailties and emotions had been trained out of him so early in his life that no one, *no one,* knew the pain he endured.

Tired was one of those feeble, ineffectual, altogether human modes he rarely indulged. But *tired* accurately described the state of his mind, and he knew it. He was bone-tired of policing this backwater hellhole, and weary to his core of manipulating fools and cretins the caliber of Oral Jenner—and even Michael Tallent, for whom he had a great deal more respect. Hatred, to be sure, but respect, as well.

A psychiatrist would deem him certifiably insane, and he knew that, too. Brilliant, but insane.

Tallent would die for his role in dismantling Joseph Preston's penetration of the precious U.S. intelligence community. Danziger almost laughed aloud. *U.S. intelligence.* A contradiction in terms—an oxymoron if he'd ever heard one. But Danziger had almost as little regard for foreign intelligence—particularly the KGB—as he had for the American dolts, for eight years ago, they had abandoned their operative mole, Joseph Preston, to his fate. But they had paid.

Danziger knew that the KGB knew that he'd penetrated even their computer files because, singlehandedly, he'd ruined the covers of seventeen separate operatives. *Perestroika* and *glasnost* probably seemed to the KGB the lesser of evils compared to losing agents the world over.

Revenge was of the highest order in Danziger's priorities. It had taken him years to draw the threads together, years of subtle manipulation. Years of waiting, but the curtain was rising on the final act of the life and times of Roy Danziger. Tallent and the Widow Preston and her bastard brat would live until control of her numbered Swiss account fell to Danziger.

He coveted her money as a means to an end—getting himself out of this hellhole once and for all. For all his genius in penetrating intelligence computers around the globe, he'd never managed to invade and then manipulate those of banks. Even if he had, he'd still have taken the time to destroy Tallent and his whore.

Nothing would give him sweeter satisfaction than to place the Tallent's bastard brat into the hands of those who would shape and mold him in the image and tradition of Joseph Preston—the ultimate measure of Danziger's revenge.

ERIC AND MICHAEL STRUCK out on foot for his construction site at the first light of dawn. The heat grew so intense later in the day that the cool mornings were the only reasonable time to work. Dawn was Michael's favorite time of day; typically, Eric didn't give a fig what time it was if he could be with Michael.

Bree breakfasted on the remains of Eric's scrambled eggs and toast, and planned her morning hours. The deputy's name and an address were only the first items she intended to pursue, but the Department of Motor Vehicles wouldn't open until nine. By that time, the bulk of the morning lab work would be done and it'd be far more useful for her to go to the lab after lunch.

She called the hospital, and despite the list of problems that began with the flame photometer acting up, her lab technician advised Bree the workload was mercifully light. Offering a quick-fix suggestion for the instrument problems, she promised to be in after lunch.

She helped Martha with the dishes, took a shower and was pulling her hair into a French braid when Patrick let himself in the front door and called out for her. Hurriedly, Bree tucked the end of the braid under, pinned it and went to the top of the stairs.

"Young man," Martha scolded icily from the kitchen door, "the doorbell is fully functional. Have you no better manners than to walk into someone else's house?"

"This *is* my house," Patrick spat out. "Tell her, Bree."

Bree sighed. The sight of him sickened her—she could have killed him for betraying her. No less angry with him now, she knew it was far safer to keep quiet.

"Martha," she said, "this is Patrick's house. But, Patrick, while I'm living here, paying you good money every month, you have no business walking in like that. I've asked you a hundred times—"

"Bree, I have to talk to you," he interrupted, glaring pointedly at Martha. "Alone."

Resentfully, Martha eased her apron off and stalked upstairs. Bree made a point of squeezing the elderly lady's hand as she passed by her.

"I don't have very much time, Patrick. I have to go to work. What is it you have to say?"

He watched until Martha had closed the bedroom door behind her, then came toward Bree. He saw her stiffen as he reached out to touch her hair and so pulled back his hand and jammed it into the pocket of his pleated slacks, disappointment rankling in his eyes. "Damn it, Bree, I'm sorry if I've given you any cause to mistrust me so. I—I *love* you. You know that."

He'd given her every reason to mistrust him, and she'd scratch his eyes out if anything he'd done ultimately caused Eric any harm. But she had neither the time nor the energy to get into this old news with him. "I know, Patrick. What is it you wanted to say to me alone?"

Encouraged by her acknowledgement of his affections, Patrick grew more animated. "I . . . Eric . . . I know . . ."

A shiver passed through Bree. "You know what, Patrick?"

"I know who his father is!"

Shock took hold of her first. But she knew that anyone seeing Michael and Eric together would finally guess that Michael had fathered Eric. She couldn't help the bitter smile molding her lips. Was there anyone left in Colorado who didn't know who Eric's father was? "Is that all?"

Flushing angrily, Patrick scoffed. "No, that's not all—not by a long shot! Look, Bree, I—I know this must be horribly embarrassing for you—that I know the son of a bitch raped you—"

"*Raped* me?" she cried. "Is that what you think, that Michael raped me?"

"Nothing else can account for your pregnancy by that monster," he said stiffly.

"Patrick, where did you get such an idea?"

"Bree," he implored, reaching out to her again, "you don't have to pretend with me! I *know* you, and even though he assaulted you in such a heinous, disgusting manner, the fact that he is Eric's father leaves a woman of your compassion incapable of driving him away—which is why I must help you!"

Staring at Patrick, Bree wondered how he'd come to such a sick, twisted conclusion. She was unaware that laughter bubbled from her lips until he grabbed her by the elbow.

"You see? Bree, you're hysterical! I can only guess how living with this shame must have eroded your self-esteem! Don't you see how critical is your need, don't you see how he's driven you to the brink of emotional disaster?"

"Patrick, stop it!" she commanded, jerking her arm from his clutches. It would have been a far saner thing to do to show him the door, but Bree was beyond reason anymore when it came to Patrick's delusions. "Michael is Eric's father," she said, "but not because he raped me. I begged him to make love to me, Patrick, begged him."

"That's precisely it, Bree," Patrick whined. "You were *desperate*—"

"Not so desperate, Patrick, that I didn't know exactly what I was doing. Michael Tallent is ten times the man you'll ever be—a hundred times the man Joe Preston was! Have I made myself clear enough for you, or shall I tell you how I still feel when Michael touches me?''

His face darkened with rage, Patrick hurried to the door and banged it open. "I'll see him in hell if he touches you again, Bree. You're not in your right mind and haven't been since he came here."

When the screen door slammed shut on Patrick's threat and angry departure, Bree collapsed onto the couch. She'd let him goad her. She'd gone too far, taunting him with how she felt when Michael touched her. But in all the hours since she and Michael had arrived home last night, she had only to close her eyes to share that kiss again or to hear Michael's quiet declaration.

I don't want to die, sweet Breez. I want to live long enough to see if I'm really falling in love with my son's mother all over again.

His words had stunned her. Her own heart did the rest. She took one deep breath, smiled through tears wavering in her eyes and allowed herself a few moments to regain her composure. She'd only just discovered that in her heart, she wanted to hear Michael calling her "sweet Breez" for a very, very long time.

HE WAS HALFWAY DOWN THE street before Patrick was clear-minded enough to realize that he'd forgotten in his furor to play his lone ace. In his pocket was still the name of the attorney Michael Tallent had hired to take Eric away from her.

UFQ-9307 BELONGED TO ONE Roy Danziger—but it was only by the wildest of coincidences that Bree discovered that. The Department of Motor Vehicles computers demonstrated the same symptoms of tampered-with programming that Blessing's had—only the DMV employees had no idea what was causing their problems.

The license plate was of no help, but a '65 black Mustang was unusual, and one of the DMV employees knew someone who knew someone else who was into antique cars and had once owned a black '65 Mustang himself. It took two short phone calls to come up with a name.

"Roy Danziger," the clerk serving Bree said, her brow furrowed in concentration. "Come to think, Danziger's one of the county deputies. Want me to ring up the Sheriff's Department?"

"Is there any way I could just get his address so that I could mail him a—a thank-you note?"

"A thank-you note?"

"He changed a flat tire for me in the middle of the night," Bree said, improvising quickly. "I was just exhausted and didn't catch his name, but I don't want to bother him if he's on duty...." *Stupid,* she thought—how likely was it that she'd remember a license plate and not a name?

Occupied with checking her telephone book, the clerk didn't catch Bree's inconsistency. "Here it is. Danziger, Roy." She recited a phone number and address that Bree wrote down on a scratch pad the clerk gave her. "It's probably one of them houses that backs up to the river."

Thanking the clerk profusely for her help, Bree left. Within twenty minutes, she found that Danziger's address *was* one of those houses that backed up to the Colorado River. Lime green stucco, more a cottage than a house, it was all but hidden by an enormous, unkempt weeping willow tree. It also appeared to be vacant. Morning glory vines covered the mailbox.

Bree sat parked for a long time across the street from the ugly, crumbling little cottage. It seemed a sure bet he'd never lived here. She should have known nothing was this simple. On the other hand, perhaps she had known at some subconscious level. Could she have driven alone to this address if she'd truly expected to find Danziger here?

Probably not. Michael wouldn't believe she'd done anything half so stupid as risking coming alone, either. But there were things, clues ... feelings—call them all instinct— edging around the periphery of her thoughts that she couldn't ignore. From the moment she'd recalled the *Twilight Zone* episode that reminded her so viscerally of Joe Preston, she'd had those feelings. Her dread only fed her fierce determination to stop the Hatter's threats and his reign of terror.

She had a name to go on now, and nothing left to lose.

She started the car's engine and drove to the market for a picnic lunch to share with Michael and Eric—and because it was the location of the nearest public phone she could think of.

Deputy Danziger, she was informed by the switchboard operator at the sheriff's office, was on vacation.

No one answered at the telephone number that the DMV clerk had given her, either. In fact, the line at the cottage had been disconnected.

THE SOUND OF ERIC'S laughter mingled with Caruso's baying and the hissing of geese as Bree carried her plastic bag full of cold cuts and frozen goodies down the incline to Michael's half-constructed house.

There had been times in her life, Bree thought, when only the childish peals of her son's laughter had prevented her from going quietly insane. Somehow, it was frightening now to discover that even Eric's laughter couldn't banish this darkness. Who in creation *was* Roy Danziger?

Bree quelled the mounting anxiety in her heart and called out cheerfully. "Ham, turkey, pastrami, bologna, corned beef! Anybody interested?"

"Cheddar, jack, Swiss, Velveeta or mozzarella?" Eric's voice came back at her from what would eventually be an immense living room window.

Bree smiled, enjoying the small ritual they shared. "Actually, it's bologna and cheddar on day-old rye. I spent all my money on M & M's Blizzards from the Dairy Queen. Guess there's no takers here, huh?"

But Eric was through his sandwich and spooning Blizzard bites in record time. He began alternating bites of his frozen treat with feeding the geese from the loaf of stale bread Bree had bought just for them.

As she sat next to Michael in the shaded portion of the house, Bree nibbled on her sandwich and waited for Eric to get engrossed enough with the geese so that she could talk freely.

Legs stretched out in front of him, Michael sat with his back against an inner wall. He'd taken off his tool belt, but Bree smelled warm leather on him and knew he wore his shoulder holster. Eric probably thought it as much a part of Michael now as his carpenter's tool belt. How far they'd come, she and Eric, Bree thought, from the innocence she'd strived so hard to preserve.

Michael reached for the banana pepper the market deli had put in with his sandwich and nudged Bree's foot with his. When he had her attention, he didn't mince words.

"Which of the deputies owns the Mustang?"

"Danziger," she answered. "Roy Danziger. But the DMV computers went down as soon as my request went in. No one seemed to know what had happened, but it sounds like the kind of sabotage Blessing discovered."

Without a hint of discomfort, Michael ate the blisteringly spicy pepper and nodded. "So how did you get the name?"

"One of the clerks knew someone who was into classic cars—'65 Mustangs aren't that common. I guess the guy who had the car sold it to Danziger and remembered the name. We just got lucky."

"Yeah," Michael acknowledged. "Real lucky. But since the computers were down, they couldn't give you a residence address, right?"

"Danziger was in the phone book," Bree answered blithely, handing Michael his Dairy Queen Blizzard. "Here—eat this. I can't stand to think what that banana pepper is doing to your digestive system."

Michael would have reminded Bree of his iron constitution, but he had the feeling she'd gone to Danziger's place and he had to spend all his energy containing himself. "And?"

"And...I went there— Now before you get all uptight—"

"Save it, Bree," he interrupted. His voice was angry and low. His plastic spoon cracked in the dessert he set aside. "It's obvious that nothing happened, since you're still alive to talk about it—but *damn it,* that was a half-witted thing to do!"

"I told you I wouldn't sit idly by, Michael, and I meant it. I didn't go there to confront him or—"

"Don't tell me why you *didn't* go there, Bree. Try explaining why you *did*—what in hell did you hope to accomplish?"

"I wanted to see that Mustang. I wanted to see if I could just get a look at him or get a feeling from where he lived about who he is," Bree explained, her voice rising with nearly every word. "So what if we have a name, Michael? That doesn't tell us who he is or what he wants, or even if he is the one we're looking for and not just another pawn!"

For several moments, Michael sat in silence, wishing that Bree did, in fact, have some sense of who their enemy was. He trusted her instincts more than ever, and he supposed he owed her an apology for being so quick to anger over her going alone to the address she'd discovered. But he didn't want her in danger, and he wouldn't apologize for that.

He cared—a great deal more than he could attribute to her being Eric's mother. The scent of her perfume snagged his attention; the sound of her determined words plucked at his conscience. He wanted to know what she'd learned at Danziger's place—it stunned and upset him that his feelings for Bree were coming ahead of reasoned responses to the dangers they faced.

Before Michael could reorder his priorities and ask what she'd learned, Eric came running in with an unwieldy-looking hook tied to a thick rope, and asked if he could "go fishing." Michael had tied the huge hook to the end of a rope so Eric could dangle it from the second-story window, pretending to fish while he snagged bucket handles.

"Your fishing makes the geese go crazy—"

"Yeah," Eric agreed, his eyes sparkling. "Ya ought to see this, Mom. They can't figure out what's going on when the hook bangs into the buckets!"

Michael ruffled Eric's hair and then lifted him through the stairwell hole to the second floor above. "I'll go up with him, Bree. I'll show you the upstairs if you want to see it. We can talk while Eric's playing with his rope and hook."

Michael lifted her through the same hole, and she dutifully watched as Eric lowered his hook, stirred up an impressive commotion, and then set to the serious work of snagging a bucket.

Michael climbed through behind her with a practiced ease, then flexed his shoulders to adjust the holster beneath his shirt. Leading the way a short distance from Eric, Michael laid a two-by-eight pine scrap down over the wood frame of a benchlike structure. "Want to sit?" he asked Bree.

Looking interestedly around, she sat. "Where are we? What is this I'm sitting in?"

"The master bedroom," he answered, his gaze stuck to Bree's wide, blue eyes. Was it the color of a delicate flush he saw at her throat, or only his sun-baked imagination? "You're sitting next to the fireplace, on the wood box. There's a dumbwaiter behind you for hauling up the wood. The bathroom and walk-in closets take up that end of the house. And where Eric is playing is his . . . room," Michael said, finishing awkwardly.

Bree didn't hear the word *room* over Caruso's baying, the geese squawking and Eric's laughter, but she'd heard it coming, and had expected as much for a long time. Whatever happened, Eric would need a room at Michael's place. . . . She swallowed hard and smiled to keep herself calm in the face of Michael's plans for Eric.

"Patrick thinks you raped me," she blurted.

It was the wrong thing to say—the worst possible thing to say here, in Michael's master bedroom. Blushing furiously with the sudden intensity of Michael's gray eyes on her, Bree hurried on. "He knows that you're Eric's father, and he thinks the only possible explanation is that you . . . assaulted me."

Michael said nothing and only looked at her. The truth was—and they both knew it—Eric had been conceived in love and mutual respect and, admittedly, more real passion than by all rights the situation should have allowed.

Were she a doe sighted in the cross hairs of a shotgun, Bree couldn't have looked more vulnerable to Michael. Her admission of Marquet's moronic assumptions was like tinder, igniting memories neither of them could erase or even control . . . memories of the way it had really been when Eric was conceived . . . sweet, visceral memories. It was all Michael could do to keep his hands off her.

Bree was equally desperate to thwart the flames licking between them. "I think you're right about Danziger manipulating everyone."

Getting up from the makeshift bench, she paced toward the framed headers of the bedroom window. "I was thinking on the way over here that it would have been simple for Danziger to put in that phony call to the sheriff in Ouray—claiming to be Croker holding hostages. I—I just . . . I still don't know how he would know where my cabin is, but—I guess he could even have followed me once and I just didn't know."

Michael crammed his hands into his jeans pockets. "What did you find when you got to Danziger's place?"

"It's a little, green-stucco cottage. No one has lived there in a long time, Michael. So if that's the address the county personnel records have—"

"We're back to square one," Michael concluded grimly.

Despite the glaring heat of the noonday sun, Bree shivered. Coming to her from behind, Michael put his arms around her. A few moments ago, his touch would have been too much, too sexual. Now, holding her expressed feelings far more dangerous between them than the chemistry. The shelter of Michael's arms expressed caring, compassion. Protection.

Bree shivered harder, for this danger was as great a threat to her in its way as the Hatter was to her life. She trusted Michael, but she couldn't let herself depend on that.

She loved him, but she couldn't think of that.

Instinct had betrayed her. Patrick had betrayed her, and when she thought seriously about it, if Patrick Marquet was the best Henry Reinhardt could do for her, she'd have been better off going it alone.

Michael wasn't among those who had betrayed her. She'd only just discovered trust again, and it was god-awful hard to get over that—the elation just wouldn't go away.

FROM A VANTAGE POINT OFF the highway above the old peach grove, Patrick Marquet watched them through high-powered binoculars. The brat, Eric, was content to bedevil the geese and the damnable baying hound while Tallent

pawed Bree, whispering into her ear. Stroking the flesh at
her inner elbow, Tallent's hands, Patrick noticed, were mere
millimeters from her breasts....

His sensibilities offended once again, Patrick became
convinced that Bree had slipped beyond any semblance of
sanity. Even if he'd remembered to show her the name of the
attorney Tallent had hired to take Eric from her, she
wouldn't have seen Tallent's treachery. The only possibility
for distracting her from Tallent now lay in her son. Patrick
envisioned so traumatizing the brat that Bree's attentions
would again center on Eric.

The next time, Patrick vowed to himself, the very next
time the brat saw those geese, they'd be dead. Stone
cold...dead.

Chapter Nine

At four-thirty that afternoon, Sister Mary Alice Rourke called for Bree from St. Stephen's and asked her to come by the school for a short conference. The last of her work nearly done, Bree agreed. She had a few remaining specimens to culture, but in all, they took her only another ten minutes. Bree let the hospital operator know she'd be taking emergency calls, then tossed the beeper into her purse, locked up the lab and left.

The moment the lab was behind her, Bree's thoughts returned to finding Danziger.

She thought for a while about whether she knew anyone at the utility company whom she could approach for information. With the kind of high-tech computer necessary to penetrate Blessing's operation, Danziger had to have electric service somewhere. Of course, he could have service under the name of some phony business. Worse still for purposes of finding him, Bree supposed, Danziger might have a generator of his own, just as she had at the cabin above Ouray. Still, it was worth checking into.

But then, stopped at a traffic light behind a pickup whose driver was talking on a cellular car phone, Bree thought about the telephone company.

Again, supposing Danziger had such a computer, he *had* to have a modem to access Blessing's computers. She grew excited with the possibility that Blessing could follow such a connection back to the point of origination. All else failing, surely there would be phone-company records to establish long-distance charges to Blessing's computer center!

On her way to St. Stephen's, Bree changed direction and drove toward Michael's house site. Perhaps he had an idea about gaining access to phone-company records. She parked the Eagle just off the highway and walked down the small slope.

Both Michael and Eric had on Walkmans now, and both were engrossed, their heads bent together over some project. The geese intercepted Bree well before she reached the house; she'd grown adept at shooing them away.

Busy practicing with a hammer and nail, the tip of Eric's tongue stuck endearingly out the corner of his mouth.

Busy holding the nail for his son, Michael's arms surrounded Eric as they stood together at a saw horse.

For a moment, the stab of pleasure in Bree for Eric's sake was as sweet as anything she'd ever known. Michael's highly muscled limbs surrounding Eric's coltish ones made her hesitate. For hours, working in the lab, she'd acknowledged to herself how important this man had become in her life in a few short days—how vital in Eric's life.

Now, she owed herself another acknowledgement. She hadn't driven back here only to speak with Michael about computers and finding Danziger. She'd come because it was time Eric learned Michael was his father.

When Michael looked up, her gaze was snared by some powerful, compelling emotion in his pewter gray eyes. Awareness of him made her feel teenage awkward, silly.

She'd been caught out, looking at him the way a woman in love looks at a man, and she knew it.

She smiled, and Michael grinned. Then Eric missed the nail and got Michael's thumb instead. Michael's knowing smile turned rapidly into a startled grimace, and it was all he could do to bite off a curse. Bree laughed aloud and gestured "shame on you" at him, one index finger brushing the other. He whipped off his Walkman and pointed fingers at Bree. "You think it's so funny, you come over here and hold the nails." But his voice contained no anger, and Eric giggled happily.

Bree smirked and made eyes at Michael that Eric wouldn't understand for a few years yet. "The way you were smiling at me, you'd have hit your own thumb, bud."

"The way *you* were smiling at me, I'll have nothing left for fingers inside of a week," Michael returned, his voice nearly as raw as the look in his eyes.

"That'd be a real shame, Tallent," Bree taunted back softly, meaning every word, mesmerized by the fire she was playing with here.

"You guys gonna jaw all day?" Eric interrupted, pulling off his own Walkman. "I'm learning how to hammer, here, Mom!"

Michael cleared his throat, put Eric's headset back on and held up another nail. "Remember what I told you now," he urged gently, "look at the nail—don't take your eyes off it to watch the hammer. Okay?"

Eric nodded and began hammering intently.

Michael looked up again, dividing his attention now between Bree and keeping the nail straight. "Where were we?"

Lips pursed, her smile seemingly unquenchable, Bree's expression told him he knew exactly where they had been. "I have to run over to St. Stephen's. I thought maybe you'd want to take Eric out to McDonald's and . . . tell him."

By degrees, Michael straightened. He knew instantly that she meant he should tell Eric, now, that he was his father, and he was stunned. Every time he felt the wallop of sheer physical attraction between them, Bree inspired something still stronger in him, some latent, almost alien emotion far more noble than lust.

Reminded this noon of the passion in which Eric had been conceived, Bree made him want more than anything to protect her—in a fairly primitive manner for being a civilized man. And in the midst of a little sexual banter, she'd made him straighten up and think . . . respect.

He knew how scared she was that Eric would hate her for her lies, that she'd lose him emotionally. The decision, her selflessness, only made Michael love her more.

No doubt about it, he thought, more than a little warily, he was, indeed, falling for his son's mother all over again.

Squeezing Eric lightly on the shoulder to get his attention, Michael suggested his son take a break—maybe get a Coke from the camper icebox and play fetch with Caruso for a while. Bree snagged Eric for a quick hug and told him she'd see him later, after he and Mike had dinner.

"Alone?" Michael croaked after Eric scampered away. "You want me to tell him alone?"

Bree shrugged. "I know you'll be fair. I have to go over to the school anyway." She saw something like gratitude or admiration rising in Michael's eyes. She didn't want to think about why she'd done what she'd done in giving Michael the go-ahead. She didn't want to think about Michael having to be grateful for something so basic as the right to be his son's father, either, so she changed the subject quickly.

"Michael, I was thinking, if there really is no way to track Roy Danziger—did I tell you they told me he's on vacation?—anyway, if we're really at a dead end, wouldn't the phone company have a record of long-distance calls?"

Adjusting to her change of subject, Michael had no trouble following the drift of her thoughts. "Sure. Danziger would have had to use a modem to access the naval-intelligence computers. He could have planted the loop on the deputies months ago, though—"

"Still, there would be records. Could you flash your old ID again, tell the phone company you're investigating computer fraud and demand to see their records?"

"Probably not, Breez. They'd ask for a warrant—"

"Which, I bet, Blessing could fax to you within twelve hours."

"You're forgetting, I'm not empowered to serve a warrant."

"Michael, think! Blessing wants this maniac, too. If he could get a federal search warrant, do you think he'd give a fig whether *anyone* ever found out you weren't empowered to serve it?"

Michael had to admit that no matter what the obstacles, Blessing would overcome them if it meant neutralizing the threat to national security that Joseph Preston's avenger represented. And Bree's idea to check the long-distance records ought to confirm or clear Danziger as their Mad Hatter once and for all. Any call to the computers in Virginia from Grand Junction, Colorado, had to be their man.

Reaching out to touch her cheek, Michael complimented her plan. "Sounds like our best bet, Breez."

Bree nodded. "I have to go now, or Sister Mary Alice will give up on me. Will you call Blessing this afternoon?"

"Yeah. I'll find a public phone somewhere when I take Eric to dinner. We're better off presuming your phone is tapped, and this will only work if Danziger, or whoever we're fighting, never knows—which means we're limited to public phones."

"Well," Bree said, backing slowly away, "I'll be going. I'll see you back at my house later?"

"Later," Michael confirmed, his gray eyes trained on her as she walked backward. But when she had turned and made her way very nearly out of earshot, Michael called to her. "Bree?"

She turned back, and even from that distance, knew that Michael saw the tears gathering in her eyes. The next time she saw Eric, he would know Michael was his father.

"Thanks."

Bree smiled tremulously, but by the time she'd reached the car, her tears had faded unshed. She needed every bit of her composure to face the formidable Sister Mary Alice Rourke, the nun in charge of Eric's school, with the necessary changes in his records. Changes to reflect Michael Tallent as Eric's father, which meant explaining the lies she'd told years ago.

Sister Mary Alice was waiting at the door when Bree drove up. Statuesque in her shortened version of a religious habit, thin as a rail and perceptive as she was eagle-eyed, Sister Mary Alice put her arm around Bree's shoulder as they walked toward the office. "Have you had a nice summer, my dear?"

In all the years she had known Sister Mary Alice Rourke, Bree had never known her to inquire idly about anything. Did the nun already know about Michael? Perhaps Sutterfield had told her. "It's been . . . interesting, Mary Alice. A lot of changes. I've meant to come see you. Is there some problem?"

They'd reached the school office, and the nun indicated Bree should sit. Curiously, Mary Alice didn't sit behind her desk, but instead pulled her chair around near Bree. Before she sat, she plucked a file from her desk and held it to her chest. "I don't know if there is a problem as yet, Bree, but I have received some papers which I presumed you would wish to see. However, if you've something to tell me, by all means do so first."

Bree drew a deep breath and proceeded to set the record straight. "Eric's father isn't dead, Mary Alice. He's alive and living now in Grand Junction."

Unless it really mattered, Bree told the nun, she wouldn't go into all the history that had caused her to enroll Eric with a deliberately inaccurate history. In the thick of her apologies and explanations, Bree stopped and smiled self-consciously. "Feel free to stop me, Mary Alice, when you've heard enough...."

"My dear, I am not so surprised as you may think—at least, not since I have had time to think about the papers that were waiting here for me when I returned from my small vacation. Here—" she pulled an envelope from Eric's file and handed it to Bree "—perhaps if you read this, you'll see what I mean."

The return address on the envelope read Grissom, Dirks and Panteel, Attorneys at Law.

PATRICK HAD NEVER COUNTED himself a violent man. He knew a gun when he saw one, but doubted quite sincerely that he could distinguish a shotgun from a rifle. It hardly mattered in any case. Shooting those geese might well draw unwelcome attention.

By the same token, though he had an ax and could use it, he doubted that he could get close enough to the geese to be effective with an axe. Or maybe he just wanted to avoid thinking of the blood an ax would spill.

He had examined and discarded numerous possibilities to carry out his intentions and had settled, at last, upon poison. Then he discovered that he couldn't just go out and buy a poison that was immediately fatal upon ingestion. The world had become too environmentally conscious to offer such a poison for sale without the buyer producing a permit.

Patrick couldn't wait for the cumulative effects of more readily available mouse and rat poisons, and so he'd given up that choice altogether.

The only thing for it was to find an executioner other than himself, and so Patrick had called Johannson Farms, which locally produced chicken, as well as domestic turkey, pheasant and goose for grocery chains and restaurants. Speaking with the proprietor, Patrick made up a story he was really quite proud of. In fact, the elegance of his improvisational solution impressed him very much. Claiming to be Michael Tallent, he explained that he had purchased four geese to guard his building site, but just today, the geese had attacked a neighbor child. He wanted the geese destroyed, he said, but left on the property so that he could bury them. He'd become quite attached to those birds and couldn't bring himself to cause their demise.

The proprietor had agreed, after some ten minutes more of Patrick's impassioned pleas coupled with promise of handsome payment, to send his son by the building site after the close of business. If his son found no one there but the geese, he'd wring their necks—otherwise, Mr. Tallent would have to call back again.

Patrick was elated with the success of his story, and confident. Didn't Roy speak all the time of chance favoring the prepared mind?

Patrick couldn't watch the executions. He was fascinated by the promise of dispassionate violence, truth be told. *Truth be damned.* Patrick smiled at his clever sleight of words—truth be told; truth be damned. Later, he'd tell Roy Danziger how *he himself* had wrung the necks of Tallent's geese.

Truth be told; truth be damned.

Addressed to Sister Mary Alice Rourke, Director, the missive from Grissom, Dirks and Panteel was signed by Hamilton Grissom and included a copy of Eric's birth certificate. Insofar as Michael Tallent was named on the birth certificate as the child's father, the letter said, and insofar as Mr. Tallent wished to acknowledge paternity of the child Eric, and insofar as the child's mother had obtained a passport for the child under a name not even her own...

Bree lost track of the "insofars" and "wherefores" and the "rights of paternity" that followed. A small breath of alarm curled in her, but she read on, determined not to allow vague, nameless fears to overshadow the faith in Michael she'd only just found. The import of the letter was that Michael wanted St. Stephen's voluntarily and immediately to place his name on any and all records necessary to assure that every matter concerning his son be referred to him, emergency or not.

Finished reading, Bree glanced at the date of the letter and handed it back to Mary Alice along with the rest of the file. "This must have come as quite a shock to you, Mary Alice. I'm very sorry."

"I was truly stunned, Bree. This letter says Gregory is an assumed name for you, as well?"

Bree nodded. "My name is...was Sabrina Preston. Mary Alice, this letter is five weeks old. Michael must have seen this attorney even before he...contacted me."

Her lips pursed in disapproval, Mary Alice waved the letter from Grissom at Bree. "Yes, the letter is several weeks old—I was out of town, remember? But what kind of man goes behind the back of his child's mother in such a way as this?"

"He was very bitter that I kept Eric's existence from him, and his from Eric," Bree answered softly. How curious to be put in the position of defending Michael's actions! "In some ways, Michael is a very hard man, Mary Alice, but...he had a baby daughter once, named Abbie. Her mother, Michael's wife, Daisy, was my best friend."

"What happened to them?"

"Daisy fell asleep at the wheel of her car and drove off a bridge. They drowned. It was awful, Mary Alice. Abbie's breathing was never dependable her first year, and the pediatricians had just taken her off a nighttime breathing monitor.'' The memory of that awful time tore at Bree. She'd never before or since had such a close friend as she'd had in Daisy Tallent, and Abbie had been Bree's goddaughter. It was Daisy who'd first called Bree by the name Michael used even now—Breezy....

''Michael and I tolerated each other for Daisy's sake. I didn't like him very much then—he had such a hotshot, conceited way about him.'' After all these years, Bree still couldn't think why, in comparison to Joe Preston, Michael had seemed so arrogant. According to Daisy, it was simple as pie: Michael was the best, and he knew it.

''After Daisy died, I spent a lot of time with Michael— talking about her, talking about his little girl, just filling up the enormous hole Daisy had left in both our lives. He loved being a father, Mary Alice, and I knew that. It makes him crazy that I knew how much children meant to him and that I could keep Eric from him.''

''I'm certain that you had your reasons, Bree. And I understand—he is a man who loves his children. But surely he must know the importance of a mother?''

Bree sat a little straighter in her chair, somewhat bewildered at the wariness in herself. ''I don't know what you mean. The letter sent to you doesn't say that you may not contact me or that only Michael—'' The look in Mary Alice's eyes—was it pity?—stopped Bree.

''Hamilton Grissom is an old classmate of mine, Bree. Can you imagine that? Thirty years ago, back in Iowa, we went to the same Catholic grammar school.... Anyway, he included a handwritten note to me—of things I'm quite certain he could not put into an official communication.'' She passed the note with Grissom's embossed initials to Bree.

Reluctantly, she took the note. There was a lethargy about her own movements that frightened her, an unwillingness to let go of the gentle euphoria of trusting Michael Tallent. With every spidery-scrawled word, Bree wanted more to throw the note away.

Mary Alice, I find this case extraordinary, to say the least! My client, Mr. Tallent, is prepared to force a custody suit should the child's mother cross him—despite the near impossibility of winning such a suit. I have never before encountered such circumstances, however, and with the current trend toward upholding the father's rights, the mother's actions in failing to notify my client of his son's existence may very well weigh heavily against her in court. Have you a feel for this?

Fondly,
Ham

Her faith in Michael, so new and bright and fraught with possibility, faltered badly. The pressure in her chest made it nearly impossible to breathe. This very afternoon, Eric would learn the truth…from Michael. Dear God, what had she done?

WHAT SURPRISED PATRICK most, hours later when he kept his dinner appointment at the Hilton with Roy, was the deterioration in his friend's appearance. He'd wondered whether Roy was suffering excessive stress when he'd burned his flesh like that; now Patrick was sure of it.

"Roy, my dear friend, you are looking quite exhausted. Is there anything I can do for you?"

Danziger could think of any number of things Patrick might do—the kindest suggestion being to take a long walk off a short pier. His usefulness in the scheme of things was wearing exceedingly thin—about as thin as Danziger's humor where Patrick Marquet was concerned. "I am feeling a bit under the weather," he said, "but I can't think of a thing you need do for me."

"Are you sure?" Patrick queried, anxious to repay Roy in some small measure for all he had done.

"Quite." Danziger grimaced, and he supposed Marquet took the expression for a reflection of his not feeling well. It was. It was far, far more, as well—pure, unadulterated scorn for present company.

Patrick sipped at his white wine and, gratified by its bouquet, began telling his news. "Poor Bree is on the verge of madness under Tallent's spell. I—I killed Tallent's geese this afternoon. Wrung their necks. I have to get her attention again, Roy," he said, hurrying to explain, seeing in his friend's eyes a hint of incredulity. "The brat was fond of those birds—he'll doubtless be quite upset. Bree will see the ugliness—and once she does, she won't be able to avoid seeing the ugliness in Tallent. When she does, I'll be there, just as you have predicted all along, and when she does—" Patrick stopped suddenly, self-conscious and alarmed that he hadn't quite stopped speaking when he'd been done.

Danziger knew madness. He was as familiar with the solace of madness as he was with the jagged edges of his pain in the real world. He moved back and forth between reason and madness himself now, with an ease and prowess beyond the ordinary, and because of that, he knew it was Patrick and not Sabrina Preston on the brink of irreversible insanity. How else could Marquet suppose that slaughtering those geese would make her look favorably upon him? "Have you had a chance to tell our little widow of Tallent's custody intentions?"

Patrick frowned at the memory of his having botched that particular revelation. He had the most peculiar feeling that Roy no longer approved of him. "No. Didn't I tell you? No, I hadn't—I came to the most insightful conclusion, thanks to your information, and I was eager to pass that along to Bree—''

''What insight would that be, Patrick?'' Danziger lifted his wineglass, inhaling its aroma over the sensory-numbing medication he had administered himself.

''That Tallent assaulted her—sexually, of course. How else does one explain the brat's existence?''

Betrayal explains it, you fool. Simple, sordid betrayal. Truly appalled at the ludicrous leap in Patrick's logic, Danziger could barely restrain himself from ridicule. ''I see. And what did she say to that?''

''She laughed,'' Patrick blurted out. ''I told her she was nearing hysteria and that I didn't blame her for the shame she must feel that I knew what Tallent had done to her. That's when she said she had begged him to make love to her, pleaded with him!''

Patrick felt his rage somehow mirrored in Danziger, and comforted himself that his earlier feelings of disapproval from his friend had been in error. ''She said he was ten times the man I am,'' Patrick scoffed, the anger in him growing again, ''and a hundred times the man Joseph Preston ever was.''

The whore! Control of himself very nearly overloaded Danziger's system. How dare she compare Michael Tallent to Joseph Preston? His lungs lacked oxygen and his head pounded violently, but the speed with which he recovered control reminded Danziger how very, very good he was.

''My friend,'' he urged smoothly, supplying just the insipid advice necessary, ''forget these absurd slights to your masculinity. I have some excellent news for you, if you think you can possibly afford to absent Grand Junction for a day or two.''

Like a Siamese fighting fish confronted by its own image in a mirror, Patrick thought, Danziger had seemed to puff up to awesome, threatening, even murderous proportions—but the image receded so quickly that Patrick was unsure what it had meant.

"This is not a good time, really, to leave—"

"Ah, but the reward! As I've often told you, I know people who know people in high places. Martin Calabrese is willing to look at directing your project, Patrick."

Patrick choked on his fish. "Calabrese?" The name was synonymous with films of stunning intensity and power. Even the possibility of a chance to work with the famous director made Patrick's heart pound. But suddenly, Patrick wondered why it was that a Mesa County sheriff's deputy knew, or even had access to, Martin Calabrese.

Anticipating the doubt flitting across Patrick's eyes, Danziger handed him a piece of paper with a 714 area-code phone number. "Of course, you will wish to check on my information. This phone number is unlisted—the Calabrese beachfront residence. He's en route home from Italy as we speak. Try the number, Patrick. Try it now."

Patrick followed the direction of Roy's implacable eyes to the pay telephones at the restaurant entrance. Threatened by the almost menacing tone of Roy's voice, Patrick knew he should never have doubted. Now he had little choice but to make the call he already believed would connect him with Martin Calabrese's home. Still, Danziger was a nobody. How had he come by this phone number?

Skepticism helped Patrick regain his composure. He left the table with a strong measure of dignity, reached the phone, punched numbers, read off credit-card numbers and turned so that he could see Danziger while the phone rang. A housekeeper answered Patrick's sharp questions with all the right information. Due in yet this evening, Mr. Calabrese had been vacationing on the Italian Riviera.

Pleased, Patrick smiled and gave Roy a thumbs-up gesture.

Gratified, vindicated before this little worm, Danziger grouped his fingertips, brought them to his lips and let his fingers burst apart. Marquet smiled wider. Danziger nearly laughed. He'd known all along only Marquet would see good wishes in the gesture meant to kiss him off.

By this time tomorrow, having told Bree that he'd be off to Hollywood, Patrick Marquet would be dead. Courtesy of Danziger.

The whore would pay even sooner. In spades, courtesy of the KGB lackey.

Chapter Ten

Michael chose a filling station close to the small downtown area, both for the public telephone near the door and because it had a beat-up old pinball machine inside for Eric to play at while Michael placed his call to Virginia.

Blessing answered on the first ring, which meant that he was in his office at home.

"I'm calling from a public phone—"

"Wise move," Blessing interrupted. "Telephone taps are almost certainly child's play for our man—perhaps monitoring Bree's calls all along. I'd wager my pension on it."

"Such a loss," Michael cracked. His back to the wall at the pay telephone, standing within two yards of Eric, Michael went straight to the point. "What do the hackers tell you?"

"The programming loop that comes up with every inquiry into Mesa County personnel records is a so-called computer virus. I'm told that this one was planted at least twenty-eight days ago, but no more than thirty-five days. We have no interactive interference, which—"

"Means it's almost impossible to trace or follow a modem back to the culprit," Michael concluded. Eric managed five hundred points on one steel ball, and Michael exchanged a jubilant high-five slap of the hands with him while continuing his conversation.

"Precisely. Almost impossible," Blessing agreed.

"What about a computer search of phone-company records? There have to be long-distance charges from somewhere in Grand Junction—or at least Colorado—to your computers."

"We've tried. I'm told the phone company's accessible memory on your end has failed for the entire Grand Junction area."

For a moment, Michael just dropped the receiver from his ear in overwhelming frustration. About the same time, Eric ran out of quarters. Michael dug into his pocket for a few more coins, then stuck the phone back between his shoulder and ear. "That leaves only the taped backup copies of the long-distance usage records—right here in Grand Junction. I'll need a search warrant, Carl, and some ID."

"I'm facing some real . . . jurisdiction problems here, Michael." Blessing said hesitantly.

"Jurisdiction! I'm bailing *you* out and trying to keep bodies alive here, and you have the nerve to spout jurisdiction at me?"

"I'm perfectly aware how ridiculous that sounds—"

"I doubt it!" Michael snapped.

"Compared," Blessing continued, "to the national security threat that we are faced with—not to mention your lives. Nevertheless, I am not willing to try explaining all this in a Congressional hearing, which is what happens these days, Michael. I am answerable. I could call in a few markers and get a federal warrant—"

"Forget it. Just forget it. I'll figure something out from this end. But let me tell *you* something, Carl." Michael had had it with everything—knowing so little, wanting so much. Trying to keep Bree and Eric alive—and Martha and others he hadn't even met—all the while, coping with an enemy he couldn't name, much less find.

"I figure you're stonewalling me, old man. I figure you sent me in here blind. I don't know what you know or why you did it. But if this thing goes down bad, you're answerable to me...*first*. Answering to a Congressional committee will be the least of your worries."

Then Michael hung up, afraid if he didn't break the connection, he'd slam his fist through plate glass—or something else stupid enough to scare the hell out of Eric. Which was, of course, the last thing he wanted to do. The last of the pinballs escaped Eric's furious flipper action and fell through.

"Darn! Could we play together this time? I could take this flipper and you take that one? Please, could we?"

Michael elbowed Eric's shoulder conspiratorially. "How about we come back again someday and play together? I don't know about you, pardner, but I could eat a dinosaur."

"I could, too," Eric answered, an equally conniving smile on his face.

They weren't three bites into their burgers before Michael discovered what Eric's connivance was all about.

"Is my Mom pretty?" he asked.

Grateful for the bite of sandwich that made a quick response impossible, Michael mentally congratulated his matchmaking, devious-minded seven-year-old for a brilliant ploy. No matter how transparent the question was, images of Bree still flashed in Michael's head, and he was reminded of exactly how pretty he thought Bree was.

He'd already figured out that straightforward was the only way to handle Eric, and so he nodded, took a swallow of his strawberry shake and answered Eric's question. "Yeah. I think your mom is real pretty."

Eric nodded solemnly. "Kinda thought you did."

"She a good cook, too?"

"You *know* she is," Eric answered, close to figuring out his matchmaking was coming as no surprise to Mike.

"And *you* know your mom is pretty, so let's not kid each other, okay?"

Eric nodded, and a greater determination came into his eyes. "Okay, let's be straight."

Michael's opening had come. He couldn't believe how fast his mouth went desert dry—or that he'd go cotton mouthed when he had his chance. "Eric, your mom and I haven't been straight with you. We're both very sorry for that. You've always wanted to know about your dad—"

"I don't care about my dad," Eric said, interrupting excitedly, his burger forgotten. "I mean, I want *you* to be my dad, so if you think my mom is pretty and all, and you marry her, then you *will* be my dad and I won't be an orphan anymore like Little Orphan Annie wasn't an orphan anymore when Daddy Warbucks adopted her!"

Touched to his core, Michael swallowed hard and tossed three-quarters of his second sandwich back into the box, just as Eric had done with his sandwich in his excitement. "Eric, there are . . . things between your mom and me. We were very good friends once, but a lot of things went wrong and it's hard now to remember the good instead of the bad."

Nervously, Eric twirled a French fry back and forth in his ketchup. "Does that mean you won't ever think of gettin' married to my mom?"

"I don't know, Eric." Lord, why was it so hard to say? *I am your father.* "The thing is, we don't have to get married for me to be your dad."

"You don't . . . ? You don't!" Swallowing hard, scared to death to misunderstand, Eric jumped to his feet. "You mean you *are* my dad? My real dad?"

"Yeah," Michael croaked. "Your real dad."

At first, confusion lit Eric's eyes, a sort of wait-a-minute-why-didn't-I-know-this-before wariness that Michael suspected would come again. But in the next moment, Eric gave in to a seven-year-old's delight at having gotten exactly what he wanted, no matter how.

Talk about your smiles. Michael hadn't ever felt quite the kind of uncomplicated joy he did as when his son launched himself into his arms, knowing for the first time that they were father and son.

But the joy was not so uncomplicated, and Michael knew it. Eric deserved a family—not a mother here, a father there and conflict all around. Family.

What a hypocrite, Tallent, he mocked himself. He'd told Eric they oughtn't be kidding each other when he was only kidding himself. He'd been thinking maybe... maybe he'd ask Bree to marry him.

And it wasn't only because Eric needed a family.

BREE LEFT MARY ALICE Rourke's office at St. Stephen's in a state of shock. She held the Eagle's keys in her hand. She could smell the roses on the trellis by the door and she could see for herself that the earth still revolved about the sun. Reason told her no court in Colorado would take her child from her, no matter how many lies she had told.

But Colorado had never dealt with Michael Tallent.

Bree got into her car, switched on the ignition and backed out of her parking place, all the while remembering what it was to deal with Michael when his principles were violated. She'd told Mary Alice that Michael was a very hard man in some ways—which didn't paint the picture by half. As a mole, spying on behalf of the KGB, Joseph Preston had violated all of Michael's moral standards. It had taken enormous integrity and persistence to discover and expose his best friend for a traitor, but to Bree's knowledge, Michael hadn't once flinched.

Now it was *her* lies clashing with Michael's values. Above all else, she'd raised Eric to tell the truth, but because of the choices she had made, Eric didn't even know he had a father who was alive. A lie Michael couldn't tolerate.

If Michael wanted Eric, he would have him. He had told her that from the first, and maybe because she wanted so badly to trust Michael, Bree was scared.

She drove toward home in a sort of haze and found Martha alone there. The elderly lady had fixed a cool chicken salad and was just settling in to watch her favorite PBS program when Bree came in. Martha hadn't seen Michael and Eric, but she knew, because Michael had been so thoughtful as to call her, that "the men" would be having dinner out.

Bree dished up a small serving in her kitchen and tried to eat a bit of Martha's wonderful curried chicken salad. She could swallow only a few bites, for anxiety had her stomach in knots. Michael was hard, but never cruel, and it had been thoughtful for him to call Martha. But Bree mistrusted even his kindnesses now.

Michael's honor and integrity wouldn't allow him to just take Eric and leave her to her fate with Joe Preston's avenger. No, he'd stick around long enough to see her out of this scrape and when it was all over, he'd take Eric away.

A few hours ago, his smile had made her melt. A few hours ago, she'd have trusted Michael Tallent with her very soul. Now, she knew she had done just that in letting him speak alone to Eric.

She wished Michael had never come to Grand Junction. She couldn't help caring for him, for the kind of man, even the kind of father, that he was, but he had it well within his power to destroy her.

Scraping her salad into the disposal, Bree rinsed her plate, stuck it in the dishwasher and went to change clothes. She had to find Eric.

When she found him, tears were pouring down Eric's cheeks and he was shrieking in outrage. Like a kite whipping out of control in a windstorm, Eric's little fists flailed wildly at Michael.

Panic and fury at Michael flooded her, and a dozen crazy possibilities, like kidnapping, sprang to her mind. She slammed the car door and raced down the slope toward Michael's half-built house, ready to gather Eric into her own arms and take him away. But when she saw the geese lying on the ground, their heads at awful, unnatural angles to their once long, elegant necks, she understood. It wasn't Michael or anything he'd done that had caused Eric's hysteria.

Someone had killed the birds, and Eric had loved those geese as much as he loved Caruso.

The grizzly horror struck Bree nearly as hard. Her stomach lurched and she went cold all over. Michael finally got hold of Eric and held him tightly to fend off the ugliness a little boy shouldn't have to handle.

Bree sat beside them on the ground and fought back tears that had as much to do with Eric's torment as with the poor, dead geese. For a moment, she even forgot the threat of Michael's custody demands. "Who could have done this? Who could be so cruel?"

Michael only shifted Eric in his lap and, eyeing the twisted bodies, shook his head disgustedly. Eric's heartbroken sobs eased away gradually. Cradled into the welcoming bulk of Michael's chest, the rage went out of him. Bree's heartbreak seemed only to get worse because the longer Michael held Eric, the more insecure she became.

"Let me take him home, Michael."

He seemed to consider her request before letting his head down so that his chin rested against the top of Eric's head. "Think we better bury the geese. What do you say, pardner?"

"Michael, please . . . this is . . . Eric doesn't need to—"

"Mom! We gotta bury 'em!" Eric shouted, darting out of Michael's lap. His eyes were nearly raw from his rubbing, and the tendons stood out in anger on his flushed little neck.

Bree clapped a hand over her mouth to keep from overreacting or reacting badly. "Eric, honey, I didn't say the geese don't have to be buried—"

Eric jammed his fingers into the pockets of his jeans and kicked belligerently at the dirt. "You didn't say Mike was my *dad,* either."

If Eric had accused *her* of killing the geese, Bree couldn't have been more stunned or more upset, and though she opened her mouth to speak, there seemed absolutely nothing to say. She clamped her lips shut again and turned accusing eyes to Michael.

To his credit, he seemed surprised at Eric's frontal attack as well—but Michael wasn't left without anything to say. Kneeling in front of Eric, he took his son by the shoulders. "That was a little bit out of line, pardner. Remember, I told you we were both really sorry we hadn't been straight with you?"

"Yeah," Eric said, the belligerence gone out of his posture. "Sorry, Mom."

Bree's jaw ached, so tightly had her teeth been clenched together. "I know, Eric. I'm sorry, too, for not telling you. But I think you should come home now. It's almost dark, and—" Bree could see the resistance flooding back into Eric the geese still had to be buried, after all. "Michael?"

Staring at Bree in the deepening twilight, unable to figure out why she was making such an issue of taking Eric home, Michael suggested Eric go the camper and bring back some blankets in which to wrap the poor geese. When Eric darted off to do that, Michael turned back to Bree, his fingers crammed into his jeans exactly as Eric's had been a few minutes ago.

"What's going on, Bree?"

"I don't want him to stay," she snapped.

"Well, what you want isn't the only consideration anymore, is it?" he returned. "When a pet dies, Bree, you bury it. Every kid knows that."

"And when pets are murdered because a kid's parents are the targets in some deranged global intrigue?"

"The geese still need to be buried." But although he knew Bree had a point and he was curious about her global-intrigue remark, her overly defensive attitude concerned him more. "What happened, Breez, to make you so tense and angry?"

Bree dragged a hand through her hair as she watched Eric emerge from Michael's camper with a pile of blankets. The sun had just dipped over the western horizon, and a sudden chill in the air made her hug her bare arms close to her body. "Mary Alice Rourke had a letter from Grissom, Dirks and Panteel."

Uneasiness began moving through him. "Mary Alice Rourke—the principal at Eric's school?"

"Yes, Michael. The principal at St. Stephen's got a letter from your attorney."

Michael nodded. The fireflies were beginning to come out and he wanted to get the geese buried soon. "A letter asking that my name be put onto Eric's school records. Right?"

"Along with a personal note from your lawyer to Mary Alice. Grissom said you are serious about forcing a custody suit."

The accusation in Bree's voice took away Michael's breath. How could she believe, how could she even *think* that he'd try to take Eric from her? An hour ago, Michael had been thinking there might be enough between himself and Bree to make a go of getting married and being a family.

"We ought to be beyond these accusations, Bree. I thought maybe after Ouray, you trusted me. I thought I let my thumb get hammered this afternoon because you were making eyes at me. Was I wrong?"

She didn't have an answer for that, any more than she'd had one for Eric. Yes, she'd learned to trust Michael, and yes, she'd been making eyes at him. None of that mattered; he'd gone to an attorney to gain custody of her son, and talk was cheap.

Disappointment in Bree's inability to sustain a little faith in him gripped Michael to his soul. What possible chance did he have with a woman who had been burned as badly as Bree? It was a wonder she could trust another human being at all.

Michael wanted even more than trust from her, not less, and he seemed pretty damned unlikely of ever getting it. The worst part was, he couldn't even blame her.

He turned away and called to Eric, who'd been arranging covers on the dead geese. "Your mom is right about going home," he told Eric. "Now, before you get all upset, I want you to help me later with their grave markers, okay? Because markers are the most important things."

Sensing this compromise was the only one, Eric quickly agreed. Michael tousled his son's hair and then backed away, his eyes pinned on Bree's. He might never get the full measure of her scant trust, or even less, her love, but he couldn't help telling her how it was with him. If he'd wanted only Eric, he'd have taken the boy weeks ago and left Bree to her own devices with the Hatter.

"Take him home, Bree. And think about this. If I wanted things the way you're so ready to believe I want them, I'd already be long gone with the goods."

Bree swallowed as she took Eric's hand. "With or without the Hatter?"

"Believe it." Michael nodded and his eyes never left hers until she turned away.

Bree had been scared before, a hundred times since Joe Preston had been discovered as a traitor, in a hundred different ways, but she'd never been more scared than now. Michael Tallent wanted her as much as he'd wanted Eric or he'd have taken his son and gladly left her to her fate.

She'd told Mary Alice what a hard man Michael was, only she hadn't truly believed it until now. Paradoxically, he was as ready to die for her as for Eric, and that frightened her. She'd never in her life known that kind of compassion. She dared not call it love.

AFTER HE HAD BURIED the geese, each mated pair in a single grave as he'd promised Eric, Michael debated whether to drive his pickup truck to Bree's house or to walk. Time to think that a walk would afford tilted the balance in favor of leaving the truck at the building site. He went inside the small camper, collected the last of his clean clothes, as well as a shotgun and his binoculars, stuffed them all into a duffel bag, then stepped outside again.

The silence in place of the usual guttural geese sounds hit Michael hard, and he realized how attached he'd become to those birds. He remembered to pick out some wood scraps suitable for grave markers and started out in the night toward the ridge above Bree's house.

There was the off chance that the geese had been killed by vandals, but it didn't seem likely. Michael sensed that the Hatter was getting bored now of the cat-and-mouse games. Until the slaughter of the geese, the avenger had had to take no overt action to keep the terror rolling. He'd simply taken brilliant advantage of situations as they arose, such as the escaped prisoner's presence in the mountains near Bree's cabin.

The sheriff's deputy, Danziger, seemed the common factor, connected not only with Patrick Marquet and Tom Sutterfield, but with the Mustang that followed Bree for no other reason than to intimidate. Until they could find Danziger—and his ability to stay out of sight seemed highly suspicious now, too—there was no hope of stopping him.

Hiking over the hills, Michael thought about the various tactics for getting into the phone company tomorrow—cover stories he might offer for examining records in search of modem contacts made to Blessing's computers.

If they didn't get a break in identifying Danziger soon, it might be too late.

When he reached the ridge above Bree's neighborhood, he dropped his duffel bag and, checking the safety on the shotgun, sat looking for someone else observing her house. For all his scrutiny, he detected nothing out of the ordinary, nothing even vaguely threatening—except that Marquet was leaving by Bree's front door.

Straightening, every muscle in his body tensed for action, Michael watched as Bree waved goodbye. Marquet waved, too, then got into his Mercedes, turned on the engine and rolled down the power window next to him, as if to say something more to Bree. Michael pulled the binoculars from his duffel bag and focused immediately behind Bree.

No one. For an instant, his muscles went slack with relief. Then Michael realized exactly how vulnerable they all were, and his relief evaporated. The visitor might have been Preston's avenger and not Marquet. From now on, Michael realized, none of them could afford to be alone.

He focused the binoculars inside the Mercedes and noted the expensive leather suitcase and what looked like a suit bag. Cursing himself for having left his truck, because he couldn't follow Marquet, Michael waited to see which direction Patrick took when he got to the highway.

The Mercedes turned eastbound, and though Michael lost sight of the car for a moment as it passed behind a hill, he picked out the distinctive taillights again just as the car approached the bridge spanning the Colorado River.

Lowering the binoculars, Michael started to get up when he heard an echo that sounded vaguely like an explosion. He glanced back; the pit of his stomach seemed to fall away. He jerked the glasses back up in time to see Patrick Marquet's Mercedes, shooting flames fifty feet into the air, go off the bridge and crash into the river.

Even the tremendous splash of river water failed to stop succeeding explosions.

FOR A LONG TIME, Eric and Michael worked in the garage on the grave markers. Eric knew exactly where to find a hammer and nails because Michael had given him a child's size tool belt a couple of weeks before. He also knew that he could find a partly used can of paint in the cabinet by the back door.

Bree sat on the stair riser just outside the door of the garage with her cup of orange pekoe tea, waiting to see their work. Eric held up the marker he'd worked on and asked what Bree thought.

He had used his water colors to paint an outsized Rest In Peace on the marker, and beneath, he'd printed the names of the geese he'd called George and Martha—after the nation's first President and his wife. Painted flowers trailing down the side were a little smudged, but all in all, it was a wonderful marker, and Bree told him so. She could see the approval in Michael's eyes, but the phone rang then before she could see the marker Michael had painted.

Martha had answered the phone by the time Bree got back into the house. "Sounds like the hospital, Bree. Are you on call tonight?"

Nodding, Bree patted Martha's hand and reminded her that she'd taken call duty tonight because her suspension was over. Answering the call, she learned Martha was right. The nurse in charge was calling to relate emergency orders for lab tests. The intensive-care patient needed blood examinations—oxygen levels, electrolytes and liver-enzyme studies right away. By the time Bree hung up the phone, Michael and Eric had finished in the garage and were walking into the kitchen.

"The hospital?" Michael asked.

From the moment he'd walked in the door tonight, Bree had sensed an intensity about Michael that seemed almost violent to her. The raspy tone of his question confirmed her opinion.

"Yes. That was the ICU calling. I'll be just an hour or so." She turned to go upstairs and change out of her running shorts.

"You're not going anywhere, Bree."

She knew Michael well enough to know this was no ridiculous macho power play; still, she resented it. "The patient's treatment will depend on blood-test results, Michael. I cannot simply say I will not go."

Bree could see the anger flaring in Michael's pewter-colored eyes, but he slapped the paintbrush into the kitchen sink, started the tap water streaming over it, then cuffed Eric playfully on the shoulder. "Better hit the showers, pardner."

Eric grabbed a soda from the refrigerator and ran up the stairs to his room. Having a real father around seemed to motivate him to cooperate.

Michael began to wash his own hands under the sink tap. He had to tell Bree about Marquet's fiery death if he expected her to understand why he would stand here all night refusing to let her out of the house. Until now, he hadn't thought of a way to tell her. He reached for a kitchen towel. Leaning against the counter, he dried his hands. As an entrée, he asked, "What was Marquet doing here tonight?"

"He came over to tell me he was flying out tonight to Hollywood—some big-time chance to break back in. Michael, I don't have time for this right now. I have to go in—"

"Patrick is dead, Bree. Some kind of explosives or incendiary bullet hit his car. I saw his Mercedes go off the bridge in flames, and then there were several more explosions."

The color drained from Bree's face. She sank down in shock onto one of the kitchen chairs. Michael thought he should still have been a little horrified himself at knowing someone had assassinated Patrick, but he wasn't.

All he could think was that he'd wanted and half expected Bree to come into his arms for a tiny bit of comfort and she hadn't. It didn't matter that he loved her. Bree had become incapable of needing anyone.

He'd never seen quite the iron control that Bree exercised. Yes, she'd been shocked, but no tears, not one, escaped her over the news of Patrick Marquet's death.

The horror multiplying over and over again inside her, Bree wanted Michael to hold *her* as he had held Eric when they'd discovered the dead geese. For one insane moment, Bree felt a childish hysteria rising in her, enough to make her want Michael to hold her through the nightmare.

Instead, she pushed the grief and panic aside and denied even to herself that she needed Michael or needed to be held. First the geese, and now Patrick had been killed, and she understood why Michael had told her she wasn't going anywhere. But there *was* no one else to call to the lab, and a critically ill patient's life depended on her getting there and turning out some results.

"I'm going, Michael. I have to go. I'd be no better than Danziger—or whoever murdered Patrick—if that patient dies because I was afraid to go to the hospital."

Michael scraped the back of his hand against whiskers he hadn't had a chance to shave since morning. He knew Bree thought he could be heartless, and just now, he knew why. He'd choose Bree's safety over the life of the hospital patient any day. She wouldn't make that choice herself, and unless he was willing to forcibly stop her, he knew she'd go.

"I'll take you, then," he conceded at last.

"And leave Eric and Martha here alone?"

"They can ride along."

"Eric needs to get to bed. Think about it, Michael," she said, reasoning with him. "The Hatter has killed the geese and Patrick both—it's in keeping with his style to sit back now and let the horror sink in. I have to go—now—or it won't matter." She turned again to go get out of her shorts and into a skirt. Michael followed her and stood at her bedroom door while she changed.

He caught one tiny glimpse of her panties and acknowledged to himself how fiercely attracted to her he was. The relentless truth was, he'd forgo his attraction in a minute if he could ensure her safety. "Do one thing for me, Breez? Call the intensive-care nurse."

"Why?"

"To make sure the call is legitimate...and to see if it's one of Sutterfield's patients that you're being called out for."

Reaching behind to tuck in the ends of her sleeveless blouse into the skirt she'd put on, Bree nodded her agreement. She felt threatened—and not half so brave as she'd let Michael think she was about going alone to the hospital.

She took a deep breath and dialed the direct number for the intensive-care unit while Michael stood leaning against her doorjamb. "Theresa, Bree Gregory. I'm about to leave home, but I couldn't remember whether the patient was in the unit...." Pausing while the charge nurse confirmed the patient was in her unit, Bree slipped into her white huaraches. "Thanks, really—oh, and is this one of Sutterfield's cases...? No... Shipley. Okay. I'll be there in ten minutes."

Bree hung up the phone, picked up her purse and walked toward Michael at her bedroom door. Stopping short because the way out was blocked and Michael wasn't moving out of the way, Bree felt a bolt of awareness pass through her that she couldn't ignore.

"Satisfied?"

She'd meant was he satisfied with her call to the hospital, and Michael knew it. But the danger they were in, escalated by the hour, made them both powerfully aware that it was their lives at stake. That they had so much to lose in the love neither of them had spoken of.

Michael knew there was no way to keep Bree from seeing in his expression that, in more ways than she'd meant, he was far from satisfied.

Still leaning against the doorjamb, his hands in his back pockets, Michael bent forward and down and touched his lips to Bree's. In less than a second, the kiss was over, but neither of them moved, and their breaths mingled for a moment more. "Be careful, Breez. For Eric... for me. Be careful."

THE FLASHING LIGHTS OF half a dozen emergency vehicles were a beacon in the night from the moment Bree turned the Eagle onto the highway. Guessing that the bridge from which Patrick's Mercedes had plummeted would be closed to traffic, she drove in the opposite direction to take the Hedlands Parkway Bridge over the Colorado River. She knew the reality and the horror of Patrick's death hadn't begun to sink in, but right now, it took every ounce of nerve she had to drive to the hospital alone. For all her bravado with Michael, Bree was badly shaken.

Seven minutes later, she pulled into the circular drive at the hospital, got out of the Eagle and locked it, only to find a paunchy older man in wire-rimmed glasses and dressed in the uniform of a security guard at her elbow.

"Ms. Gregory?" he asked.

"Are you new here?" Bree snapped, not recognizing the guard.

"Officer Weininger, ma'am, and yes, I am new to Grand Junction. Someone called and asked that security escort you in and out of the building tonight."

Bree took a deliberate step backward. Maybe her tolerance for strangers in uniform had just run out—or maybe the guard's statement that *someone* had called security reminded her that *someone* had also called the Ouray sheriff's office, triggering the sharpshooters' attack at the cabin. For whatever reason, Bree didn't want this man within a country mile of her.

"Officer Weininger, I suggest you just go about your job of keeping this facility safe. If I want an escort, I'll call for it."

"Hey, fine, lady. Whatever you want," Weininger said as he backed away.

Seeing the **man's** confusion, Bree almost regretted her outburst. He watched until she passed through the automatic doors. Bree was grateful that the guard had ignored her brush-off. She picked up the lab key at the admissions desk and exchanged greetings with the night operator-receptionist just as she had a thousand other nights on call. And as she walked down the familiar darkened hallway to the lab, Bree chided herself for her lingering anxiety. The door to the lab was locked and there were no lights on inside. Everything was just as she had left it this afternoon.

Everything but the muffled whine of the walk-in freezer alarm.

Chapter Eleven

Annoyance should have overcome Bree's skittish nerves. The insistent pitch of the freezer alarm, unheard and useless in this deserted hallway, rang through the locked laboratory door. Several thousand dollars' worth of ruined test kits and chemicals was all she needed now.

But none of that quite mattered. She hadn't left that freezer door open when she had departed the lab this afternoon, which meant that someone else had been inside. Someone with no business being there. A power or mechanical failure could cause the alarm to pitch its warning tone, but an open freezer door was certainly the most likely explanation.

Feeling vaguely uneasy, Bree turned the key in the lock and the bolt sprang back into the door, the muffled metallic thud echoing like a gunshot. She told herself it was the activated alarm that made her hearing more acute, but every nerve, every sense in her body fired warning messages at her. Nothing was as it seemed to be.

Get out. Get help. Don't go in there alone.

Bree swallowed hard. Such good advice... and for several seconds she actually listened to the voice of reason urging her away because Patrick was dead, and so were the geese—and because she didn't want to die. But the logic in that seemed so visceral, so absurd. A woman didn't die in a small-town hospital's lab in the middle of the night except, maybe, in B movies.

Most women didn't get to be the widow of a KGB mole, either, or a sitting duck in the wrong pond. Gritting her teeth, Bree pulled her key from the lock.

The laboratory door swung open too easily. She could see that the freezer door *was* open and the light inside it was out. Tiny hairs raised on her arms. She took a step inside the lab. Despite the usual odors of cleansers and ethyl alcohol, the smell of death permeated the stale, noise-filled air.

Flipping on the overhead lights, Bree moved quickly to shut off the alarm and close the walk-in freezer's door. Only then she saw a goose dangling from the light fixture in the freezer. One of Michael's geese. One of Eric's pets. Bree clapped a hand over her mouth and instinctively moved back. The goose had one light, flesh-colored foot, and one black. Crudely plucked, its head and beak and twisted neck still dirt covered, this one hung upside down from its albino foot. Her stomach heaving, Bree forced panting breaths to stave off the sickness.

One moment and then another went by while the cruelty registered in her. Shivering violently even before she stepped into the freezer, Bree thought for a fleeting instant how single-mindedly intent she was on getting down the ravaged goose. Rationally, she knew she was in terrible danger herself, but it was impossible for her to leave Eric's pet hanging there.

Despite the cold, Bree forced herself to take one more step inside the freezer. Her limbs seemed stiff and unwilling to cooperate. The cord tied to the wire bulb protector was done in a simple square knot. One more step and she could untie the knot and let the goose down. If only she could get rid of the bitter, metallic taste in her mouth!

Her heart pounding painfully, Bree took another step, but her purse, still hanging from her shoulder, began to fall; it was then, catching at the shoulder bag, that she caught movement behind her out of the corner of her eye. One brutal shove sent her crashing down onto her knees, while at the same time, the shadow of a long-handled, bladed instrument hurtled toward her.

"No!" she shrieked, and hurled herself away from the violent shadow. Too late, she realized she was not the target at all. Instead, an ax poll smashed into the safety handle on the inside of the freezer door.

Bree screamed as the handle broke off and fell to the floor. Struggling to her feet, she lunged at the door. If her attacker managed to shut it against her with no functioning safety release, there would be no way out. She would freeze to death.

"Dear God, can't anyone hear me? Can't anyone hear the damn alarm?" she cried.

In response, her attacker—she had vague, splintered impressions of dark gray clothes and a wrist sprinkled with blond hair above work gloves—slammed the ax at the alarm box, silencing its shrill warning.

Bree struggled with every bit of her strength against the door closing. Her bare knees ached from hitting the floor so hard, and her hands felt raw. The freezing cold sapped her strength with every passing second, and she had almost nothing to use for leverage against the superior strength of her attacker.

Millimeter by millimeter, the door closed tighter. If she had a chance at all, it had to be now. Her whole body shivering, she forced herself to stop shaking and relax, to gather the last dregs of her strength. She took one very deep breath, leveraged her body against frozen metal shelving and pushed against the door as hard as she could. For one glorious, gratifying instant, the door opened wider, tantalizing her with a bigger slice of light. But then, rebounding against her, the door slammed shut.

"No! No!" Bree cried out, furious with herself. The freezer had gone completely dark, and the echo of the door latching mocked her. Defeated, Bree backed away until the head of the goose brushed her shoulder. Instantly, her body wrenched away from that contact.

She fought the terror. She had to think, she had to act, to keep awake, to fight off the effects of the cold. There would be terrible consequences to losing control now, like the deadly euphoria of hypothermia.

You could freeze to death with a smile on your face....

No! Not after everything she'd been through. Forcing movement and purpose on herself, Bree groped blindly in the dark until her hand encountered the body of the bird. *Get it down....* She made herself ignore the way her stomach heaved, and forced her hand to follow the bird's nearly frozen body upward to the cord tied around its foot.

Untie the knot, she ordered herself. But now, her fingers growing colder, even loosening the simple square knot seemed beyond her. A tear fell onto her cheek, warm and wet or she'd never have felt it at all. She dashed it away with the back of her hand.

Getting out was surely more important, and she could pound at the door and scream for help until she froze or someone opened that door, but she would get Eric's pet goose down first if it was the last thing she did ... ever did.

Time lost meaning for Bree in the utterly dark and silent freezer. She'd have sworn she could hear the telephone ringing, endlessly ringing, but she supposed it was only her imagination or wishful thinking. She had no idea how long it took to get the knot loose, but by the time she had, her fingers were numb and raw.

She allowed herself one moment to slump against the door and wonder how soon the ICU charge nurse who had called her in would begin to get concerned and call someone.

Her one languid moment expanded into another, and then another. Bree knew she should keep moving, but somehow, nothing seemed so important. At a level of awareness she couldn't hold on to, Bree knew that this was what hypothermia did to you, letting you relax when relaxing was the last thing you should do, letting you feel peaceful and euphoric when death lurked near enough to grab you. But there seemed nothing she could do, nothing she wanted to do... nothing that needed to be done.

Her thoughts were scattered. Was it Sutterfield who had done this to her, had he called her in and then trapped her and left her to freeze to death...? Poor Patrick... Poor simple man.

The ax. She remembered the ax now, the one her attacker had used to break off the inside door handle. It was Michael's ax.... Of course, it made sense... someone had unearthed the goose and taken Michael's ax at the same time.... Sutterfield? There was no question in her mind, fuzzy and unfocused as it was. Sutterfield had to have ordered tests on another doctor's patient to get her into the lab where he could get at her away from Michael.

Michael. Eric, the child of her heart. Bree could no longer feel... anything... nothing but the gentle, euphoric warmth emanating from inside her, thinking of Michael. Not the memory Michael, but the real man, the man himself.... *Call me Tallent, Bree, if it helps you keep it straight in your head....* Smiling whimsically to herself, Bree curled up next to the door.

I'm in a bit of trouble, Tallent, she thought. *If you're out there...*

THE SWEET OBLIVION of her hypothermia shattered.

From some great distance, she could hear the sound of people rushing about working over and around her, voices...Michael's voice. "I'm here, Breez. I'm here. You're fine—you'll be fine...."

Soft-spoken Michael. She wanted to open her eyes and see for herself that he was there, but she couldn't. It didn't matter. No one in the world had a voice with quite the same hushed, imperative...sensual timbre that Michael Tallent had. But her fingers and toes, wrists and ankles, even her ears and cheeks throbbed with the stabbing of thousands upon thousands of needles as her flesh gradually warmed, and his being there couldn't change any of that.

She'd never known anything like that pain, never, and she knew that she was passing in and out of consciousness...so that when her eyes opened and it was Sutterfield's eyes she saw staring through the emergency treatment room door, she cried out. But in the next instant, the face in the window was gone and Bree couldn't remember how vivid the vision was, or even *if* it was....

She quieted, and for a long time just closed her eyes, resting, her teeth clenched against the pain of her flesh warming again, listening to Michael murmuring encouragement to her. Michael... In her half sleep, Bree forgot Sutterfield's eyes in the window and smiled.

"What is it?" Michael asked. "What's making you smile?"

"Tallent," she croaked. "Not Michael. Tallent."

Michael's heart pounded erratically. "What does that mean, 'Not Michael Tallent'?"

Didn't he remember? Didn't he know? *I'm in a bit of trouble here, Tallent....* Bree shook her head in confusion; why didn't *he* remember what he'd told her or what she'd said to him? "You had to be there, I guess...." At last, her eyes opened to find Michael's at a level with hers where she lay on the emergency room gurney. "What time is it?"

His dear, pewter gray eyes rose to glance at the wall clock behind her. "Almost 3:00 a.m."

Fear hit Bree's veins about the same time she felt the stabbing pain of her thawing flesh easing a little, and she rose onto one elbow. "How long have Eric and Martha been alone?"

"Four or five hours." The glimpse of her naked breast as she lifted herself onto her elbow took Michael by surprise and his palms went suddenly damp. Her clothes had been stripped off her—he'd helped and felt nothing but the pressure to get her out of her clothing and into a warm, circulating bath. But now that she was out of the bath and he knew she'd survive, now that only the pile of warm blankets covered her, now when she moved like that and he caught a glimpse of her breast—now the need of her filled him.

He'd almost lost her.... It took all his concentration to clear his thoughts and to give her an answer.

"Eric and Martha are fine. As soon as I found you locked in the freezer, the police were called. Not the sheriff," he said, anticipating her fear of anyone associated with the Sheriff's Department. "The city police. They have no connection with the sheriff or Danziger. There's a detective outside the door waiting to talk with you, and an officer was assigned to watch your house."

Bree tried to sit up and get off the gurney. Discovering quickly the extent of her weakness after hypothermia, Bree crumpled onto her back. "I want to go home, Michael. We shouldn't leave them alone. I—"

"Bree, you can't expect to get up and walk out of here—"

"Why not? What is there you're not telling me?"

Michael shook his head and stroked a lock of her silvery blond hair behind her ear. He'd almost grown used to her hair being this color. "Nothing, Breez. Nothing. You've only got a tiny spot of frostbite on your forehead...here, and on two of your fingers, here. But the police want to talk to you and—"

"I'm going home, Michael." Wariness curled in her like the overpowering feeling she'd ignored when she went into the lab against her better judgment. She clutched at Michael's hands, willing him to understand. "I have to go home, don't you see? Something terrible is happening! Where are my clothes?"

Michael exchanged glances with the emergency room nurse, then gathered both of Bree's hands in one of his and stroked at her forehead with his other hand. The nurse, who Bree knew only slightly, spoke directly to Michael.

"This kind of irrational fear is to be expected in the aftermath of hypothermia. She could be confused and disoriented and suffer delusions for several more hours yet."

Frustrated, angry and hurting, Bree fell back on the gurney, stared at the ceiling and sighed heavily. "We could all be dead in *several more hours,*" she hissed, her voice low and urgent.

"Look at me, Bree."

She did as he asked and prayed he could see in her eyes that she wasn't suffering delusions at all. "Don't patronize me, Tallent. I know who I am, who you are and that something very bad is going to happen if—"

"Get her clothes," Michael said, directing the nurse while meeting Bree's eyes.

"Sir, I'll have to check this with the doctor—"

"Get her clothes," Michael snapped. "I'm taking her out of here in five minutes, with or without them."

Gratified that Michael had trusted her intuition so quickly against the nurse's warnings of paranoia, Bree smiled. Though even that small effort to smile cost her precious energy, Bree sat up on her own. "I'll get dressed. Can you get rid of the cop?"

Tuned in to every nuance of Bree's words and expressions, Michael knew exactly what it was costing her to get up and move on her own so soon after she'd been near to dying. For weeks now, he'd been telling himself that he respected that strength. Now, by the tightness in his chest, he knew he loved her for it.

He wasn't happy to be taking her out of here, away from medical attention, but he also had to respect her instincts. He'd known Bree a decade ago when they'd both been married to other partners and would have sworn he truly *knew* her.

He'd only just learned. The lady had the instincts of a street fighter and the grit to listen to them. So when she sat there with her cornflower blue eyes huge in her pale face and asked him to get rid of the policeman, he found a way.

He supported her against his body as they made their way out to the car, then lifted her into the passenger seat of her Eagle. Michael drove toward her home as fast as he thought he could get away with, as aware as Bree was of the dangers looming all around them.

Plucking at threads in the gauze taped over her frostbitten fingers, she could feel the toll the freezer incident had taken on her body.

"How did you know to come after me?" she asked.

"I called to make sure you'd gotten to the hospital safely."

So the telephone she'd thought she heard *had* been ringing. Despite her assurances, Michael explained, he'd been worried.

"I tried for half an hour to get an answer at the lab. When I couldn't get you, I had you paged—still nothing." Michael hesitated, his expression grim in recalling the sequence of events for her. He shifted the gears and pressed the accelerator to the floor. "I made Martha and Eric promise not to answer the phone or the door, and we turned on every light in the house."

"You came then, and found me?"

Michael nodded. "The night operator called in someone else to do the lab work you went in for. It was an orderly in the emergency room who called the police."

"Was it you who called security? Some new guy—"

"Yeah." Michael grimaced. "Where the hell was your escort when you got trapped in the freezer?"

"I told him . . . I sent him away. He didn't come in with me."

"You *what?*" Michael swore darkly, and the muscles bunched in his jaw beneath the heavy black shadow of his whiskers. "Bree, why in the hell—"

"I was scared, Michael! I'd never seen that security guard before, and all he said was that *someone* had called. Well, damn it, *someone* called the sheriff in Ouray, too, and we both know how that turned out!"

Knowing she had a valid point, Michael raked his fingers over the knot in his shoulder. "Sorry, that thought never crossed my mind. . . . Do you think that security guard—"

"No."

"How can you be so sure?"

"He was dark complexioned. The one who closed that door on me had blond hair on his wrists. . . . I saw Sutterfield, Michael."

"When you were locked in the freezer?"

"No," she answered, her eyes focused not on him now but somewhere in the distance, as if she was concentrating very hard. "Afterward, looking into the treatment room."

"While you were just coming awake?"

Bree nodded.

"No possibility you were simply seeing things—that it was . . . an illusion?"

"No."

Michael stopped at the light on the intersection of Broadway and First where Bree had noticed the black Mustang following her. "Breez, how the hell can you be so nonchalant? Sutterfield was outside the door looking in and you just—"

"I'm not worried about Sutterfield, Michael! Maybe he locked me in, but maybe the whole incident was a ploy to get us both out of the house—to get to Eric and Martha!"

"There's a squad car sitting in front of the house, sweetheart. If anything had happened, we'd know—"

"But the Hatter said no cops, Michael! If he sees the squad car, all bets are off!"

Michael nodded, aware that calling police into the picture blatantly defied the Hatter's rules. "Alerting the police is what ordinary people do, Breez. The orderly had no way of knowing it might put anyone at greater risk."

"Did they have to send someone to the house?"

The light changed. Michael put the clutch in, shifted to first and nodded to Bree as the Eagle sped into the intersection. "Standard procedure, I take it, to cover the house of a crime victim."

"But—" Whatever had been on her mind fled, for as Michael slowly followed the curve of the westbound road in the glare of the sunrise, a small figure on the road startled and dashed off to the side. A figure the size of a small boy. *Eric* . . . "Michael, stop!"

"What the hell?" he demanded, jerking his head around, trying to see what they'd just passed.

"Michael, stop," Bree cried. "That was Eric!"

"Eric? That was . . . that couldn't—" Though he hadn't seen clearly enough to dispute her, Michael wondered for a split second if the nurse hadn't been right in predicting continuing delusions for Bree. But she jumped out of the stopped car and plunged down the side of the small ravine, screaming Eric's name.

By the time Michael got out of the car and reached the edge of the ravine, he saw that it was Eric scrambling up the hill to Bree, crying incoherently, tears streaming down his face.

In spite of her own lingering weakness, Bree grabbed Eric into her arms and ran back up the hill, though brush caught at her skirt and scrub oak scratched her bare arms. She collapsed at the side of the road, cradling Eric and stroking him to ease his sobs. "Eric, my God. Eric."

Michael went to pull the car a little farther off onto the shoulder, then sat down beside them. The sight of Eric's bare feet, bloodied and bruised below his pajama bottoms, almost made Michael gag. Bree asked the boy what had happened, but for several long moments, he was still incoherent through his tears. When he could finally explain, the story he told was worse than anything Bree had imagined.

Eric said that a man with a big gun like the one Mike wore in his holster had come knocking on the back door, warning Gramma Martha that he'd torch the place if she didn't send Eric out. According to Eric, she'd sent him out the front door instead, telling him to run until he couldn't run anymore.

Michael and Bree exchanged anxious glances as traffic on the highway began to pick up. Her nerves already stretched to the limit with Eric's terror and headlong flight from home, new alarm for Martha's safety flooded Bree.

Michael scooped Eric out of Bree's lap. "Come on, let's get you to the car, little buddy."

Scrambling to her feet, Bree followed. "Wasn't there a policeman in front of the house, sweetheart?"

Eric nodded, his little chin quivering.

"And did he follow you when you ran away like Gramma Martha said?"

Eric wiped his tear-streaked cheek on her shoulder. "For a little while, Mom—in his car, but I lost him." Then, seeing the troubled expression flickering between his mom and dad, Eric asked, "Was that all right? He was the one who was so mean to you when I ran away before."

"You bet it was all right, pardner," Michael reassured him. He helped Eric into the car and then got in himself as Bree closed her door.

Michael knew it was Martha who was still in greater danger, whether the policeman had stayed nearby or not. The effrontery of the Hatter coming to Bree's house under the very noses of the police only meant Preston's avenger wouldn't hesitate to harm Martha, as well. The stakes kept escalating. Pushing the Eagle to eighty miles an hour down the highway toward Bree's house he feared they would be too late to prevent anything happening to the elderly lady.

Michael carried Eric inside to bathe and disinfect the cuts on his feet. It was Bree who found Martha, fallen off the back porch steps with a note clutched in her hands.

"Oh, Martha!" For a second, gaping in horror at this last evidence of the lengths the Hatter would go, Bree was paralyzed. She took the note from Martha's hand. Bending low to kiss Martha's cheek, to reassure the unconscious woman, Bree took a moment to listen for Martha's respirations and to get a count of her thready pulse, then whirled and ran for the telephone to call for an ambulance. While she dialed 911 and waited, Bree skimmed the note in her hand.

Greetings, Michael and Breezy-whore,
   You're getting close, but don't you know, CLOSE only counts in horseshoes and hand grenades, and sometimes, SOMETIMES, not even then. You are too late smart, as my old German grandmother used to say. Catch me if you can.

                                                            Danziger

From the main bathroom where he was bandaging Eric's feet, Michael heard Bree's anguished, muffled cry. Leaving

Eric to finish the bandages, he took the stairs three at a time. He read the crumpled note by the telephone, then found Bree hovering over Martha by the back door. In the distance, they heard the wail of an approaching ambulance.

Anger suffusing him over the brutality to a helpless, brave old woman, Michael crouched on his haunches across Martha's body from Bree and reached out to stroke Bree's cheek. "Will she be okay?"

Bree shook her head. "I don't know. She's probably got internal injuries, maybe a broken hip... I don't know."

Crouched low, his fingers steepled between his thighs, Michael drew a deep breath. "Breez, you know we have to get Eric out of here, don't you? Out of Grand Junction—out of the country, if we can."

Bree looked up from Martha's chalky white, still unconscious face and struggled to hold back the angry quaver in her voice. "Of course, we do. But where, Michael? Tell me that. Where can Eric go that this madman won't find him?

"You know everything about that note he left in Martha's fingers reminds me of *him,* don't you?" she cried, thinking of Preston. "The words he used, the arrogance, the ego. Joe may be dead, Michael, but the evil in him won't die! Someone else just came along to wreak Joe's revenge and pick up where Joe left off. So you tell me, where do we send Eric that—"

Shaking Bree's shoulder, Michael harshly interrupted her outburst. "I don't know, Bree. To my parents, maybe. But wherever, he'll be safer than he is here. We should never have kept him here this long."

"I know that!" Bree snapped, more angry at their foolishness for having kept Eric exposed to danger than at Michael for pointing it out.

"Mom," Eric cried plaintively from behind the screen door. "What's wrong with Gramma Martha? And where are you sending me?"

Bree drew an agonized breath and looked at Michael. She could stay in Grand Junction until her name was cleared and Joe Preston's avenger was caught or killed. She could handle Michael's presence in their lives and even Eric's sniping at her for the lies she'd told him about his father. She could bury geese and even keep herself together after what had happened first to Patrick, and then Martha. But she didn't know how to tell Eric she had to send him away from her.

EIGHT HOURS LATER, at two o'clock that afternoon, Bree stood sipping hot tea by a window in the telephone company's conference room. Carpeted in a sturdy, forest green shag, the room contained an oval oak table surrounded by ten chairs.

Bree hardly noticed. Eric was gone.

Michael had called the Denver-area phone-company offices and managed to collect an impressive array of upper managers' names. Then, under the guise of a regional-office auditor, with a subtle combination of name-dropping and charm, he'd managed to get exactly what he wanted out of the locals—a comfortable place to work and the promise of a printout of all long-distance records covering the period Blessing had suggested. Keeping it simple by the use of her maiden name, he'd introduced Bree as his associate, Sabrina Huntley.

The problem was they had nothing as yet to audit. Michael sat in one of the side chairs, drumming his fingers lightly on the table. Only peripherally aware of all Michael's machinations or of her surroundings, Bree stood at the window overlooking the parking lot and the Toyota Camry Michael had rented at the airport.

Eric was gone and until she had something else to concentrate on, Bree's thoughts kept returning to the past, frenzied hours.

She'd gone in the ambulance with Martha to St. Mary's Hospital. Both of the elderly woman's hips had been broken in the fall she'd taken, and Bree had waited until the orthopedic surgeon took Martha to surgery.

Then they'd buried the geese properly. Michaél had managed to retrieve the goose from the police, who'd removed it from the lab, and safely back into the pillaged grave. Never the wiser, Eric had set out the grave markers. And that was the first Bree knew the names Michael had given the other pair of geese. John and Priscilla.

Where fear and foreboding had failed to provoke her to tears, Michael's romantic allusion to the lovers in Longfellow's *Courtship of Miles Standish* made her cry. Eric thought her tears were for the dead geese.

By eleven that morning, Michael had dressed in the only business suit he'd brought to Colorado, and Bree in the most conservative, businesslike dress she owned. At noon, they'd put Eric on a private plane bound for Aspen, Colorado—and from there, to an international connecting flight Blessing had arranged. Bree had no idea how Michael had handled telling Eric he'd have to fly away and go visit grandparents he'd never even met—she'd been with Martha at the hospital then. But Eric went around spouting a line from the movie *Annie,* and for the second time in one day, Bree had been reduced to tears. *"'A child without courage is like a night without stars.'"*

A private jet would fly Eric to Sapporo, Japan, where Michael's parents were summering. They would look after their new grandson.

Pain threatened her like a talon at her throat, but she couldn't afford to indulge the overwhelming sense of loss in separating so completely from her child. The only way to get Eric back was to put an end to this nightmare.

The only way to do that was to find Preston's avenger and put an end to him.

By one o'clock, they had rented a car at the airport to make it look as if they'd just flown in from Denver to perform the audit. Bree drove her own car but parked a few blocks away, and rode with Michael in the rented Camry to the phone company offices. Michael even gave the supervisor on duty the rental car keys as a subliminal kind of evidence that they had, indeed, just arrived in Grand Junction. His attention to detail paid off. Management believed what it wanted to believe; Michael and Bree were accorded VIP handling.

They needed desperately to find an address for Danziger's operations in the long-distance records at the phone company, but the tapes needed to be brought out of storage, logged, loaded, accessed, printed.... Bree could have screamed over the delay.

Michael shrugged out of his suit coat and sat watching Bree. She'd done far better than he'd have ever guessed in putting Eric on that flight. Michael had to wonder if, keeping her emotions so tightly leashed, Bree might not crack under the pressure. He was as anxious as she to get at the long-distance records.

The search would give them something positive to do, some recourse in the deadly game Preston's avenger had set into motion. Despite the strain, Bree had things on her mind Michael wanted to discuss.

Leaning back in his chair, he crossed his arms over his chest. "Tea any good?"

Bree shrugged. Michael thought even that gesture an improvement to her rigid, tension-filled posture.

"Just tea, nothing extraordinary."

"Breez, yesterday you said something about the geese being slaughtered because we're the targets in some deranged global intrigue. What made you say that?"

"Whoever killed the geese, whoever is behind *all* of this, had to have known Joe," she said simply, still staring out into space. "Maybe Joe recruited him. Maybe they worked together. Even Blessing says no one has made such hash of his computer security since Joe. Maybe Joe was his mentor, his contact with the KGB, and he got cut off when Joe died. If he had even half Joe's ego, Michael, he'd have been outraged to be cut off like that . . . to suddenly become an unwelcome nobody."

Michael got out of his chair and went to check at the door. Apparently satisfied, he closed it again. "That's pretty close to what we've guessed all along. What makes that an international intrigue? If the guy was cut off because Joe was killed, presumably he's been operating on his own ever since."

Bree paced near the window. "What would Joe have done in that position? What if he'd been the one left behind, and he knew who had betrayed *his* mentor?"

"Come after us," Michael answered unequivocally.

"Exactly. So what if the KGB knew about him? What if they knew, sooner or later, he'd come after us and create an international incident? What if he'd tampered with their computers as well as Blessing's? The KGB hasn't gone out of existence just because U.S. relations have become more cordial. Now more than ever, they can't afford a maverick agent like this guy would have to be."

Nodding, Michael saw the elegant logic in the scenario Bree had contrived. "That would explain Sutterfield, wouldn't it? The KGB pops up in Grand Junction, finds the most vulnerable, exploitable resource in Sutterfield and sets him up like a little tin god. In exchange, all he has to do is report to them if I ever show up or if anyone ever puts the screws to you."

"I'm not sure it explains Sutterfield at all. If he was only supposed to report back to some KGB contact, why did he turn on me the way he did that morning in the hospital? Why act like we haven't been friends—at least as the parents of boys who have been friends since they were in diapers together? Why set me up for the big chill in my own lab freezer?'' Bree shook her head. ''It just makes me crazy to think that someone Joe knew and trusted is even near—''

Bree broke off as a woman came through the conference room door, a stack of computer printouts six- or eight-inches thick in her arms and an apology on her lips.

The ingratiating pitch of her voice caused Michael to escort her to the door in short order. With equally ingratiating thanks so syrupy Bree almost choked, Michael promised to let the flirtatious woman know if more help were needed.

When the woman had gone, Michael took one long moment to appreciate Bree's teasing smile.

Bree thought Michael's answering grin made the room seem suddenly a lot smaller. More intimate than it had seemed five minutes ago.

''Are you always such a charmer?'' she demanded, dampening her suddenly bone-dry lips.

''Only when it pays.'' Michael's grin faded about the same time as Bree's tongue swept over her lower lip, and he shoved the printouts to one side. ''I can think of better uses of this table, Bree.''

Heat streaked through her like lightning down a kite tail. Nothing would happen on this table. They had hours of work in front of them, a connection to find, an address to come up with. Their success was a matter of life and death.

All the same, she suddenly knew how very urgent, how very real the attraction between them had become.

Life-and-death real.

Chapter Twelve

At 9:00 p.m., Martha was deemed stable enough to be moved out of the intensive-care unit and onto the surgical ward. Bree followed, poured herself a cup of coffee in the lounge off the nursing station, and returned to Martha's new room, to the easy chair an orderly had moved in for her.

She'd nearly completed a third pass through the thick sheaf of computer printouts, searching for the complicated long-distance transactions Michael had explained to her. By the time she'd left the phone company with the data under her arm, they'd only begun to discover how complicated the search for Danziger's place could be.

The work day ended and most of the staff left the building. Area codes 804 and 703, representing all of Virginia, had revealed less than fifty calls originating in Grand Junction. None connected to Blessing's computer-operations center.

The carryout Chinese dinner was great, but the building janitorial staff came and went before a search for District of Columbia area code 202 calls also failed to provide them a clue.

Undiscouraged, Michael was in his intellectual bailiwick. Code cracking had once challenged his mental prowess every day of his life, and he'd missed that more than he knew. Teaching linguistics didn't quite cut the mustard.

So when it became clear that Danziger hadn't made direct connections with Blessing's computers, Michael's interest was piqued when Bree's heart sank. Bad enough, she worried, that Danziger might be using one of the smaller long-distance competitors. Michael discounted that possibility—industry estimates said this company still had the lion's share of the long-distance business.

Yeah, they *were* dead in the water if Danziger used another service. Michael simply played the odds and focused on the hitch he could solve.

"There has to be at least one intervening computer, Breez," he explained, "which when accessed, acts as a camouflaging link to an end computer—in this case, Blessing's operations computers."

Michael was in luck; the evening supervisor turned out to be somewhat of a hacker herself, a woman only two years out of the Massachusetts Institute of Technology.

Aware that the supervisor had been told they were auditors out of Denver, Michael gave the woman a story about tracking down fraudulent usage. She was only too willing to try reordering the tape data.

Concerned about Martha, alone and vulnerable in the intensive-care unit at St. Mary's, Bree wanted to take a while to check on her. If Michael had been any less preoccupied with the complicated search, she knew he'd never have agreed to let her out of his sight. He consented only after she promised to stay at the hospital until he came to pick her up. He didn't want her out alone after dark.

She left Michael to explain her departure to the phone-company supervisor however he could.

Hours later, weary to the bone, her muscles aching and cramped from hours of inactivity as she pored over page after page of numbers, Bree was tempted to put the accordion-fold sheaf of printouts aside, close her eyes and nap until Michael arrived. Given her stint in the freezer at Mesa

Memorial and the wrenching separation from Eric less than twelve hours ago, it seemed a wonder to her that she could still be even marginally alert.

The problem was, she had fifteen or twenty pages more to go, searching for one of half a dozen patterns Michael had described to her. She couldn't stop now for the smallest catnap. She would either find the pattern of long-distance transactions in these past pages or not. Not finding it was vital information by itself, because it could rule out possibilities they need no longer consider.

She adjusted the lamp so the light wouldn't disturb Martha, then reached out and patted her fragile hand. Tissue soft, thin enough to see every tiny vein, Martha's skin was cool and dry. She was feeling no pain, and for that, Bree was eternally thankful. The old dear was sleeping soundly now, snoring occasionally in her drugged state.

At last, Bree sat back in the easy chair, curled her legs beneath her and opened the fanfold printout to the page where she'd left off. Painstakingly, for her weariness seemed to be cutting into her concentration now, Bree reviewed in her mind the criteria she was searching for. Asterisks, and the symbols @, #, ? and $$ in given combinations meant one thing in one situation, something else in another—all were important. Then, with the use of a small, six-inch ruler to run down the columns, she began.

She'd done the same thing for hours. Hours of staring at numbers and symbols that made her eyes blur and water. Now, within moments, the combination of characters and numbers she sought popped out at her. Her heart skipped a beat or two, but Bree didn't trust her eyes or herself to be right. Sitting a little straighter in the easy chair, holding the ruler tight to that line, she took her eyes off the page, closed them and then looked again.

Nothing had changed. It was a little like getting the winning numbers on a lotto ticket and not quite believing what you were seeing. But this was only one pattern. Only one. What were the chances it was the right one? Shivering—more intensely alert than cold—Bree took a pen out of her purse and carefully drew a line beneath the pattern of characters. She circled the page number, put a star by it and then followed the printout line back across the thirteen inch paper to the column listing the customer account name.

BlackBird Enterprises.

Her heart seemed to fill her throat. BlackBird Enterprises. For some inexplicable reason, the name summoned up UFQ-9307 and a black Mustang to her mind. She flinched at the warning signals resonating from still deeper levels of her subconscious. Shakily, Bree closed the pages carefully in their fanfold and reached for her coffee cup.

She needed to search no more. BlackBird Enterprises was the one—it had led to Danziger. She took several sips of lukewarm coffee, breathed deeply and forced herself to acknowledge that the connection to Danziger was to be expected. Exactly what they'd hoped for.

Perfect. Only getting this close to the maniac extracting Joe Preston's revenge seemed to paralyze her. She wanted to burn the printouts. She wanted to find Michael, fly to Japan, collect Eric and have the three of them fade into some anonymous far-eastern rice paddy. The instinct to run was as strong in her as the day she'd taken the private jet Henry had provided for her to escape even his protective environs for a corner of the world as small and inconsequential as Grand Junction, Colorado.

Pacing the confines of Martha's small room, Bree felt trapped, hopeless as an animal caught in a vicious snare. No matter what she did now, she couldn't win. If she ran, she'd be found, only to suffer this terror again. If she told Michael where he could find Danziger and the two confronted each other, neither of them would give in before the other was dead.

The effects of the pain medications seemed to be wearing off, and Martha began to whimper in her now-troubled sleep. The anguished sound dragged Bree out of her thoughts. She turned back to Martha's bedside and pressed a cool cloth to her sweat-dampened brow.

It was Martha's dear, creased face twisted in pain that finally acquainted Bree with the unadorned truth about herself. She was done with the pain of her lonely and vulnerable existence, done with the lies. She wanted Eric back, and she wanted to spend the rest of her life being a woman to the extraordinary man Michael Tallent was. It was really that simple. She had no choice but to show him the address she'd discovered.

Bree stroked an unconscious tear from Martha's pale and weathered cheek and vowed that the old woman would never suffer like this again. Gathering the printouts, her pen and purse, Bree switched off the lamp and blew Martha a kiss, then went to the nursing station to request Martha be given another pain shot.

She didn't think until she reached the parking lot about Michael's conditions—that she stay with Martha until he arrived. But he hadn't come or called, and she had no way of reaching him with the answer they so desperately needed. They couldn't afford the luxury of wasted time.

Determinedly, Bree set out across the lot toward the Eagle. The night was still unusually warm. A hot breeze rustled the leaves of trees all around, carrying with it the familiar scent of the river only a mile or so away. Shifting the printouts to her other arm, Bree reached into her purse for her keys, unlocked her door and got in. Again she shifted the papers, this time from her lap onto the passenger seat, and closed her door.

When it shut solidly, Bree let her wrists flop over the steering wheel, sat back and breathed a sigh of relief. From behind her, a gloved hand suddenly locked her door.

The cool barrel of a gun lodged at the base of her skull and the sound of soft, evil laughter reached her ears.

"People who take chances should pay, don't you agree, sweet Breez?"

Fear shot through her on a rush of adrenaline. The taste of it made saliva pool in her mouth, turning her muffled cry of alarm into a ridiculous gurgling sound. Emotions vied in her. Anger, hatred, spite, disbelief, even consternation that she would not only pay, but die for the foolishness of getting caught like this. Hatred won out when she heard Michael's endearment "sweet Breez" coming from her captor's vile lips.

"Danziger." She knew it was Danziger; another wave of pure chemical shock flooded her. Beside her was the print-out identifying his location in the city. All he had to do to know how close they were was to force her to turn the pages until he saw the entry she'd so carefully underlined. *BlackBird Enterprises*.

Automatically, her eyes flew to the rearview mirror to see what he looked like, but the hand holding a pistol shot out and crashed into the mirror, shattering it to bits. Bree cried out and threw her hands up in front of her face as shards of the mirrored glass flew in every direction.

"Don't be stupid, *sweet Breez*, or you won't last out the next five minutes. You got that, huh?" He lifted her hair from the back of her neck with his gun.

Rage rose in her, countering the fear, and Bree clamped her teeth shut against crying out. "Don't call me that again."

"Well, well, well. The little whore has a backbone, after all—" he jammed the pistol to the top of her spine "—until I blow it into a thousand little pieces." She felt the gun barrel sweeping lightly over her flesh then, toying with her neck. Bree froze and her breath locked in her throat.

The cold pistol rounded to the front of her neck...
burrowed beneath the collar of her egg-shell silk blouse.
Slipped lower, straining the fabric. A small button popped
off, and Danziger's hot wrist dangled on her shoulder so
that the gun barrel stroked the top of her breast.

His harsh whisper changed then, to a murmur more per-
suasively, deceptively kind. "Don't make me pull the trigger, *sweet Breez*. We wouldn't want to spoil your body for
friend Michael, now, would we?"

Tears of pure rage threatened to spill. She couldn't answer him without her voice trembling, so she said nothing.

"Would we?" Danziger said threateningly, the heat of his
breath against her ear.

"No. No!"

He laughed again and sat back, letting the pistol trail over
her. "Well, then. Friend Michael's little investment in you
is saved. Perhaps we can get down to business now."

"What do you want?" Frantically, she looked for something, *anything* to fight back with, or a way to get out before he killed her, but he clearly knew what she was
thinking.

He didn't sit forward again or jab the pistol into her flesh,
but simply warned her in his eerie, grating whisper. "Remember, our agreement—nothing stupid. Are we agreed?"

"Yes." Her hands wrapped tightly on the bottom of the
steering wheel, Bree drew a deep breath. If she were very,
very careful not to turn her head, perhaps she could get a
glimpse of Danziger in the side-view mirror. "Who are
you?"

She could hear the angry, rapid-fire thumping of his heel
against the floor before he answered her. "You know,
Breezy-whore, that's what really turns my crank." A muffled bullet sang past her ear, through the window, and exploded the side mirror.

Shivering violently, Bree clapped a hand to her ear. She could still feel the heat, the incredible force of that bullet speeding by, but at the same time, she realized that there was no amusement left in Danziger's voice, no self-satisfied smirk that he had the best of her, only rage. *You know, Breezy-whore, that's what really turns my crank.*

Exhaustion and fear of this monster were taking their toll, and Bree fought to remember what question she'd asked to throw him into such a cold-blooded rage. *Who are you...?* Who are you? That was it. Why did he think she would know? What made him believe she *should* know?

One torturous moment of silence went by, and then another. She didn't want to know why his silence threatened her more than his rage. Some intuition told her Danziger was in enormous pain, but she had no idea where that vague impression had come from or why. The nervous thumping of his heel stopped, and when he spoke again, his voice was nothing more than a harsh, thready whisper.

"All mine, Breezy-whore. Every little indignity." He laughed then, almost musingly. "I've been policing this backwater hellhole for years, and even I couldn't believe how easy it was to con those imbeciles in Ouray."

Staring out at the streetlamps casting light in circles that didn't quite reach the car, Bree felt the bile rising in her throat. She'd been right—Danziger had known precisely how to go about arranging the maximum damage in Ouray. She couldn't help the tear that seeped out of her eye, but she was damned if she'd give him the satisfaction of seeing her wipe it away.

"Michael's geese?"

He laughed yet again. This time, Bree heard the crazed, deadly timbre. It was that strain in his voice that confirmed her thought that he suffered some physical pain. And if he were in pain, maybe she had a chance.

"Your dear friend Patrick offed the geese—or claimed the kill, at least. But I offed Patrick," he concluded softly. There wasn't a shred of remorse in his voice.

Over her heaving nausea, she asked, "And Martha?"

"Just a warning, Breezy-whore. Just a warning. You see, the cops came around," he grated out, "and I had to use the back door, which, as you might guess, I despise."

"Don't you want to know why Ouray happened?" he continued. "*You left town.* You knew you shouldn't have left town, and I had to bring that home to you—so to speak. Home..." He paused then, and when he spoke again, his harsh, jagged taunt was venom-laced and utterly lethal. "Where is your bastard brat, Sabrina?"

Her heart simply stopped. Danziger's question and the use of her full name shocked her on so many levels, it was impossible to think. She felt the hard, twisting thud of her heart, but her mind refused to work.

He knew Eric was gone. How could he know?

Eric must be nearly to Sapporo by now, but she could neither lie nor tell the truth. Either way, she'd broken the rules—Eric was gone, beyond Danziger's power to hurt him.

Or so she thought. She said nothing of where Eric had gone. "What do you want?"

"What do I want? More than you can deliver, whore," he snarled.

"Why are you doing this, then? Who are—"

He jammed the pistol into the flesh behind her ear again. "We'll start with the fortune good old Henry left you," he said, his tone strangely flat. "Transfer all funds from your numbered Swiss account to mine and we'll begin to call it even."

"Money?" she cried. "All of this has been about money?"

"All of this has been about driving you to your knees, *whore*... you and *friend* Michael," he spat out. "Terror is such an amusing, gratifying method of extortion—soothes the savage breast, you know."

Nothing of his brutal sarcasm escaped Bree. He wanted the money; but first, he'd wanted to play his deadly terror games. He was insane—completely, irrevocably mad.

No matter how she'd wracked her mind, she couldn't imagine a man so loyal, so tenacious . . . so *fanatical* as to exact a dead man's revenge. Joseph Preston's revenge. But it suddenly made terrible sense to her. Danziger, whoever he'd truly been in Joe Preston's secret life, could gain her money, the ambassador's legacy, and at the same time, rip away whole strips of her emotional skin with this campaign of terror.

If money was all he wanted, if money was all it took to be free of this monster... Could she truly believe he'd take the money and leave them in peace? A tiny ray of hope glimmered, like moonlight racing up and down a single long strand of a spider's silk.

"I'll telex orders to transfer all the money in the morning."

His constant whisper made her skin crawl as if alive with spiders spinning silk strands. "That's not all, *sweet Breez.*"

Her fingers compulsively stroking against the steering wheel, Bree flinched inside as she did every time Danziger infused "sweet Breez" with such bitter hatred. It made no sense to her, none at all. But she waited to hear what else it was he wanted from her, never dreaming he'd strike her emotional jugular in a way he had only when the sharpshooting team had attacked her cabin.

"Suppose you just drive on down to Ouray in the morning and get the deed to your little hideaway."

"Why?"

His laugh brought her throat to a close. "It won't be yours anymore, then, will it?"

Her breath caught in her throat. Ouray. Her cabin. Her sanctuary. Her home. She felt the insult, knew the injury, the rape Danziger intended in stripping her of the cabin. She treasured her linens, yes, and the cameo locket Michael and Daisy had given her, and all the pictures of Eric.

The cabin in Ouray was the safe harbor of her fugitive heart, and Danziger knew it.

"I can't—I don't have the title. It's not even in my name."

Danziger swore vilely. "You're confusing me with someone who gives a damn, *sweet Breez.* I don't care how you do it. I want title transferred to the same Swiss account to which you're going to transfer the money—by one o'clock tomorrow."

She'd see Danziger in hell first. "That's not enough time." Given time, given even the rest of this night, she and Michael had a chance of stopping him.

Again, his hoarse whisper turned conversational. "Would you care to see another photograph of mine?"

He had to lean forward again to dangle the photo over her shoulder. She hated the enforced proximity, but she would not take the photo or cower in any way.

"The background is a bit of a problem—the skies were all overcast in Aspen this afternoon, but—"

Aspen.

Eric.

Against impossible odds, Danziger knew exactly what she'd done with Eric! She snatched the photo dangling above her breast and turned it over. There was Eric, grinning as he did only in times of massive uncertainty, the tooth he'd lost only three days ago missing. He was dressed in the clothes he'd worn this morning. She recognized in the background a Learjet aircraft and the airport in Aspen.

She recognized the skull and crossbones etched over Eric's precious little face.

The silence in her head was numbing. As if her body had already spent every emotional response and dram of chemical agents, Bree felt nothing. "If anything happens to him, I will—"

"Your bastard son, you mean," Danziger cut her off. "And something will happen to him—something very unpleasant and...permanent, unless you do exactly as I say. Exactly. When and where I say.

"If *friend* Michael comes anywhere near me, he's a dead man. If anything happens to me, your bastard brat dies."

BREE SAT IN THE CAR FOR long, silent moments after Danziger got out and faded somewhere into the night, staring at the full, blood-red moon. Danziger hadn't cared if she saw him; she cared. She didn't want to see him.

She couldn't *not* watch. He made no effort to walk in any direction but the one in which she could see him until he disappeared. She noticed the slight limp, as she had the night she and Michael had spotted him with Patrick. The limp seemed more pronounced to her now, but maybe she simply didn't remember how obvious it was. She never saw his face, but her eyes were glued to him until the darkness swallowed him up.

She had no explanation for her contrary fascination and the deep unease that swamped her. None but that, were he Joe Preston himself, Danziger couldn't have harbored more malice for her.

She judged him to be over six feet tall, with dark blond, almost brown hair, and powerfully built—broad-shouldered, trim hips and lean. Her age or older, there was not a trace of a paunch on him. His arrogance made the limp seem more threatening than debilitating.

She couldn't take the information she had on him to the police. She could tell Michael nothing of this because if she did, Danziger would kill him—and Eric, as well—before the moon rose again.

She made her decision very deliberately. She'd go back to Martha's hospital bedside, and when Michael came, she'd act as though she'd never discovered BlackBird Enterprises in the printouts, that she'd never left Martha's room. Sooner or later, Michael would come for her, and when he did, she'd plead such exhaustion that she couldn't drive home. She had to keep Michael from seeing her car, because if he did, he'd also see the shattered side-view mirror and know that something had happened.

She tucked the scrap of paper with the number of Danziger's Swiss account into her billfold. Bundling together her purse and the printouts, Bree got out of the car and abandoned it without locking the doors. Her legs carried her toward the hospital, though she couldn't guess how they still functioned. She felt limp and powerless. In spite of that, there was no doubt about what she had to do. By the time Michael knew that she'd bowed to the extortion, the game would be over.

Danziger wanted her money; he'd have it. Danziger wanted title to the mountain property; he'd have it. Terror was only a game. As he'd said, a quite efficient method of extortion. Deed to her beloved cabin was the final measure of his revenge; he would simply lock it away in some safety deposit box and title would forever after hang in limbo. He'd told her. Her money would get him out of Grand Junction to whatever he considered civilization. In style and complete anonymity.

The night watchman greeted her in some surprise over her return and opened the door. Where had he been? Where had any of hospital security been when Danziger had blown away her side-view mirror?

Bree bit her lip to keep from demanding an answer to those questions. Might as well begin now with the guard and before she had to face Michael to keep her own counsel. From this moment until Danziger took the title and proof of her bank transfers, she had to be very, very careful. Michael was no fool. Just fool enough to go after Danziger, even if it meant getting killed himself.

Before she made it halfway across the lobby, she heard Michael's voice. "Breez?"

She whirled around, thinking fast. Tears bit at her eyelids. He was so impossibly good-looking, so dear to her, so like Eric in every way.

He strode toward her and took the heavy printouts from her arms. "Breez, you look like death warmed over. What's happened?"

Michael, he'll kill you both if I answer that question.... Had he seen her walking back from the Eagle? She wasn't at Martha's side, and it was impossible now to say she'd never left. She shook her head. "Nothing has happened. I— I was about to leave when I remembered I should wait for you. Michael, I'm so tired. So tired..."

As if the bulky printouts weighed no more than a paperback novel, Michael held them to his side and caught Bree about the shoulders with his other arm. He pulled her close, and Bree let herself go limp against his body.

She'd grown used to him in jeans and chambray work shirts large enough to conceal his weapon. Now, he still wore his business suit. The jacket was beautifully cut, so well done that it camouflaged his holster and gun without flaw. He'd never looked so handsome.

She rested her cheek against his warm, broad chest, and the silk shirt carried the scent of him, the scent of warm holster leather. The gun had come quickly to mean safety to her. She'd grown used to that gun. Now, it became a potent symbol of why she must not tell him about Danziger.

Michael's gun invited his own death, and Eric's. *He'll kill you both, Michael. I have no choice....*

He felt the shuddering of her body, and pulled her closer, burying his face in her precious, flyaway hair. He preferred the sable color he remembered so well because the silvery blond only emphasized the pallor of her skin when she was tired.

Another woman would still have been in a hospital bed recuperating from the hypothermia she'd suffered. Michael swore at himself for pushing Bree so hard. He'd had no choice but to drag her along. He didn't dare leave her alone, vulnerable and unprotected.

At last, taking a deep breath, Bree pulled back a little from him. "Did you . . . were you able to find anything?"

His arm still around her, Michael turned and guided her toward the door. The tightness around his lips told her he hadn't found BlackBird Enterprises.

Michael shook his head. "I'm close, Breez. Real close. Maybe in the morning . . ."

Whatever else he said, Bree lost, for in her mind his words echoed the note Danziger had stuck in Martha's hand. *Close only counts in horseshoes and hand grenades, and sometimes . . . not even then. . . .*

The same dire sense of disquiet she'd experienced when Danziger walked away confronted Bree again. Confused by elusive, uneasy images, Bree couldn't quite seem to draw a proper breath.

Michael halted them both just outside the hospital doors. "Bree? Did you hear me?"

She shook her head, as much to clear the confusion and unease as to confess she hadn't heard.

He cursed softly. The shadows beneath her eyes looked more like bruises, and he knew he had no business expecting even a show of alertness from her. She'd been through hellish conditions in the past twenty-four hours. Tenderness welled in him. He wanted to take her home and take her to bed and make such love to her that she would forget, even for a little while, that Eric was gone and that Danziger was still out there waiting for them.

He lifted a strand of her hair from her forehead and gently pushed it back into place. He had to know. "Did you find anything in these?" he asked, indicating the thick fanfold of printouts.

Bree swallowed hard and her eyes darted away. Lying to him hurt. Losing him if he went after Danziger and was killed for his trouble would hurt far, far worse. "No. There's nothing, Michael. Nothing at all." Then she looked back up at him, because telling the truth was so wrapped up in what could be seen in another's eyes, and she had to make him believe her.

Michael saw only the weariness in her eyes and nodded with his own fatigue. "Could be I was wrong playing the odds. Maybe Danziger *is* using a smaller long-distance service."

Bree's chin lifted a tiny bit. For an instant, Michael thought he saw consternation flicker across her eyes, and he started to ask her why when she dampened her lips with her tongue.

His question died on his lips with that tiny gesture. The need of her was on him like lightning on a firefly. For the first time, he noticed the tiny button missing from her blouse. He noticed because there in the diffuse light of the moon and street lamps, he glimpsed the swell of her breast and a wisp of peach-colored lace.

He'd seen the sudden doubt in her eyes. Her simple lie, that she'd found nothing, grew more complex the moment he accepted it. He wasn't wrong. He'd been absolutely right about the computer modem codes and everything else.

Lies were like that, Bree knew. Mushrooming. Entangling. For one brief moment, she doubted the wisdom of her decision, but only this lie could save Michael and their son.

She'd licked her lips because they'd gone so suddenly dry with doubt. The instant Michael caught her in the act, she felt awareness reverberating between them. The instant his eyes found the missing button and the breach in her blouse, her nipples tightened. Heat flashed over her skin, making the night air feel chilled by comparison.

"Michael—"

"Bree—"

Neither heard the hospital doors opening behind them. "You folks need me to call you a cab?"

Bree recognized the reflexive movement of Michael's hand toward his gun. Midway to his weapon, he hesitated and instead, jammed his hand into his pants pocket. His eyes never left her. She took a step back and dragged her fingers nervously through her hair. The way he looked at her, the way his look made her feel, so feminine, so... beautiful, gave her the excuse she needed to stay away from her car. "I... Michael, I don't want to drive home alone."

He nodded, acknowledging both his own desire for her and her need to be with him. Answering the security guard, he said, "Thanks, but no." He took Bree's elbow and guided her in the direction of the rental car, unlocked the door and helped her in.

He drove without speaking. The tires whined as he pulled off the highway into her neighborhood.

"Michael, I—"

His ardent, hungry glance quelled her. His eyes strayed again from her lips to the missing button over her breasts. If she'd thought his driving had lessened his awareness of her, she discovered now that she was wrong. Everything about the way he looked at her was heated, promising. A thrill passed through her that had only to do with him.

He pulled the car into the driveway, jerked on the emergency brake and shut off the engine in rapid succession.

Grabbing up Bree's printout, he came around the front of the car in time to help lift her out, then escorted her up the stairs. The scent of the peach orchard over the bluffs filled the night air, and the need between them soared.

Michael followed her in, dumped the fanfold of papers into the nearest chair and turned to Bree as she closed the door. Two steps, maybe three, separated them. Michael closed the distance. Slowly. Her back to the door, Bree watched his eyes. Moonlight streamed through the picture window. There wasn't enough light to read the intentions in his eyes.

He kissed her, and her hands crept beneath his suit coat. Need furled, then exploded in him. For the first time in eight years, he pressed himself fully against her, wanting her to know how badly he wanted her.

He wanted her to remember the way their bodies fit together.

God help her, she remembered.

He kissed like a man starved, and Bree found an overwhelming hunger in herself. Pinned to the door, the fullness of her breasts flattened against the hard wall of his chest, she felt his rigid, palpable need, and she remembered.

But Michael broke off their ravenous kiss and leaned his forehead against the door next to hers, gulping in deep, desperate breaths.

"I won't do this if it's going to be a one-night stand again, Breez. I can't. I need to know you understand that."

She wanted to promise Michael that this night would not be the only one, but if Danziger wanted her dead, she wouldn't survive another night.

She needed Michael's loving as much tonight as she had eight years, four months and seventeen days ago. She told herself that if this were the only night they were ever to have, at least Michael would have Eric to remember her by. Eric... and this one night.

And so she kissed him, and her lie grew still more entangling. "No, Michael. Not only for tonight."

Chapter Thirteen

He had no idea what time it was when he heard the Mickey Mouse phone ring. Or even why he heard the damn thing. Sutterfield had been working on a drunken stupor for hours and hours—ever since he'd seen Bree Gregory on that gurney through the small square window in the door of the emergency-treatment room.

He'd put her there.

The guilt gnawed at him like a dog gnaws a bone. Ceaselessly. He couldn't believe, after all, that he'd done it. He'd managed to lure Bree into the lab. He'd taken and then replaced the lab key while the night clerk fetched coffee for him. He'd dug up that dead goose from its grave and hung it inside the lab freezer and then left the door ajar.

Sutterfield couldn't believe, no matter how much single-malt Scotch he managed to get down his throat, that he'd ever agreed in the first place to do those things, to have any part in terrorizing a woman he respected.

He'd made mistakes in his time, but he'd gotten along on a lick and a promise all his life, and he could credit most of his mistakes to that predilection. This one belonged to his fear of losing everything.

Only one man had ever contacted him in regard to his mission with Bree Gregory. Only one purpose had ever been assigned him: to keep tabs on her and report when and if a man called Michael Tallent came into her life.

He still didn't know why, and he didn't care. It didn't matter. For the rewards, the job had been a cakewalk.

Then the order to set her up for disciplinary action had come from his contact, and the same morning, the letter from Tallent's attorney arrived, asking for information that would support a custody suit against Bree, which was why he'd told her to watch her back. He'd tried to warn her. He didn't pretend to understand the things going on around her.

He understood even less the "or else" orders from Danziger. "Unearth the dead geese," he'd been told. "Make sure the whore finds one hanging in the lab freezer, and then make sure she keeps it company for a while...."

He'd played in golf foursomes with Danziger. He'd shared drinks with Danziger in the Bookcliffs Country Club. A county sheriff's deputy didn't go around dispensing orders for such lawless, cruel actions!

But Danziger had, and he'd done so over the Mickey Mouse telephone that only the contact had used before. Sutterfield was convinced that if he didn't do those things, his wife and son would keep the other dead geese company.

He cared about every possession he'd accumulated. He loved the house, treasured the antique juke and doted on his BMW. His son Sutterfield loved more than life itself.

He thought that phone call was probably the single most sick joke he'd ever heard of. How had Danziger even gotten hold of that phone number? Sutterfield didn't believe there even were dead geese, but when he found them in fresh graves, then he believed. *Do those things or Scott will die,* he'd told himself.

Well, he'd done them, and now the cursed phone was ringing again.

Stumbling half-drunkenly across the length of the house he loved, all he wanted to do was rip the cord out of the wall and trash the designer phone he'd once thought so clever. Instead, he answered it.

This time, the caller was not Danziger, but the man to whom Sutterfield had answered all these years. Sutterfield said nothing, only listened, and by the time the call was disconnected, he'd become stone-cold sober. He'd just been released from any further responsibility where Bree Gregory was concerned. Released, that was, with one last mission he didn't understand.

BREE WOKE WELL BEFORE morning broke—with tears seeping down her cheeks. Though the tears came as a surprise to her, she understood them very well. She had never in her life spent a more precious night than this one, or known more compelling emotions. Now she had to leave this bed where, with Michael, she had known such exquisite pleasure.

Perhaps, forever.

A frown of subconscious disapproval touched his face when she moved carefully out of Michael's arms, but he slept on, and Bree crept quietly to the bathroom. She sponge-bathed in order not to wake him with the sound of the shower, and in the dark, dressed in a comfortable chambray skirt and a dotted Swiss blouse.

Michael's gun, holstered on the floor by her bed, gave Bree a moment's distress. She considered taking it or the clip to slow him down. But she knew where to find Danziger; Michael didn't. She couldn't leave him without protection of his own. Instead, she took the keys to the Camry and to his pickup truck from his coat pocket.

For a while, he might believe she'd gone back to the hospital to be with Martha, and if she were very lucky, she'd get back to Danziger with proof of the bank and deed transfers before Michael found him.

She stared for no more than a minute into Eric's room, and a lump settled in her throat. Like Michael's gun, her son's empty bed spurred her on to her purpose. The sooner Danziger gained control of her money, the sooner he'd have reason to abandon the game.

When she left, taking only her purse, she let the Toyota Camry roll down the slope of her driveway. Angling so that the car would begin rolling downhill in the direction of the highway, she let out the clutch near the first intersection, and the engine turned over.

She would drive as far south toward Ouray as Montrose, then stop and telex her bank in Switzerland with instructions to transfer funds from her account to Danziger's. Given the eight-hour time difference between Colorado and Geneva, she had to manage the transfer by no later than eight o'clock this morning.

She stopped at a convenience store on the way out of town to fill the car's gas tank and to get a cup of coffee. The first rays of sunlight came over the horizon when she took her cup of coffee to the phone booth and dialed St. Mary's to check on Martha.

The nursing supervisor told her Martha had suffered through a pretty rough night, then volunteered to transfer Bree's call to Martha's room.

"No," Bree said, declining the offer, "I'm sure she's in no condition to answer the phone."

"Oh, but there's a doctor in with her now!" the nurse assured. "You could speak with him."

Alarmed, Bree transferred her coffee cup from one hand to the other and tilted her wrist to check the time on her watch. "It's only six-fifteen. Which doctor?"

"Danzer...? I think that's what he said his name was. I've never seen him before, but then, I haven't been here long."

Hopelessly, Bree grimaced. Danziger didn't miss a trick. "Perhaps I should speak with him."

The nurse promised to relay Bree's concern to the day shift nurses, then transferred the call. Danziger answered.

"Well, if it isn't the little whore!"

"Look," Bree said, "I don't know who you are, and *I don't care*. But if you do anything more to hurt that innocent old lady, I'll see you in hell."

Danziger only laughed—his cruel, humorless version. His fractured voice, that whisper, was even more unnerving over the phone. "You'll care," he taunted, "and hell would be a church picnic compared to what I've been through, *sweet Breez*. Get back here before one o'clock...unless you want the old biddy to get an air embolism in the brain she won't live through."

Her fingers in a white-knuckled grip on the flexible metal receiver cord, Bree agreed. "Yes."

"The Bookcliffs Country Club, at one, then."

God, the arrogance. The Bookcliffs Country Club! She'd rather have insisted on Martha's room, to know that the old lady was safe. Michael might go there.

Her hesitation goaded Danziger. "My way, Breezy-whore. Do or die."

The last thing Bree heard was Martha's small, helpless cry. Her own nearly echoed it. Bree got back into the Camry and headed south toward Montrose and then Ouray. Heaven help her if she couldn't find Clyde Easterday and get the deed.

MICHAEL WOKE AT EIGHT o'clock to an uncommon, almost threatening quiet. He couldn't remember the last time he'd slept so late, and though the urgency of finding Danziger was never gone from his thoughts, a satisfied smile played at his lips for the night he'd spent with Bree.

But she was gone from the bed, and the sheets where she'd been were cool. He got up and went to Eric's closet, where days ago, he'd begun to keep his clothes, and pulled on a pair of jeans. Barefoot and shirtless, he headed downstairs in search of Bree. He knew before another minute had passed that she'd left. Then he found the Camry gone, and his truck keys missing as well.

In another minute, he had St. Mary's on the telephone. A deep-seated alarm ran through him like ground water through a cave, but he was prepared to forgive the risk she'd taken by going out alone without his protection, if she'd gone to the hospital to be with Martha.

Only no one at the hospital had seen her.

God *damn* it, not again! His fist slammed the wall so hard, the phone came off its moorings and dangled by its wire. If he'd been hit in the chest with a baseball bat he'd have felt better. She'd found something, *found Danziger.* Michael knew it with every instinct in him. And still, she hadn't trusted him, after everything they'd been through.

He took the steps up three at a time, threw on a shirt, followed by his gun holster and a denim jacket. Only his fear for Bree outdistanced his anger. He knew she'd found Danziger. What he didn't know was what she intended to do or where to begin looking for either one of them.

But as he returned downstairs, knowing he'd have to hike back to his truck, he thought of the printouts Bree had taken with her the night before. Whatever she had discovered had to be there.

Forcing himself to slow down, he took the printouts to the kitchen and began searching. He began at the last page and progressed further into the printouts. He heard a car pull into the driveway at the same time as he saw Bree's marks, half a dozen pages in. He checked the code sequences and a triumph surged in him. He followed the line she'd made across the page and read the customer's name: BlackBird Enterprises.

He absorbed the address while making all the same connections in his mind that Bree had made. BlackBird Enterprises. Black Mustang. UFQ-9307. He could almost feel the visceral, gut-level horror Bree must have known. *This* was Danziger.

Wary now, he moved carefully into position to look for the car he'd heard, hoping against hope Bree had returned. Instead, Michael saw Sutterfield emerging from a navy blue BMW, wiping his palms along his pant legs.

Michael drew his automatic before the door bell rang, and had the gun barrel aimed at Sutterfield's head through the screen door in another instant.

"Short and sweet, Sutterfield. Where's Bree?"

His hands palms outward to Michael, Sutterfield shook like a leaf. "I don't... I don't know."

"Like you don't know anything about hanging a goose corpse in the lab freezer?"

"Yeah, well..." Sutterfield hesitated, his eyes glued to the gun barrel pointed at his face. "That's what... there's more than that to explain—if I could just... could I come inside?"

Sensing the truth in Sutterfield's plea, Michael pulled out of his spread-legged stance. Sutterfield backed away, and Michael kicked the screen door open, never losing dead aim at Sutterfield's head. "No, but we'll go for a little ride."

Gesturing Sutterfield back to his car, Michael got in the passenger side still without losing his aim at Sutterfield. "If you know where she is—"

"I don't. God's truth, I don't."

"And Danziger?" Michael asked. "You know where he is?"

Eyes wide with surprise, Sutterfield swallowed nervously and shook his head. "All I know is, Danziger ordered the freezer incident."

"*Incident?*" Michael said mockingly. "Is that what you called attempted murder?" But he saw Sutterfield pale to the point of passing out, and Michael needed the man coherent to get out of him whatever he'd come to say. Bree could be facing any terror alone right this minute, but Michael had the gut-eating feeling he'd better hear Sutterfield out. "Drive. I presume you know how to find my place?"

Nodding, Sutterfield started the car. "I have to tell you—"

"Spit it out," Michael interrupted. "You've been watching Bree for years, haven't you? What was it? Money? Your house? Your BMW? How many BMWs for betraying Bree?"

Sutterfield grimaced silently, then found his voice. "Three... four BMWs. But, it was never only the money. I'd made minor... actionable surgical errors, and my malpractice insurance was being dropped at the same time a multimillion dollar suit was filed. The suit was settled out of court."

"In exchange for what?"

His eyes focused on the road, Sutterfield answered in a flat, emotionless voice. "They wanted to know everything Bree did, everyone she associated with. I think they especially wanted to know if you ever showed up."

Something sharp and ugly and dangerous twisted in Michael's chest, a gut-level perception of possibilities his mind refused to consider.

"For years," Sutterfield continued, "nothing happened. After you showed up, things started getting... crazy. I was ordered to make a stink over her remarks in my operating room so that Jenner would slap her with a suspension— Jenner is such a fool.... And I got a letter from a lawyer named Grissom looking for any information which would help you gain custody of Eric. That's why I told Bree to watch her back. I set her up in the freezer, too, only it wasn't them this time—Danziger ordered that."

"*Them who?*" Michael insisted, his voice more deadly than the automatic still pointed at Sutterfield.

"The KGB. Imagine that," Sutterfield complained bitterly. "Some...some arm of the KGB. Last night, I got another call. They were never interested in Bree, but they always believed she'd draw someone else here." Sutterfield shrugged. "I don't...I don't have any idea what this is about, Tallent, or who they're after...."

Michael did. His heart began pounding, hard, hard, harder, and if Sutterfield said anything else, Michael missed it. Bree was never the target, only the lure. Pieces of the puzzle began falling into place, and his fear for her multiplied a thousand times.

Only the traitor Joseph Preston had motivation enough to track her so far, so doggedly, and then, only if he believed Bree had betrayed his secrets to Michael. Wrong, but that hardly mattered.

Joseph Allen Preston himself had to be alive.

At the turnoff into the old orchard, Michael put his automatic back into its holster and directed Sutterfield to pull over. He got out of Sutterfield's shiny new BMW, closed the door and then crashed through the passenger window with a single blow of his elbow. Better the window than the stool pigeon's neck.

Sutterfield just sat there, staring straight ahead, shaking like a leaf in a stiff wind. Michael looked through the shattered window, his rage and contempt thicker than blood. "What's it like, selling your soul to the KGB?"

Sutterfield popped the clutch and floored the accelerator in the same instant. Michael watched the BMW careening away, then he ran down the slope toward his construction site. Rage and fear for Bree consumed him. He ignored other warnings going off in his head like so many buzzing flies. He could hot-wire his truck, but without his keys, he had to break into the camper.

There were signs. There were always signs of tampering. Somewhere beneath the rage, Michael knew he ought to be a little less angry, and far more careful. Every instinct in him, every primitive rudiment of survival warned him against breaking into the camper—but the duffel bag with his ammunition was locked in there.

He had to get to Bree, and he had to be able to protect her. He got the door open, and in that same splinter of time, knew he'd set off a heat-sensing explosive. At the very last possible second, some powerful, self-protective premonition assaulted him, and Michael hurled himself out of the camper.

The first explosion triggered the next. A chain of detonations were fueled higher and hotter by the ammunition he kept inside. Sparks rained down on his unfinished house, and then the house exploded, hurtling splintered beams in every direction. Flying debris rained down on Michael's body and head.

But in the moment before he lost consciousness, Michael knew the explosions would end without igniting fires that might summon help. Preston's methods were faultless.

His last conscious thought was of Bree, the woman he loved beyond life, walking straight and unwitting into Preston's clutches.

Just one of the hundred and one ways to die.

BREE PULLED THE RENTED Camry into the lot of the Bookcliffs Country Club at nineteen minutes past one o'clock. Shakily, for her tardiness, she parked the claret-colored, four-door sedan at the end of a row of cars, switched off the ignition and took several deep breaths.

Danziger appeared out of nowhere, his body close enough to the car that she couldn't see his face, and with the butt of his gun, he smashed out the side-view mirror as he had her Eagle's. With the gun, he gestured for her to unlock the doors, and when she released the power lock, he got in behind her and dealt a blow to the rearview mirror.

"You're late."

"I know that!" Reaching deep within herself for control, Bree held up title to the mountain property and the transaction codes given her by the bank in Switzerland to document the transfers. "It's a four-hour round trip to Ouray. You have what you wanted." It had taken her two hours just to find Clyde Easterday, and another hour to get the title signed over and notarized.

"Oh, and I'm supposed to be a nice extortionist and let you go now, is that what you thought, sweet Breez?"

"Yes," she snapped, staring straight ahead, "that's exactly what I thought."

He laughed. "Drive, Breezy-whore. It ain't over yet."

She heard the crazed timbre of Danziger's haunting, ragged whisper, and she began to understand how naive she'd been to believe this nightmare would end with his extortion demands fulfilled. He meant to kill her. She'd had no choice. To save Michael and Eric, she'd made the only choice possible. If only she'd trusted Michael eight years ago.... Oh, God. If only she'd trusted him then. Regret all but crushed her spirit.

She'd done it again.

She'd left Michael, and left him in the dark because his life and Eric's were at stake. Danziger would betray her and kill them all anyway.

"I said, *drive!*"

At Danziger's insane scream, Bree swallowed hard. The thought occurred to her to drive into a concrete embankment at a hundred miles an hour. She'd die, but then, so would this monster. Eric and Michael, at least, would live. Michael, whom she should have trusted... Whom she should always have trusted. *I'm sorry, Michael... so sorry.* The bitter irony of her apology to the memory Michael filled her. She swore to herself that she'd survive this monster.

"Where?" she asked Danziger.

He gave her terse directions to what she recognized as the location of BlackBird Enterprises. His words were clipped. Harsh. She could see peripherally that he was holding his head, and she knew he was almost over the edge with pain. Tiny rays of hope lit up the darkness in her. Michael might find the address she'd so carefully marked in the computer printouts. And if Danziger was hurting badly enough, he'd make a mistake.

God in heaven, let him make a mistake.

She drove. Her destination took no more than eight minutes to reach. The building appeared to be an abandoned two-story, windowless warehouse. There were no other buildings within three miles of it. Bree got out of the car first, followed by Danziger, his gun in the small of her back.

"Up the stairs, whore," he snarled.

Her hands clenched at her sides, Bree walked toward the building and up the stairs. Danziger handed her a key from behind. As she took the key, she noticed the pale blond hair on his knuckles and the shape of his hand. Despite her shaking fingers, she managed to get the key into the padlock and the padlock off the door. Shoving the gun tighter against her back, Danziger forced her inside.

She stepped onto a landing. There was an open door to her right, through which she could see a kitchen deep in dirty dishes and pans. The landing continued in front of her for about six feet, and then a set of stairs descended into the yawning space of the warehouse. Her pupils adjusted to bright sunlight outside, she could see nothing until her vision accommodated the deep gloom.

Behind her, Bree heard Danziger throw a light switch. Below her, eerie in the darkness that surrounded it, a vintage jukebox lit up, and Danziger's demented laughter filled the deep silence.

The truth took Bree like a fire storm takes down a forest. Ravaging her wits. Consuming her oxygen before she could drag in even one breath. How could she have failed to guess, to know?

Sheriff's Deputy Roy Danziger was none other than Joseph Allen Preston.

Heat swarmed all over Bree, and then cold dread. She hadn't even seen his face yet, but she knew. She'd believed him to be dead. She'd never dreamed, never in her deepest, most desperate nightmares had imagined that he lived. She'd been wrong. This man was Joe Preston.

Somehow, he'd survived. The evidence was all there, parading through her mind at high speed like a seventy-eight-r.p.m. record playing on an antique jukebox.

The marked photos that had reminded her at some primitive level of Joe's obsession with that *Twilight Zone* episode. Joe would long ago have seen Eric's resemblance to Michael and grown to hate her still more for the unwitting betrayal of having given birth to Michael's son. He would remember and ridicule Michael's "sweet Breez" endearment. And he'd left that cryptic note in Martha's hand. *...Close only counts in horseshoes and hand grenades, and sometimes, SOMETIMES, not even then. You are too late smart, as my old German grandmother used to say....*

Joseph Preston's maternal grandmother was German.

Bree clutched at the stair railing for support. Shuttled back and forth from a maximum-security prison to his trial, Joe Preston's government transport had been firebombed. But he had somehow survived.

Bree had witnessed the firebombing, first in person, and then a dozen times more on television news reports. Experts of every jurisdiction, from the CIA to the local police, had speculated on the possibility of Preston escaping that conflagration. Every one of them swore, both then and later for the record, that Joseph Allen Preston had been blown to bits too tiny for forensic identification.

Bree had believed them. Had believed Joe Preston was dead.

But Danziger was Joe Preston, and he'd designed a trap so cunning that even Michael had walked right in. The greeting from the transcript of the tape Blessing had given Michael echoed in her mind. *Preston is dead. Long live Preston.*

Clutching the wooden railing, horror reverberating in her, Bree sank to the landing. Still, she hadn't seen his face. "How?"

Joe's laughter ended on a bitter bark. "How what, Breezy-whore? How did I survive that firebombing? Not without a price." From against the wall still behind her, he picked up a rope.

Jerking her to her feet, he pulled her arms back hard so that her hands were behind her. She fought him. She tried kicking out, scratching and pulling, but his maniacal strength overcame all her efforts. He wrapped her wrists with the coarse hemp rope, then knotted her hands together and let the end of the rope drop. He bound her ankles and then shoved her back down onto the landing.

"Not without a price," he repeated. "I had friends, Breezy-whore, to arrange a trade in the entourage of limousines. I rode in the press car, two vehicles behind the one they firebombed."

He left her, tied up at the wrists and ankles, helpless to move off the landing. His limp pronounced, he walked down the stairs and turned so that she could see him. "Got it now, whore?"

Like a wraith from her worst nightmares, she saw now that this man was Joe Preston. The shock of recognition, of seeing him alive, took her breath away. But though he still emanated enormous power, his pale blond hair was thin and lifeless, and he seemed shaky . . . splintered. His charismatic green eyes now seemed lit with an insane glint.

Her fingers struggling against the ropes that bound her wrists, Bree asked, "The press car? Who died in your place, Joe?"

"John Rector McCarthy, United Press stringer, 1976 to 1983. The fool walked like me, talked like me, *looked* like me, and wanted a story real bad. Locating such doubles is S.O.P. for an agent mole of the KGB. McCarthy got his exclusive only hours before he died. Never saw a byline, naturally."

Naturally. Another man's life ended so that Joseph Preston could live on. Bree's sense of reality, already shaky, grew even more tenuous. His heartlessness sickened her and made her feel forever sullied. "How can you be so cold-blooded, Joe, about the death of another human being?"

He sat beside the jukebox at an old Formica-topped table with his feet up on another chair. Idly rubbing the handle of his handgun against his temple, he smiled mirthlessly. "I paid, *Breezy-whore.* Paid as you never will, even when I kill you."

She knew by the limp, by the way he moved and held his head as if it might explode—even by the fractured whisper of his voice—that Joe must have come close to dying himself. That he must still suffer headaches as enormous as his willpower to survive.

He knew nothing of her will to survive.

Instinctively, she sought ways to anger him, to increase his stress, to somehow aggravate his headache. To defy his monstrous ego seemed her only chance at surviving. At last, she understood why it had so enraged him that she hadn't known who he was.

"What are you waiting for, Joe? Kill me, now. That's what you're going to do anyway, isn't it?"

On his feet now and pacing near the silent but lighted jukebox, he smiled up at her. "I've waited three thousand days for this moment. Why should I rush it now, when *friend* Michael hasn't even arrived yet?''

"Where is he?" she blurted.

"Where is he?" Preston said, mocking her. Rage warped his expression. He picked up his automatic handgun, took very deliberate aim at her... and fired.

Chapter Fourteen

Michael came to consciousness with a blinding headache. The fear in him for Bree was worse.

He had to overcome the punishment his body had absorbed from the construction debris hurtling in every direction. Standing up took every bit of his concentration. Blood still seeped from a head wound, and for a moment, he wondered if he had a chance in hell of getting to Bree before Preston killed her. But revenge was Joe's game, and Michael knew better. Preston would wait for him.

Preston wouldn't survive this day.

Michael hobbled to his pickup, pulled himself into the seat and jerked hard on the steering wheel housing to get at the wiring. Fiddling as much by feel as sight, he managed to start the truck.

A half mile away from the address of BlackBird Enterprises, Preston's place, Michael saw the rental Camry Bree had driven. His heart faltered as he thought of her alone and confronted by Preston again.

Eight hundred yards farther, he shut off the pickup. He wouldn't give Preston the warning sound of a running engine. But then he heard the blast of an automatic handgun. He jerked his shotgun off the rack behind his head in the truck cab and took off running.

He was within two hundred yards when he heard another gunshot reverberating madly in the warehouse. He saw the door standing ajar at the top of the stairs. A third shot rang out. He knew, then, that Bree was still alive, because shots spaced like that were meant not to kill but to intimidate.

He had to find another way in.

SPLINTERS ERUPTED FROM the balustrade and tore at her flesh. Bree clamped her lips against rewarding Joe with her screams and just stared at him.

Joe's pacing near the jukebox grew more agitated. If he'd meant to take the edge off his mounting frenzy by firing at her, Bree knew he'd failed. "Where is Michael, Joe?"

His lips curled in contempt at her. "I left his place crawling with heat-sensitive explosives. But if I know Michael," Preston snarled, "*and I do know friend Michael,* he survived that one."

Bree forced herself to focus on Joe instead of on the things he said to bait her. He was masterful at disguising his pain, at playing the role—he'd have had to be masterful to get away with living a mole's double identity. But the tightness around his eyes and lips betrayed him. Masterful, not perfect. She had to find a way to force a mistake on his part.

An edge as jagged as the splintered baluster laced Joe's laughter, and he tossed his gun aside. "Some music while we wait, Sabrina?"

Turning to the jukebox, he made his selection. Bree recognized the Beatles in the first measure and the song "Blackbird" by the third. The music made her throat lock up, or maybe it was Joe's fractured, toneless singing. To keep her shredded control, Bree began counting measures with the music.

She lost track when Joe kicked the jukebox into silence. The expression on his face was one of unadulterated hatred.

"Free," he snarled. "Like it says in the song. *I've* waited for this moment."

Near the outer limits of any imaginable control, Bree gritted her teeth and forced herself to answer his taunt with one of her own. "You already said that, Joe. Three thousand days, you said. You're beginning to repeat yourself."

Her harassing seemed only to strengthen him. Ignoring her taunt, he strolled casually back and forth where before he'd paced like a caged animal. "When this is all over, I think I'll turn your brat over to the KGB. He can grow up to be a second-generation mole. Don't you think that will round things out nicely?"

Forcing herself past the image of her son in this monster's hands, Bree contradicted him with the first thing that came to mind. "I think you would be crazy to do that! It was the KGB that set up that firebombing, wasn't it? They betrayed you in the end," she taunted softly. "Why would you do that?"

He didn't like being caught in a contradiction. He despised it. "*Why* rarely matters," he snapped, then laughed humorlessly. "Isn't that what Blessing always says? Why, you want to know? Simply because you would hate for your bastard spawn to wind up a traitor to his country."

The thought sickened her, but Bree refused to play the terrified victim. Like a shark reacting to the scent of blood, if Joe sensed weakness in her, he'd move in fast for the kill. She couldn't afford to let her emotions show.

"Go ahead, then," she dared him. "Kill me, kill Michael, take Eric and hand him over to whomever you like, Joe. Eric will be better at it than you ever dreamed of being."

This time, her taunt hit a raw nerve. "Whoring bitch!"

Working her bonds against the fragmented wood, Bree fueled the tension rising in him every time she turned his words against him. "I was never unfaithful. I was only with Michael once, and only after you died."

"I am not dead! I never died! I will never die!" Rage twisted his features, and he grabbed up his gun again and took calculated aim once more. Another baluster splintered to bits, pelting her with sharp, force-driven slivers that tore into her blouse.

In the echoing blast of the gun, Michael hurtled through the ground-level door across the expanse of the warehouse floor from Joe, his shotgun aimed at Preston. But Joe still held the Magnum on Bree, and he began to smile. A slow, twisted, sick smile. "Speak of the devil, *sweet Breez*. Here's your lover now. Welcome to the party, old *friend*."

Outraged by the reality of Joe Preston alive, Michael stared at the jukebox. The irony of the jukebox... From Joe's tract house in Virginia Beach to the Buckhorn Bar in Laramie to a deserted warehouse in Grand Junction, Colorado.

A juke was the most powerful symbol of evil Michael knew.

Quickly, thoroughly, Michael evaluated the seemingly futile situation. He knew where Bree sat on the landing and in relation to the door, that she was bound at her wrists and feet, that the balustrade around her had been systematically blown away. And that her cheek was bleeding.

He loved her. He just wished she had it left in her to trust him. Once again, she'd failed to trust him. She'd known where to find Preston and had come alone. But he loved her, and if he once really looked at her... *Don't lose it now, Tallent. No Rambo tactics guaranteed to get us both killed.*

Michael confronted the man he had long ago counted a friend. "You've played me for a fool once too often, Joe. It's over. The party's all over."

Joe never took his eyes off Bree or his gun. "The party's not over till *I* say it's over. You could blow me away, but I'll take *sweet Breez* with me, and I don't think you want to risk that, now do you, Michael?''

From his angle, though Bree had gone quite still, Michael could see that she had worked through part of the rope binding her hands. Nodding imperceptibly at her, Michael answered Preston in the most soothing tones he could muster. "I'd rather none of us get killed, Joe. Put down your weapon, and I'll put down mine."

Preston laughed. "You first, old *friend,*" he answered, his grating whisper a taunting imitation of Michael. "Now—before I blow Sabrina to kingdom come."

Michael had no alternative. He knew Preston would kill her before he'd threaten again. Kneeling slowly, Michael skidded his shotgun across the waxed concrete floor of the warehouse. He stood back then, waiting.

Preston answered by firing again, this time into the stair riser just below Bree, and this time, she did flinch. "Your holster, Michael. Don't make me ask again."

His own heart pounding, his head throbbing, Michael disarmed himself. "That's it. What more do you want, Joe?"

Preston finally lowered his gun. It didn't escape Michael that his arms shook as he did so. On the other hand, Preston seemed to regain his jovial, lording manner. "I want you to explain to Sabrina how it was between us, Michael."

Watching for the slightest chance of jumping Preston, Michael edged toward him. In a hundred years, he'd never have believed Joe to be alive. And yet, everything about the events he'd engineered—from sending those skull-and-crossbone marked photos to Blessing's home to the travesty in Ouray—everything pointed to him.

"I don't know what you're talking about, Joe. How is it between us?"

Bree's wrists burned; splinters had gouged her flesh from her neck to her back and arms, but Bree sent Michael every mental encouragement to keep Joe talking in the hope he'd make a mistake.

"Come on, Michael, let's not be so modest, here!" Preston urged. "Tell her! Tell Sabrina how you were in it with me from the beginning. Tell her how you covered my bacon all those years I was passing information along to the KGB."

Michael felt his blood turn cold. He knew Bree had known where to find Danziger—Preston—and that she'd deliberately kept it from him. Bottom line, she'd believed more in Preston's threats than in Michael's ability to protect them. Could she possibly believe these lies?

"Tell our little whore how I survived that bombing! I couldn't have done it without you! I don't think *sweet Breez* quite believes me! Make her believe, Michael."

"Joe—"

"Make her believe!" Preston screamed, switching his aim to Michael.

Michael glanced up at Bree, sitting there at the top of the staircase, and prayed she recognized Preston's diatribe for the lie it was. Michael had never abetted Preston's treason in any way. *I have to have your trust, now, sweetheart, or nothing else will ever come close to mattering.*

Bree looked from one man to the other, knowing that Joe's outrageous claims made a twisted sort of sense—he'd have had to have a network of cronies ready to back him up or to take the blame. She simply didn't believe Michael had ever been one of them.

"C'mon, Joe. She's window dressing—that's all she ever was to you," Michael urged a little desperately. "What difference does it make what she believes? I'd rather hear how you really pulled this off."

Bree heard the subtle emphasis in Michael's words. She'd been window dressing to Joe. That wasn't true of Michael. The truth was, Michael Tallent loved her. The truth was, she loved him, and she had to believe in Michael now as she had never believed in anyone.

"He's only baiting you, Michael—I already know how it really was," she said. *I could never have believed that of you, Michael,* she thought. *I only wish I could have believed you when it would have made a difference....*

Michael's head dropped in uncommon relief. She believed him—believed in him, and for a moment, he allowed himself the respite.

How very sad to discover her faith in Michael when they were about to die.... Again, Bree swore to survive this insane twist in fate.

Sensing the pain and tension in Joe growing more severe by the second, she took the offensive with him again. "I don't understand why I was worth coming after, Joe. Didn't you have bigger fish to fry?"

"I fried them all!" he bellowed. His hand passed over his eyes, as if he couldn't tolerate even the scant light in the warehouse. "All of them, do you hear me? The KGB, Blessing—all of them, one way or another! But you! You betrayed me, both of you! I could have killed you a thousand times over. I could have had your bastard brat any day of any week."

Michael sensed the dismay rising again in Bree for Preston's reference to Eric, and he turned for the first time to look straight at her. Willing her to remain strong and calm, he spoke only to her, as if Preston had suddenly disappeared. "We were right, Breez, about Sutterfield."

"An informant?"

"For the KGB," Michael confirmed.

Her arms ached like fury, but Bree could feel her bonds beginning to slip. Aware of Preston's mounting ire at being excluded, she inclined her head in his direction. "The KGB wants him dead, Michael. They knew he'd survived, and they had to figure he'd eventually come after me for the revenge. I was the bait, you were supposed to be the executioner—I'd bet the KGB had Blessing's approval on that! What I don't get is why Sutterfield forced the disciplinary action or set up the freezer incident."

"Things weren't happening fast enough for the KGB, *sweet Breez,"* Joe said, mocking her, caught up now in revealing how he'd outwitted them all. Brandishing his gun, he taunted, "You're right. They want me dead. They thought if you were unnerved enough, you'd run—which would flush me out of my cover. Fools! Utterly predictable fools! *I* coerced Sutterfield into pulling off the freezer incident, just to show them what contemptible clods they are."

For a moment, seeing the way Joe twitched in pain and favored his left leg as he paced, Bree stopped struggling with the ropes that bound her hands. Michael stood near Joe now, his fingers tucked in his jeans pockets in a deceptively relaxed stance.

"What took you so long, Joe? Why so many years?" she asked.

"Revenge is like a fine, vintage wine—years in the making, to be savored."

But the image of pain, intense, uncompromising pain, came to Bree, and she knew that there must have been months, even years, in which the pain of the injuries he'd suffered in the bombing must have made even surviving day to day a superhuman effort. He'd hated her and Michael enough to survive. Enough to wait years on his revenge.

"And what of Patrick? Did he have to die, Joe?"

"Marquet was so besotted with you he'd have done anything to get your attention. Did you know he was planning a comeback in Hollywood?"

"Why shouldn't he? He—"

"His script exploited the terrible tale of a mole's poor, innocent widow," Preston goaded, his smile brittle as old, old paper. Before Bree could think what damage Patrick would have done her life with that screenplay, Joe went relentlessly on.

"Michael was besotted with you, too. Marquet was a born loser. The world is full of fools, Breezy-whore. What do you think it is about you that attracts them?"

Revulsion for this maniac passed through Michael, so powerful it made him shudder. "What does that say of the man who married her—about you, Joe?"

"Enough!" His own words turned against him again, Preston lost all pleasure in bragging. "Enough talk!" Flushed and ugly with his rage, he trained his gun on Michael. "Go to her, *friend.* Untie your lover and take her into your arms. It would amuse me to kill you both with a single bullet."

His hands spread wide in a conciliatory gesture, Michael edged toward the stairs and tried reasoning. "Take it easy, Joe. The party is really over if you kill us both. Let her go—"

"I'm bored with this party, Michael." Steady as a rock now, he had the gun trained at Michael's chest. "Move. *Move!*"

Dropping any pretense of placating Joe, Michael dropped his hands, as well, turned on his heel and made a broad target of his back once more. *Aces and eights, a dead man's hand,* for being fool enough to expose his back. He had a far better chance of dying this day with a bullet in his back than he had that blustery, fated day in Laramie, Wyoming.

As he walked toward the stairs, Michael thought of the taped message Blessing had delivered then. The harsh, whispering voice had promised Michael he'd live long enough to appreciate his losses. The woman he loved and the son he'd known less than a month. Preston had accomplished what he'd promised. Michael knew exactly the extent of his losses if he died today.

Sick with fear for Michael, heartsick for the years her lack of faith had cost them, Bree watched him turn and take the first stair. The second. The third. By the sixth, his pewter gray eyes were at a level with her own. His face expressionless, those eyes conveyed volumes.

He loved her.

He'd find a way. He loved her.

He'd find a way out. The jukebox flashed eerily. The silence was interrupted only by the scrape of Michael's boots on the stair risers. Apparently mesmerized with his moment, Joe was content to look on and absorb the scene he'd waited so long to unfold before him. Her teeth gritted against crying out, Bree watched Michael's eyes dart up and to his left.

In her mind, Bree saw the door leading into the apartment and understood Michael's intentions. If they could get out of the line of Joe's fire by ducking through that door, they had a chance. Lifting her chin, Bree conveyed her understanding with the barest of nods.

From the corner of her eye, Bree saw that even that small movement on her part drew Joe out of his trancelike enjoyment. In horror, she saw his arm rise, the gun aimed and the flash of light as he fired.

The riser beneath Michael's boot collapsed in the midst of the deafening shot. "*Untie her, Michael!* NOW!"

In the split second before the shot, he'd seen Bree's eyes widen in horror. He'd expected to take the shot in his back, to feel the fire and the explosion of his own flesh. Now, fighting for balance instead, Michael jerked his boot loose from the collapsed stair and thanked God for a few more moments.

He gained the landing and went behind Bree to untie the ropes. The gouges in her flesh enraged him. "That's five, Joe," he jeered. "One more bullet in that clip. You have more?"

"Plenty—but I only need one." His laughter was softly insidious, demented. "Stand up, Michael. Take *sweet Breez*. Show me how a man betrays his best friend."

"I never betrayed you with Bree, Joe. You were already long dead before I ever touched her."

"As you can finally see, Michael," Joe grated out, "I was never dead."

Bree felt the ropes fall away from her ankles, but Michael massaged her feet while pretending to work at untying the knot. She wouldn't have a chance of staying on her feet unless her circulation was restored.

"Now!" Preston flared, inflamed with the nearness of his victory over them. "I want to see an impassioned embrace, Michael, so that one of you *dies* with a bullet that has first torn through the other's body!"

Forcing himself to ignore Joe's ranting and raving, Michael helped Bree to her feet and envisioned the apartment doorway that was behind him now. Somehow, he had to turn, to get Bree nearer to the door, positioned behind his body out of Joe's line of fire.

Her feet throbbing as circulation returned, Bree's right ankle collapsed and her body dipped. Miraculously, it provided exactly the move Michael needed. Ducking around to her side, Michael grabbed her shoulders and managed to turn them both. Now he faced the door and had a chance of shoving Bree through it before the bullet passed through him and ripped into her.

At the last moment, Bree understood that he meant to take the bullet first. Protest rose in her eyes along with the cry in her throat, but Preston roared at them again, and Michael was only too happy to comply—Bree couldn't cry out with his lips sealed to hers.

Joe began to laugh, and he kicked the juke to life again. His demented laughter clashed with McCartney singing "Blackbird."

Michael enfolded Bree in his arms and kissed her, and the cry did die in her throat. The cacophony of music and Joe's laughter faded away. Her cheeks ached with that kiss. Tears flooded into tiny ducts. She'd never known anything in her life more chaste or poignant or desirous than that kiss. It touched her heart in ways she'd not been touched ever before. The intensity of her feelings reflected knowledge that they would both die in the next moment.

But Joe's laughter reached a fevered pitch, and Bree could feel the tension in Michael's body as he held her in the embrace Preston had demanded. Michael's kiss went from chaste and poignant to sexual and possessive, and in the next instant, the world exploded with the reverberating, wild shot of the Magnum handgun. She felt the slug slam into Michael's shoulder, and then she felt herself thrown from Michael's arms. Her body struck the door, and she fell through, out of the trajectory of the bullet.

Michael lay facedown and motionless no more than four feet from her on the landing above the juke. The "Blackbird" disk stuck in its groove and played *free, free, free,* over and over again as Joe laughed hysterically. Horror and rage careening through her, Bree cried out and grabbed up a metal snow shovel just inside the apartment door. She rushed through the door and with every ounce of her strength and wrath and passion to survive, she hurtled the shovel, blade first, over the balustrade at Preston.

The shovel blade caught him full in the chest. As he stumbled backward with the force of the blow, his gun, empty now of bullets anyway, flew out of his hand and clattered to the cement floor.

"Witch! Whoring witch!" he shrieked tonelessly. Fury and disbelief galvanized him into aggressive action. He grabbed a tire iron from the floor beside him, near the vintage black Mustang. Roaring in pain and anger, he picked himself up and launched his body to the bottom of the stairs.

Hovering over Michael, aware of his ragged, unconscious breathing, Bree watched in fascinated horror as Joe took the first stair. The second. The third. He held the tire iron high above his head, threatening.

Michael flinched in his insensible pain. Despite his frenzied intent to bludgeon Bree to death, Preston saw that Michael was still alive. Hatred and bitterness twisting his features, Joe approached Michael slowly. He raised his other arm, gripped the tire iron in both hands, and aimed his death blow at Michael's head.

Screaming, driven to protect Michael as he had done for her, Bree sprang at Joe. Intent on deflecting the blow to Michael, she misjudged the strength of her attack and her body slammed into Preston. He stumbled sideways. Bree fell across Michael's legs. Preston swung his arms, desperately seeking to right his posture. He flailed at the air. He screamed and grunted and swore. Bree watched in horror as his bad leg buckled, crumpling beneath him. He crashed backward into the already splintered balustrade.

As if in slow motion, Joe looked at Bree, his eyes filled with terror and malice and pure hatred. The tire iron fell from his grip and dropped away, then the handrail collapsed under his weight. The tire iron clanged as it hit the floor seconds before Preston's body disappeared over the edge of the landing.

He fell against the dome of the juke, and its eerie lights went out at the moment Joseph Allen Preston died.

Relief overwhelmed Bree and the tears she'd held off for days began to stream down her cheeks. Still, she allowed herself not a moment to indulge the emotional release. If she didn't get help immediately, Michael could die as well.

The worst, the horror was over—Michael needed her with her wits in place or he'd bleed to death. Pulling back from the edge of the landing twenty feet above the floor where Joe's body lay, Bree turned and sank to her knees at Michael's side. He was already in shock. His breathing and his pulse were thready and jackhammer fast. She feared the additional damage she might do by turning him onto his back.

Swiping at her tears, she got up and went into Joseph Preston's apartment in search of a phone. The 911 operator answered promptly. Staring at the bank of computer equipment Joe had used to breach Blessing's security and tap into dozens of phone lines, Bree had to be asked twice for the location and nature of her emergency.

By the time she got back to Michael's side, he'd regained consciousness and had turned over himself. There was a bullet hole in Michael's shirt and massive bloodstains. Bree clapped her hand to her mouth to hide her trembling from his pain-glazed eyes.

She saw Michael eyeing the broken baluster, and she told him Joe had fallen through to the cement floor below.

"He's dead, then?"

Bree's throat refused to work for a moment. "Yes. I—it looks as if his neck is broken."

Michael's eyes closed. The nightmare was over. Truly over. "Where were you, Breez?" he croaked.

Bree sat beside him and tore off a piece of her skirt to stanch the flow of his blood. "Shh, Michael. You shouldn't talk. I went to call for help."

Despite the pain, Michael shook his head. "I mean...this morning."

Then Bree understood what he wanted to know. "Joe wanted the money Henry left me—and the title to the cabin and property in Ouray. I had to go get it, Michael. I didn't see any other choice. He knew we'd sent Eric to your parents in Sapporo. I should have told you...I know that now."

To Michael, the remorse in Bree's eyes hurt more than the bullet that had ripped through his shoulder. He'd seen enough of doubt and regret and shame clouding Bree's cornflower blue eyes. He hoped never to hear any apologies from her for doing what had to be done when the only one she had to trust was herself.

He almost passed out again from the pain in his shoulder. Approaching sirens wailed in the distance, and he knew he had to tell her how he felt—now. "Eric needs a family, Breez. Both of us, and Martha, pet geese and...maybe a little sister."

It wasn't doubt clouding her eyes now, but tears. She'd forgotten how special tears of joy could be. "I hate to point this out, Tallent, but you're in no shape for making babies."

He'd forgotten what an anesthetic such joy could be, and he smiled. "Don't bet on it, Breezy-love."

"Do you think your son will like the geese or a little sister more?"

"The kid is nobody's fool, Breez," Michael scolded.

"Neither is his mother, Tallent. That doesn't answer the question."

Somewhere, Michael found the strength to reach up and caress Bree's cheek. "No. It doesn't, does it?"

But the fugitive heart had come home at last. Nothing else mattered as much.

MILLION DOLLAR JACKPOT
SWEEPSTAKES RULES & REGULATIONS
NO PURCHASE NECESSARY TO ENTER OR RECEIVE A PRIZE

1. Alternate means of entry: Print your name and address on a 3″ ×5″ piece of plain paper and send to the appropriate address below.

In the U.S.	In Canada
MILLION DOLLAR JACKPOT	MILLION DOLLAR JACKPOT
P.O. Box 1867	P.O. Box 609
3010 Walden Avenue	Fort Erie, Ontario
Buffalo, NY 14269-1867	L2A 5X3

2. To enter the Sweepstakes and join the Reader Service, check off the "YES" box on your Sweepstakes Entry Form and return. If you do not wish to join the Reader Service but wish to enter the Sweepstakes only, check off the "NO" box on your Sweepstakes Entry Form. To qualify for the Extra Bonus prize, scratch off the silver on your Lucky Keys. If the registration numbers match, you are eligible for the Extra Bonus Prize offering. Incomplete entries are ineligible. Torstar Corp. and its affiliates are not responsible for mutilated or unreadable entries or inadvertent printing errors. Mechanically reproduced entries are null and void.

3. Whether you take advantage of this offer or not, on or about April 30, 1992, at the offices of D.L. Blair, Inc., Blair, NE, your sweepstakes numbers will be compared against the list of winning numbers generated at random by the computer. However, prizes will only be awarded to individuals who have entered the Sweepstakes. In the event that all prizes are not claimed, a random drawing will be held from all qualified entries received from March 30, 1990 to March 31, 1992, to award all unclaimed prizes. All cash prizes (Grand to Sixth) will be mailed to winners and are payable by check in U.S. funds. Seventh Prize will be shipped to winners via third-class mail. These prizes are in addition to any free, surprise or mystery gifts that might be offered. Versions of this Sweepstakes with different prizes of approximate equal value may appear at retail outlets or in other mailings by Torstar Corp. and its affiliates.

4. PRIZES: (1) *Grand Prize $1,000,000.00 Annuity; (1) First Prize $25,000.00; (1) Second Prize $10,000.00; (5) Third Prize $5,000.00; (10) Fourth Prize $1,000.00; (100) Fifth Prize $250.00; (2,500) Sixth Prize $10.00; (6,000) **Seventh Prize $12.95 ARV.

   *This presentation offers a Grand Prize of a $1,000,000.00 annuity. Winner will receive $33,333.33 a year for 30 years without interest totalling $1,000,000.00.

   **Seventh Prize: A fully illustrated hardcover book, published by Torstar Corp. Approximate Retail Value of the book is $12.95.

   Entrants may cancel the Reader Service at any time without cost or obligation (see details in Center Insert Card).

5. Extra Bonus! This presentation offers an Extra Bonus Prize valued at $33,000.00 to be awarded in a random drawing from all qualified entries received by March 31, 1992. No purchase necessary to enter or receive a prize. To qualify, see instructions in Center Insert Card. Winner will have the choice of any of the merchandise offered or a $33,000.00 check payable in U.S. funds. All other published rules and regulations apply.

6. This Sweepstakes is being conducted under the supervision of D.L. Blair, Inc. By entering the Sweepstakes, each entrant accepts and agrees to be bound by these rules and the decisions of the judges, which shall be final and binding. Odds of winning the random drawing are dependent upon the number of entries received. Taxes, if any, are the sole responsibility of the winners. Prizes are nontransferable. All entries must be received at the address on the detachable Business Reply Card and must be postmarked no later than 12:00 MIDNIGHT on March 31, 1992. The drawing for all unclaimed Sweepstakes prizes and for the Extra Bonus Prize will take place on May 30, 1992, at 12:00 NOON at the offices of D.L. Blair, Inc., Blair, NE.

7. This offer is open to residents of the U.S., United Kingdom, France and Canada, 18 years or older, except employees and immediate family members of Torstar Corp., its affiliates, subsidiaries and all other agencies, entities and persons connected with the use, marketing or conduct of this Sweepstakes. All Federal, State, Provincial, Municipal and local laws apply. Void wherever prohibited or restricted by law. Any litigation within the Province of Quebec respecting the conduct and awarding of a prize in this publicity contest must be submitted to the Régie des Loteries et Courses du Québec.

8. Winners will be notified by mail and may be required to execute an affidavit of eligibility and release, which must be returned within 14 days after notification or an alternate winner may be selected. Canadian winners will be required to correctly answer an arithmetical, skill-testing question administered by mail, which must be returned within a limited time. Winners consent to the use of their name, photograph and/or likeness for advertising and publicity in conjunction with this and similar promotions without additional compensation.

9. For a list of our major prize winners, send a stamped, self-addressed envelope to: MILLION DOLLAR WINNERS LIST, P.O. Box 4510, Blair, NE 68009. Winners Lists will be supplied after the May 30, 1992 drawing date.

Offer limited to one per household.

LTY-H891

HARLEQUIN®
OFFICIAL SWEEPSTAKES
RULES

NO PURCHASE NECESSARY

1. To enter, complete an Official Entry Form or 3" × 5" index card by hand-printing, in plain block letters, your complete name, address, phone number and age, and mailing it to: Harlequin Fashion A Whole New You Sweepstakes, P.O. Box 9056, Buffalo, NY 14269-9056.

   No responsibility is assumed for lost, late or misdirected mail. Entries must be sent separately with first class postage affixed, and be received no later than December 31, 1991 for eligibility.

2. Winners will be selected by D.L. Blair, Inc., an independent judging organization whose decisions are final, in random drawings to be held on January 30, 1992 in Blair, NE at 10:00 a.m. from among all eligible entries received.

3. The prizes to be awarded and their approximate retail values are as follows: Grand Prize — A brand-new Mercury Sable LS plus a trip for two (2) to Paris, including round-trip air transportation, six (6) nights hotel accommodation, a $1,400 meal/spending money stipend and $2,000 cash toward a new fashion wardrobe (approximate value: $28,000) or $15,000 cash; two (2) Second Prizes — A trip to Paris, including round-trip air transportation, six (6) nights hotel accommodation, a $1,400 meal/spending money stipend and $2,000 cash toward a new fashion wardrobe (approximate value: $11,000) or $5,000 cash; three (3) Third Prizes — $2,000 cash toward a new fashion wardrobe. All prizes are valued in U.S. currency. Travel award air transportation is from the commercial airport nearest winner's home. Travel is subject to space and accommodation availability, and must be completed by June 30, 1993. Sweepstakes offer is open to residents of the U.S. and Canada who are 21 years of age or older as of December 31, 1991, except residents of Puerto Rico, employees and immediate family members of Torstar Corp., its affiliates, subsidiaries, and all agencies, entities and persons connected with the use, marketing, or conduct of this sweepstakes. All federal, state, provincial, municipal and local laws apply. Offer void wherever prohibited by law. Taxes and/or duties, applicable registration and licensing fees, are the sole responsibility of the winners. Any litigation within the province of Quebec respecting the conduct and awarding of a prize may be submitted to the Régie des loteries et courses du Québec. All prizes will be awarded; winners will be notified by mail. No substitution of prizes is permitted.

4. Potential winners must sign and return any required Affidavit of Eligibility/Release of Liability within 30 days of notification. In the event of noncompliance within this time period, the prize may be awarded to an alternate winner. Any prize or prize notification returned as undeliverable may result in the awarding of that prize to an alternate winner. By acceptance of their prize, winners consent to use of their names, photographs or their likenesses for purposes of advertising, trade and promotion on behalf of Torstar Corp. without further compensation. Canadian winners must correctly answer a time-limited arithmetical question in order to be awarded a prize.

5. For a list of winners (available after 3/31/92), send a separate stamped, self-addressed envelope to: Harlequin Fashion A Whole New You Sweepstakes, P.O. Box 4694, Blair, NE 68009.

PREMIUM OFFER TERMS

To receive your gift, complete the Offer Certificate according to directions. Be certain to enclose the required number of "Fashion A Whole New You" proofs of product purchase (which are found on the last page of every specially marked "Fashion A Whole New You" Harlequin or Silhouette romance novel). Requests must be received no later than December 31, 1991. Limit: four (4) gifts per name, family, group, organization or address. Items depicted are for illustrative purposes only and may not be exactly as shown. Please allow 6 to 8 weeks for receipt of order. Offer good while quantities of gifts last. In the event an ordered gift is no longer available, you will receive a free, previously unpublished Harlequin or Silhouette book for every proof of purchase you have submitted with your request, plus a refund of the postage and handling charge you have included. Offer good in the U.S. and Canada only.

HOFW-SWPR

HARLEQUIN® OFFICIAL SWEEPSTAKES ENTRY FORM

4-FWHIS-2

Complete and return this Entry Form immediately – the more entries you submit, the better your chances of winning!

- Entries must be received by **December 31, 1991.**
- A Random draw will take place on **January 30, 1992.**
- No purchase necessary.

Yes, I want to win a FASHION A WHOLE NEW YOU Classic and Romantic prize from Harlequin:

Name _____ Telephone _____ Age _____

Address _____

City _____ State _____ Zip _____

Return Entries to: **Harlequin FASHION A WHOLE NEW YOU,**
            P.O. Box 9056, Buffalo, NY 14269-9056   © 1991 Harlequin Enterprises Limited

PREMIUM OFFER

To receive your free gift, send us the required number of proofs-of-purchase from any specially marked FASHION A WHOLE NEW YOU Harlequin or Silhouette Book with the Offer Certificate properly completed, plus a check or money order (do not send cash) to cover postage and handling payable to Harlequin FASHION A WHOLE NEW YOU Offer. We will send you the specified gift.

OFFER CERTIFICATE

Item	A. ROMANTIC COLLECTOR'S DOLL	B. CLASSIC PICTURE FRAME
	(Suggested Retail Price $60.00)	(Suggested Retail Price $25.00)
# of proofs-of-purchase	18	12
Postage and Handling	$3.50	$2.95
Check one	☐	☐

Name _____

Address _____

City _____ State _____ Zip _____

Mail this certificate, designated number of proofs-of-purchase and check or money order for postage and handling to: **Harlequin FASHION A WHOLE NEW YOU Gift Offer,** P.O. Box 9057, Buffalo, NY 14269-9057. Requests must be received by December 31, 1991.

ONE PROOF-OF-PURCHASE

4-FWHIP-2

To collect your fabulous free gift you must include the necessary number of proofs-of-purchase with a properly completed Offer Certificate.

© 1991 Harlequin Enterprises Limited

See previous page for details.